# MACHETE

## A Jake Lydon mystery

# MACHETE

A Jake Lydon mystery

# JOHN OWENS

OTTAWA
PRESS AND
PUBLISHING

ottawapressandpublishing.com


Copyright © John Owens Communications 2019

IISBN (pbk.)    978-1-988437-22-4
ISBN (MOBI)    978-1-988437-23-1
ISBN (EPUB)    978-1-988437-24-8

Cover design: Glenn Torresan
Page design: Glenn Torresan
Cover photograph: Patric Fore

*To my son, Judd, who wants to wait for the movie*

*And to the past, present, and future drinking gangs*

*of Las Terrenas, Dominican Republic*

*You know that you cannot trust them*
*'Cause they know they can't trust you.*
**- Jimmy Buffet**

# PROLOGUE

Immediately before she died, she was aware of three distinct things, three sensations jolting her brain.

What she saw was the look in his eyes.

What she heard was the slight whistling sound of the silver blade as it struck her throat.

What she felt was the pain.

The white pain that stopped with the second slight whistling sound.

CHAPTER ONE

The December morning broke warm and sunny. Just like, it seemed, every other fucking December morning and every November morning so far and let's not forget all the mornings yet to come from January through April.

That is after all, the main reason I'm here. I think.

Specifically, "here" is Las Terrenas, a small, delightful, mostly touristy town on the north-east Atlantic coast of the Dominican Republic. More specifically, "here" is the expansive beach at Playa Ballenas, across the cobblestone street from the two-bedroom condo I bought last spring after three years of renting down here. As I turn away from the turquoise waters, I can almost make out Casa del Mar through the thick palms that tend to obscure just about everything in this green jungle-y place.

It's quiet now, just the way I like it.

Specifically, "now" is after a pretty tumultuous year that started going sideways for me beginning in Canada last summer and featuring near-fatal disasters in San Francisco, Toronto, Boston, and points in between. The whole shemozzle finally petered out a few weeks before I boarded a flight south at the end of October, just ahead of that magical time when the snowy shit hits the fan up north.

The plane from Toronto does this low, lazy 180-degree arc over the island before it lands. So it's coming from the south over Samana

Bay and Samana Peninsula. You can see the checkerboard rice paddies laid out, some flooded and planted, some not, before you meet the hills running down the spine of the peninsula. By that time, you're so close to the ground, that the hills and valleys are distinct, shadows and light playing off the humped landscape. You can plainly see individual palms and narrow trails leading to remote houses. Looking down from that height always reminds me of those elaborate model train set lay-outs or a museum diorama.

And then that blast of hot air greets you when the plane door opens. An instant thrill, like the sound you get when you open a new can of tennis balls. Or a beer.

And I know that over the next six months no socks will be worn. I fucking hate socks. I also know that by February, even the act of putting on insubstantial flip-flops will be a pain in the ass.

While staring at the ocean, I had contemplated my plans for the day. I might play a bit of tennis. Or not. I might go grocery shopping. Or not. I might take another stab at my second novel. Or not.

Now that I was here alone and my November and early December guests were gone, I looked forward to about five months of just enjoying the place and the people I knew here. Doing the math, I'd spent only four full months in my condo—a month and a bit this fall and just over two months after I bought the joint ten months ago. I knew that I ought to do a little decorating beyond the two large and very colourful Haitian paintings hanging in my living room. So that was the extent of my long-range thinking.

Short-term, I needed a plan for the day ahead of me. I finally settled on one. Nothing. I had determined to do nothing. And I had all day to do it.

I had even managed to convince myself that I deserved this full slate of non-activity after the murder, mayhem, and international unpleasantness of the past seven months.

But the fact was, I called bullshit on this self-justification. I knew there's a better explanation: I'm bone lazy. Pure and simple. I'm talking about being lazy about actually doing things. Thinking about things is a very different matter.

To be clear: I'm not claiming Stephen Hawking- or Noam Chomsky-type thinking, more along the lines of a steady Homer Simpson interior monologue. Despite its suspect content, my wee brain never shuts the fuck up. Even when I'm watching yet another glorious sunrise or sunset—which is about a daily thing down here—I'm rarely thoughtless. A second or two maybe, when the self-chatting stops and I nail that single moment. I figure that's all we're ever left with anyway: moments, like ol' Al Tennyson said: "that flash along the chords and go."

I was "peopled" out. I get that way. Steve Golding, my journalist pal from Toronto, had shown up on my tropical doorstep in early November and stayed for almost three weeks, finishing his book on my shenanigans of last summer. A couple of days of solitude after he left and then Alexandra arrived.

Alex had gone back to Boston a few days ago. Our re-kindled relationship had, over the week she'd spent here, "caught like a wildfire out of control until there nothing left to burn and nothing left to prove" as Mr. Seger has it.

Not too shabby for a couple of early sixty-somethings, I thought with a smile, and the only good thing that I got out of the last half year or so—besides the whack of money Steve gave me from the book rights, money I'd already spent. Oh, and bringing down a global computer hacking enterprise; that was satisfying. But other than that.

I had no idea what would happen next with Alex and me. See, we had this game we tacitly played—pretty juvenile I admit—the chief rule of which is that we were not to speak of love or commitment or any of the long-term notions that occupy normal couples. Take for example, her trip down here a couple of weeks ago. It was ostensibly to get first-hand knowledge about the sustainability of rice farms in the north-east DR in her role as an analyst for a Boston-based ethical investment advisor. Oh, and while she was down here maybe she could squeeze in a visit with an old Canadian friend who lived part-time in Las Terrenas.

For the record, we did spend close to half a day touring some rice paddies an hour or so away. To keep things distanced, I thought she should have paid me for my half-assed translation services. But it turned out her Spanish was way better than mine.

And she fit right in. As I knew she would. Starting with Alejandro, the world's best bartender™.

The only way to describe his expression as he watched us approach his poolside domain was profound surprise and joy. With just a dash of Latin lechery.

"Senor Yake! *Bienvenido!*" he said, without looking at me.

"*Hola, amigo,*" I said. "This es Alexandra."

Alejandro pretty much ignored me while he performed a courtly bow to Alex and kissed her hand. Fucking Latins.

"A drink perhaps *por la bonita*?" he suggested.

He was all smiles as he went through an elaborate and dramatic routine of preparing her bloody Mary *picante*, then mixed up usual Tanqueray and tonic as something of an afterthought.

We spent most of the week hanging around the pool and the beach but we did take a walking then stumbling tour of the town where she met—and charmed—pretty well everyone in my gang of drunken expats.

But what we never did was talk about or even allude to next steps for us.

After she left, I determined that I would not try to lure her to the DR on a more permanent basis and she wasn't begging me to move to New England.

So there it was.

I was pretty sure that whatever was going to happen next between us would feature no drama. I hate drama almost as much as I fucking hate socks. I was confident Alex felt likewise. Maybe because I was nuzzling up to sixty-one years on the planet, I just didn't get it. Where alleged love is involved, drama is exhausting and, normally, stupid. Can anyone explain the whys and wherefores of stalking old girl or boy friends? Statistically, is that a highly successful way of patching things up? Can anyone explain people who injure or kill themselves or somebody else because another human being doesn't want to be with them? Beats the shit out of me.

I gave myself hell for even thinking about these things as I crossed the road and nearly got hit by a *motoconcho,* one of the small 120 cc motorcycles that buzz the narrow streets looking to pick up fares who either don't mind or actually looked forward to having the unholy crap scared out of them.

"Snap out of it!" I said aloud but without the effect of Cher smacking Nicholas Cage in *Moonstruck.*

I had other things to do. Like nothing. Which I did. All day. And very ably, may I add.

I, of course, had no inkling that this day of pure indolence was going to be one of the last such respites for the rest of the fucking winter.

# CHAPTER TWO

After a fatiguing day of utter sloth, I was too whipped to even clean up a bit. But with evening coming on, I figured I'd go to Big Dave's, a place where gold stars for neatness and good hygiene were not ever handed out.

I made the delightful trek along the beach in front of Fishermen's Village towards the main street bar. When I first arrived in LT four winters ago, *Pueblo de Pescadores* was a row of maybe twelve large, pretty well adjoining, and decrepit wooden fishing shacks that had been converted into mid- to high-end restaurants, each accessorized by a patio facing the relentlessly fascinating ocean.

All the kitchens in these eateries ran on human-sized propane tanks with the likely predictable result that something was bound to fuck up sooner or later. Which it did. About a year and a half ago, the whole row was demolished in a series of fireballs as one after another propane tank exploded. I saw a post-blaze video of the remains on the Interweb. Except for the brick ovens of a couple of pizzerias, there was nothing left but blackened sand, concrete foundation blocks, and badly singed palm trees. Thank Christ, no one was hurt in the early morning fire, but it had put a real dent in the commercial life of the town.

To my right now as I walked along the sand were the replacements, still wooden but uniformly built, lacking the ramshackle quality of the originals. They had been had brightly painted in every pastel shade to give off that Caribbean vibe. With the sun sinking behind me, all the patio twinkle lights were on, illuminating the new wooden decks of the

French, Italian, Dominican, Chinese, and even American restaurants. The dramatic sky was now purpling up; to my left, the small waves lapped the sand smooth and spongy.

I hung a right off the beach and started up the main street of Las Terrenas, instantly struck by the study in contrasts. The quiet beach scene versus the loud sounds and noxious smells of the more or less constant stream of *motoconchos,* which jostled for road space with four-wheeled ATVs custom-fitted with wooden storage boxes. Both are perfect for navigating all the potholes and speed bumps. The ATVs are personally-owned whereas the *motoconchos* are working vehicles, two-wheeled taxis of death that for a pretty standard rate of 50 pesos—about a buck and a half—will supply enough thrills, chills, and spills as they zig and zag their way through traffic to easily equal hundred-dollar-a-day amusement park rides. Among these roaring, whining contraptions were monstrously-sized SUVs and, yes, even the occasional car.

A deaf person would be pretty well fucked down here where the use of horns is the standard form of street communication. The Dominicans are virtuosos at extracting different sounds for different messages from the same horn. A quick, single cheery-sounding beep to say 'hi' to someone they know riding the other way or walking. A somewhat more drawn out honk to express their appreciation of a pretty woman. Short softer bursts to ask you if you want a ride. Usually two beeps. Then louder, more insistent beeps to signify their emergence from a side street without looking or to warn pedestrians that they better pick up their pace crossing the road. And finally—and universally—angry prolonged blasts which, loosely translated into any language mean "Get the fuck out of my way, you goddamned moron!"

The noisy street scene was definitely painted brighter than usual because Christmas was less than three weeks away. Dominicans are crazy for *Navidad.* For sure, it's a bit incongruous to see tinsel and coloured lights hanging off palm trees and *palapa* roofs but it works somehow. You even get used to seeing Santas in shorts and sandals. I've gotten accustomed to being called Santa by the cuter-than-hell Dominican kids in grocery store line-ups. Given my long grey hair, half-assed beard, and paunch, I figure the little shits made an honest mistake.

The various shops and native diners I passed were all open, as were the small grocery stores—all coincidentally named *supermercados* in a sort of signage arms race. Their proprietors stood in the doorways and greeted me, a gauntlet of smiles, handshakes, shoulder pats, and fist bumps. I wasn't anything special. They were just uniformly sweet people who stopped hustling and hassling you when they realized you weren't a by-the-week tourist. Las Terrenas is at its core just a small town and, like small towns everywhere, when the residents recognized you and, if you weren't a dick, they were always friendly.

The real passport to acceptance down here is a decent tan. Most merchants and beach vendors left you the fuck alone when they saw the tan, figuring—correctly—that you were a longer-term resident who had already been subjected to every possible sales pitch for every possible product—or service—they had to offer.

I walked along, now warmed by the familiarity, and enjoying a little round of self-congratulation for choosing this out of the way place to hide from Canada's winters.

I did remind myself that my choice hadn't been a matter of being first-time lucky. My first winter as more or less a retiree, five years ago, had been spent in Florida which hadn't turned out all that well. Daily, I wondered what—besides superior cable television—the fuck I had been thinking to tie myself to a small condo complex in Fort Myers.

It wasn't that the other retirees around me weren't nice; they were nice. But people are *supposed* to be nice. And almost everybody everywhere *is* nice. But for casual acquaintances, fellow snowbirds, I'm also looking for not boring. These people were boring. That's not their fault, but it wasn't mine either. And it's totally on me, not them, that I rented there to begin with.

In loud voices—louder still when they were on the phone by the over-heated community pool—they seemed to discuss one of three things: their grandkids, their meds or where they were going to eat that night. More accurately: where they were going to eat that afternoon because there was gridlock at 3:59 in the complex's driveway leading to the main road as they rushed en masse to their next seniors' discount meal.

Back then, I was the kid in their arthritic enclave—at 55, a good fifteen years younger than anyone else and in many cases twenty-five years less senior. And that means that while the Summer of Love was washing over me as an early teenager, they were all working, likely married with children and houses, and likely still listening to that shit 50s music.

Sound elitist? Tough bananas. It's meant to describe how it's generally difficult to fit in with different age groups—really any group—when our experiences are so different. Except for the bit about their music. It was and still is shit.

Most were retired local and state pensioners—cops, teachers, nurses, water commission and power workers—with a disproportionate number of them from Wisconsin—sorry, Wisc*a*nsin. Except for the *Fargo a*ccents, they were normal people who'd spent normal, decent, hard-working lives getting to the point where they didn't have to shovel snow anymore.

For more of them than I care to remember, politics and religion were off the table as topics of discussion and I understand that. I was the outsider here. It ain't your country, Jake, so just shut the fuck up, will ya? And that led to more than several knuckle-biting episodes when I'd hear them talk about "that nigger Obama" as casually and as loudly as if they were debating the latest blue plate special at Applebee's or which church service they were going to attend.

Las Terrenas was different—waaaaay different. It was a buffet of different ages, accents, temperaments, and, above all, stories. There was even a wide array of different hair colours beyond the grey or bald hues favoured by the proudly self-described Florida Cheeseheads.

Nope, there was nothing I saw in Florida like the riotous Avenida Duarte, LT's main north-south street.

## CHAPTER THREE

Sooner or later—mostly sooner—all the English-speaking expatriates wound up at Big Dave's American Bar—the drinking ones at any rate. Which was most of us.

If I honestly had to list my hobbies or interests they'd be—in no particular order—talking, laughing, drinking, and smoking. That being the case for the last forty-five fucking years, I prefer settings where I can do all four simultaneously. Very few places I had ever visited fit the bill as perfectly as Big Dave's American Bar.

Dave really was American and at 6'4", maybe 250, Dave really was big but his establishment, not so much. A narrow courtyard-type patio wedged between a real estate office and a souvenir shop. In this courtyard were maybe ten white plastic tables with six chairs around each. At least, that's the configuration at the start of the drinking day. By the end of it, the chairs had been moved, tables shifted and shifted again, combined to create impromptu parties which lasted for undetermined amounts of times, people drifting in and out, coalescing and disbanding like schools of drunken fish until closing time which was generally set for whenever Dave wanted to go home.

The food was good and cheap, subcontracted to two older Mexican women who ran a small kitchen with a take-out window on one side of the courtyard. Like just about every restaurant here—or in Mexico—they wouldn't even be allowed to open in Canada or the US. And like just about every restaurant here—or in Mexico—it served tremendous food.

But Dave's real line of work was beer. He sold Presidente *grandes* for the same price as they charged at the beach for the *pecuenas* half their size. At first, I figured the great sweating green quart bottles were his loss leaders but then understood that Dave had a big box retailer's heart. Small margins, huge volume.

To ensure the sale of beer was not interrupted, Dave had installed a corrugated plastic awning at the back of the place. Nobody ever sat under it. But when a typical flash Dominican rainstorm would spring up, all the open-air drinkers performed a remarkably synchronized drill. Regardless of their level of inebriation, they would rise as one, grab their bottles and smokes, tilt their chairs over, and hustle to stand under the awning—with beer in hand—until the rain stopped, usually four or five minutes later.

Dave told me that some of his regulars were seven-night-a-weekers, which made me a dilettante, a half-miler. It didn't take me long to figure out that mere mortals such as myself could do this at most three, *maybe* four times a week.

Dave was middle-aged with a small pony tail. Taciturn, almost ill-at-ease with the merriment around him, he stayed on the edges, orchestrating it all, urging his two servers to keep circulating and selling, making sure every bottle of Presidente was wrapped in a serviette as is the inexplicable Dominican custom, every table scrubbed as soon as it was vacant, ashtrays emptied. But he was reluctant to participate. When he did, he was unfailingly warm and pleasant.

The joint was crowded which—just before Christmas and all the way to Easter—was its normal state because, in a tropical tourist town, there's no distinction between Saturday night and Tuesday night.

I surveyed the scene and again realized this confederacy of drunken foreigners was one of the things I enjoyed the most about LT.

Lacking the UN's translation facilities, the standard forms of communication at Big Dave's were English and laughter, usually at the good-natured expense of somebody else at the tables.

The long-termers were easy to spot but difficult to know. It can be a hard place for a nosy fucker like me who really enjoys finding out people's stories. The protocol here was unspoken but simple. Ask once. If you didn't get an answer, you didn't ask again. You could weasel out the declassified stuff pretty easily—past work places if any, family arrangements if any, education, and such. What you usually didn't get, beyond vagaries, were the details of the flight that brought them here and their various sources of income to support themselves once they'd arrived. But it was a happy chore to gain, over time, some understanding of the why of it all by assembling the scraps of information dropped on Big Dave's white plastic tabletops.

The other thing I discovered soon on was that everyone in our little crowd rarely used and perhaps didn't even know the last names of their fellow members.

Stuffed into the nooks and crannies of my wee brain is a bunch of trivia, one factoid being that all the financiers and politicians designing the US Federal Reserve System during ten days of secret meetings in Georgia on the exclusive Jekyll Island in 1910 also used their first names only.

Our little group wasn't quite that productive, but I'm thinkin' we had a whole lot more fun.

Sweeping Generalization #117: The long-termers down here were all running from something. Even me. But, in true Canadian fashion, the only thing I was escaping was shitty weather. I was on a six-month stretch; most of these guys and gals were permanent expats, a status that gave them the edge on us part-timers.

In my books, they deserved this position because they knew a lot more about the goings on in our town and because they had had the courage to not be in their homelands anymore. It takes real balls to pack up, sell, or abandon their former lives and countries, permanently and with no assurances beyond the target of a different and better life somewhere else. I do realize that for some—perhaps many—they didn't really have a choice to stay or go but still, they had the stones to make the move.

Here tonight as I stepped into the well-lit courtyard, I scanned the place and, near as I could tell, just about all the regulars I knew were in place in the nearly-full bar.

At first glance, the only face—and voice—missing was Sally's.

Sally Bartlett, she of Denver, had been my entree into this club. I knew Sally and her husband, Paul, because last winter—up until I bought my condo—I had rented their house while they were building another one next door. That new house was to be their full-time home in retirement while they would continue to rent out the place I was in. In the mean time, Sally had to content herself with winters here, returning to Colorado in the summer.

Blonde, 60ish, Sally was loud and gregarious, always exuding energy and confidence with a massive smile that never seemed to desert her. She was like a one-person earthquake, a force of nature. And she could always give as good as she got in this largely male crowd.

Actually, I had seen her husband just once, last year before Christmas, when he'd come down near the start of the construction project which was completely Sally's baby. My memory of him was that he was a quiet guy which was just as well. The couple would, I supposed, not have lasted 35 years together if they both had been hurricanes; it'd be a mutually destructive perfect storm. As Sally threw herself into the LT scene, she once characterized him in that flamboyantly loud voice she had as "s-o-o-o-o bor-r-r-ing." But you knew she was kidding.

Paul didn't quite fit into our beer clique, largely, I suspected because he wasn't a regular. He had a full-time job running an outfitting company with his brother that took precious urbanites on extended summer and winter camping trips into the back country near Denver. Obviously, there's a business in upcharging for the "pioneer spirit," but stopping short of recreating the Donner experience. He'd only manage to make it to the DR for a couple of weeks each winter.

That made him a lot like the guest at a party who arrives late and so sticks out because he hasn't been drinking at nearly the same rate as everyone else.

In Paul's absence, Sally had immersed herself in a variety of local causes, chief of which was setting up a sort of informal finishing school for Dominican and Haitian teenagers at the local library. Actually, she said, it was more a starting school. A lot of the girls hadn't received much of an education, but were smart and ambitious and didn't want to have babies or become hookers, two major life choices in a Dominican resort town. For the boys, she saw it as a chance to improve their resumés—after first learning how to write them. That's where I came in. Three winters ago, when I barely knew her, she took the fact that in a previous life I taught English in the Bahamas and combined it with her standard tactic of public shaming and recrimination. The result: she strong-armed me into holding ESL classes.

In my first year of coming down here, I learned to travel light, usually just my trusty bowling bag, but, thanks to Sally, that bowling bag is now crammed with 20 T-shirts that I pick up on sale in Canada at Old Navy or Giant Tiger. They're covered with designs and slogans that I don't understand but neither do the kids who turn up to my English language class at the *bibliotecha* in town. They are the poorest in a poor village and don't often go to any school. But they want the T-shirt, so most stayed, especially after I discovered that it was a whole lot smarter to give the T-shirts out after a few lessons instead of on the first day, like I did my first year.

By then, the kids were enthralled by my warmth and charm.

Sally wasn't a dreamer; she was a doer. She'd imagine practical solutions to community problems then roll up her sleeves and get busy. She cajoled Nick into leading *Basura* Days in Las Terrenas. He press-ganged expats—including *moi*—and locals into work crews that methodically cleaned up all the litter in abandoned lots, on the streets, and along the banks of the small river/drainage ditch that snaked through the town to the sea. He was a shrewd choice because when Nick—being an ex-biker and all—tells you to pick up the garbage, you fucking well pick up the garbage.

We got to feel good about doing good and the Dominican kids whom we worked alongside got 200 pesos each for picking up all the mounds of trash they had helped to create. She begged or borrowed—maybe stole, for all I knew—45-gallon blue plastic garbage barrels and then secured the city's agreement to empty them regularly.

It was Sally who had recruited a bunch of kids—and paid them out of her own pocket—to whitewash the graffiti-covered 10-foot concrete wall that separated the cemetery on the beach from the front doors of Club Jam disco across the street from it. She then ran an art contest to have the kids paint 8 by 12-foot murals of Dominican life. We all kicked in for the prizes—every art crew got one—and the results were spectacular. That took place three years ago. Since then, as she had predicted, no graffiti—not one spray-painted tag—had been added to about 200 running feet of wall.

And it was Sally's nagging voice I heard—this past fall before I came down here—that told me to do the right thing with the $200,000 I had been given by my buddy, journalist Steve Golding, for turning over to him the book exclusive chronicling the shitshow I had just emerged from. The right thing, I thought, was to buy a 2003 E-One Freightliner Pumper 1250/1000 for the hithertofore vehicle-less Las Terrenas volunteer fire department. The fire truck cost about half that, but with currency exchange, shipping from Branson, Missouri, and assorted equipment, the bill came to $198,678.

It had been delivered c/o Sally some weeks before I arrived. I had wanted the gift to remain anonymous but it didn't work out that way. Thank Christ for the merciless jeers from my drinking buddies. Unless you had been born hydrocephalic, there was no way you could get a swelled head around these sarcastic asshats.

To make sure the pumper didn't just sit there, pragmatic Sally roped a vacationing New York City firefighter into giving up two of his ten days of holiday to teach the local lads how to use it.

Most of the other regulars at Big Dave's I knew pretty well. As well as I ever would.

I probably got along best with Nick, a burly American who was about 5' 10" in either direction. Going by his numerous tattoos of skulls and revolvers and Harleys covering his well-muscled torso and arms, Nick was an ex-biker. He was from New Jersey. If you said "Joisey" in that mocking way, he'd just tell you to fuck off. And he'd mean it, his wide smile briefly disappearing. And you wouldn't ever say Joisey again. But other than that bit of touchiness, it was immediately clear that, while Nick may very well have been born to run, he was also born to laugh.

Inexplicably perhaps, he found me funnier than hell and it's hard not be in performance mode when you know you have a ready audience. Bonus: our beer-drinking routine was simpatico and there's something like instant camaraderie when you're always ordering then pissing then re-ordering then re-pissing at the same rate.

Nick told me he wasn't ever going back to the States and, like Sally, had fully thrown himself into life in the Dominican. He had become fluent in Spanish. He built three homes clustered around a large swimming pool in his walled compound, then married a wonderful Dominican woman named Yafrete who occasionally showed up with him at Big Dave's. She was beautiful and quiet and had a smile by which you could find your way home in the dark.

Nick never told me why he was in permanent exile from the US. I asked of course, but an answer was not forthcoming. Like I said, you learned to never ask again. I presumed some figurative and perhaps literal bridges had been burned during his motorcycle clubbing days. I doubted his club was comprised of weekending accountants, dentists, and tax lawyers wearing thousands of dollars of brand new leathers and accessories astride shiny new Harleys worth tens of thousands of dollars.

Nick loved all things mechanical and when he built his homes, he also had a good-sized garage put up where he spent hours tinkering with bikes—either his three or motorcycles belonging to a lot of other people who'd cover the cost of parts plus give him a few pesos.

Only when he was a grease monkey would he wear a tattered cut-off jean jacket. On its back, you could see the outline of a large patch which had once been sewn on. Maybe it had been the New Jersey Devils' hockey team logo, but I didn't think so.

At the school he dubbed Miss Sally's Preparatory Academy of Refinement, Nick occasionally taught small engine repair, pretty well a mandatory life skill in a country that runs on 120 c.c. motorcycles.

To the question of why and how he had picked Las Terrenas, Nick, rather obtusely,  said that he was not comfortable in Caberete, a couple of hours west along the north coast as though they were the only two choices on the goddamned planet. In Caberete, he told me, he'd have to wear long-sleeved shirts to hide his ink from the French Canadian Hells Angels who had decided that the town was a perfect vacation spot for their club whose Harleys were up on blocks for the winter back home.

Caberete was regarded as one of the safest towns in the DR because, as Nick put it, the Angels didn't piss in their own pool. And they apparently took violent exception to anyone who did. On the other hand, a bar owner in LT told me it was cheaper to operate in our town because there was only the police to pay protection to and not the extra levy the Angels charged in Caberete. But he also allowed that at least with the Angels you were guaranteed to get your money's worth.

Nick sometimes hung around with a skinny, red-headed Canadian kid named Jeff. While Nick was the mechanic, not giving a good goddamn what the bikes looked like as long as they ran, Jeff was the decorator, shipping box loads of cheap gee-gaws down from Canada so the bike owners could trick out their rides with plastic and metal tassels and bangles and chains and glo-bands and such.

Jeff was also a wizard with spray paint, producing intricate designs with never much room to work on the narrow *motoconcho* frames. He almost cried when I hired him to paint up the new town fire truck. He wanted to put those huge dragster flames on the side but I talked him out of it. A little too much irony—even for me.

Nick didn't appear to need the money but Jeff, on the other hand, clearly did. He had joined the Dominican legion of hustlers and dealers, always trying to make a buck because he had to. Both were off the books but, near as I could tell, everybody here was off the books. Nick must have had some money when he came down here and he made more by renting out two of the three villas he had built on his large plot of land.

As apparently naive as Nick was world-wise, Jeff had lived in Las Terrenas for three years but, owing to his freckled fair skin, he always looked like he'd just stepped off the plane. Two winters ago, I had a beer with him while he was nervously waiting for someone to show up to buy something—that's as much detail as I got—and I asked him about living here. I was particularly interested in the crime rate as I was thinking about buying.

"Some break-ins, that's about it," Jeff said, then dropped his voice. "Except a couple of months ago, a French tourist renting a villa up in the hills got broken into. He tried to stop them and they shot him."

I mentioned the break-in gone wrong to Nick.

"That was no B&E; that was a hit," he said as casually as any comment made on yesterday's weather.

There was this 75-year old Brit who was at Big Dave's every night I was there and, others confirmed, every night I wasn't there. He sat and walked with a stoop that became even stoopier with beer. He was a tall guy, rail thin, with a prominent jaw and shock of white hair he obviously self-barbered in that Keith Richards modified rooster cut. He wouldn't give his real name, referring to himself only as "Miguel." Bit by bit, he'd play a story out, with the volume of forthcoming details being directly proportional to the volume of forthcoming beers. He'd been in LT for ten years, living solely and modestly on his UK pension and government benefits. He carped incessantly about how close to the bone his financial situation was and he wasn't ever first in line to repay the beers bought for him.

The thing was, once you got past Miguel always kvetching about how poor he was (and that was a big boulder to move) he was entertaining as hell. He'd seen a lot, done a lot, and knew a lot.

"Always be curious," he had advised me, in line with my father's comment years ago: "Poor goddamned day if you don't learn something."

I was really curious about whether or not Miguel could remember any of our conversations. I like to get a beer-induced dynamo hum going as much as the next person—OK, OK, maybe a little more than the next person—but Miguel would get staven, barely ambulatory to the point that even for me he was embarrassing to watch. Dead sober, he was an ungainly man, but shit-faced he was a giant weaving scarecrow, clearing the uneven sidewalks of pedestrians as he'd meander uptown to his hole-in-the-wall apartment near the Haitian barrio.

"Why do you think we go to Mojito's?" Nick once asked me, referring to a beachfront bar our gang visited some times.

"Pretty swell view?" I guessed.

"We can get that fuckin' view anytime. We go because Miguel won't. He won't pay the extra 50 pesos a beer, says it's robbery. We all got sick of his bitching a long time ago. We need a break. And the guy gets fucked up every night. *Every* night."

You never saw Miguel much during the day; presumably he was sleeping off the nightly jag. When you did spot him in sunlight, he was usually hanging around the biggest grocery store. He seemed to know more of the locals than most of the expats. He'd always be in animated conversation with the *motoconcho* or taxi drivers or the Haitian sidewalk art dealers.

I once complimented him on his assimilation.

"That's only thanks to the sodding British Tax department which keeps me a pauper," he told me. "I can relate to these people on a socio-economic level."

He claimed he gone to school at Cambridge. Claimed he had roomed with the future prime minister of Sri Lanka. Another night, he claimed to have been on the original engineering team for the revolutionary vertical lift-off Harrier jet fighter.

"Miguel" was old enough to not quite understand the true power of the Internet in combination with an aforementioned nosy little fucker such as myself. Because the English take pictures of everything and write histories of everything, it took me less than an hour to check out his story. Why I wanted to investigate his claims is another question to which there is no clear answer.

First, I started with the former Prime Minister of Sri Lanka. Of course he has an autobiography and enough other pieces written about him to confirm his years at Cambridge and the fact that he had a roommate named Michael for one semester with whom he had engaged in Tom Brown-type school hijinks. Armed with a specific year and a college within the university, I then switched over to Cambridge class photos. There in the back row of one was the tall, gawky, lantern-jawed, and newly-minted Dr. Michael Bowering. The same Dr. Michael Bowering who was present for several photos of the engineering group at Hawker Siddeley that I found in the company's on-line archives.

That didn't of course explain how or why Dr. Michael Bowering discovered himself on the north-east corner of Hispaniola for the last decade but, judging by his humble lifestyle, if he had quit engineering to become a career criminal he wasn't very good at it. And if the British government wanted him, it wouldn't be sending him benefit cheques. So I assumed his quest for anonymity was either love- or family-related or he maybe was just bat-shit crazy. He didn't seem that unbalanced. A drunk maybe, but not unhinged. Although really, who knows?

Oddly perhaps—or not—another Brit was also a near-permanent resident at Big Dave's. About my age, Trevor was one of those Graham Greene-type Brits who loved their homeland but would not, under any circumstances, ever live there again. He hadn't set foot on UK soil for thirty years and likely wouldn't for another thirty, if cirrhosis didn't claim him first. In those thirty years, he'd lived, he said, in Venezuela, Colombia, Jamaica, Bermuda, Belize, Mexico, and the Bahamas.

Nick said that Trevor was a bullshit artist but Nick was wrong, at least about Trevor's travels. In a previous life, I made good money as a corporate PR slut that allowed me and my wife at the time to make at least two trips a winter to sunnier places. My frequent southern holidaying intersected with some of the places Trevor said he'd lived and he knew things about them that he could only have known by having been there—unless he'd spent a huge amount of time studying Google images. The crooked lighthouse in Puerto Morelos, the renovated customs building in St. George's harbour, the cost of "meat" patties on Doctor's Cave Beach, the re-location of the casino from Freeport to Lucaya.

It's a simple and wonderful fact that when you go to a lot of different places, you see a lot of different things. Comparing notes with someone else who's also been to those places is a marvellous way to make them live again. So he and I did that.

In all those places—and now, as of two years ago, here in LT—Trevor was involved in "development work," the fuller description of which never seemed to follow. It must have been a part-time job because Trevor was always in Big Dave's when I was there. Unlike Miguel, his prodigious beer consumption did not ever seem to cause drunkenness, only a very big gut.

Trevor's only constant—besides beer and "real" football—was his search for fish n' chips that would remind him of the home he would never voluntarily visit again. Trevor allowed that Rosita and Maria, the Mexican cooks in the cantina, had acquitted themselves wonderfully after following his instructions on how to make the beer batter.

From time to time, Margaret and/or Dot would be at Dave's. They formed a middle-aged couple from Ohio who had opened a B&B in Las Terrenas seven years ago. They'd bicker like any married couple but, like only some married couples, they were obviously in love, continuously happy to be free to be themselves in a place where no one gave a shit how you lived.

No peas in the proverbial pod, Margaret and Dot seemed to enjoy their vast differences. They complemented and complimented each other perfectly. Margaret was tall, severe-looking, the pragmatist of the duo, who concerned herself with bookings, budgeting, staff management, and such, while Dot was the shorter, rounder dreamer who supplied the Mariposa B&B with a New Age-y vibe that obviously appealed to a certain *Eat, Pray, Love* crowd.

Then there was Francesco whom everyone, including himself, called Frank. He was a tall, graceful Dominican property maintenance guy for several of the condo complexes in town including mine. Even though he couldn't have been 30, he ran teams of gardeners, security guys, plumbers, painters, and electricians to tend to the physical problems that come with living in the tropics—rapidly fading paint, rapidly rotting wood, rapidly growing gardens, rapidly rusting metal, and rapidly pissed-off owners and tenants.

With his cell phone constantly ringing, he really seemed to enjoy—and was good at—handling all problems great and small. He was always smiling and speaking patiently—in English, French or Spanish. I know that, faced with the same situation, I'd be answering every insistent call with "How about you fuck off? Oh, sorry, there's another call; hold please. Hello? Yeah? How about *you* fuck off?" and so on.

Unlike the foreigners, Frank was mostly open about his past. He was from the sparsely populated northeastern highlands near San

Francisco de Macoris—and when he wasn't on his cell—he told his story with pride—leaving his small and poor village for school in Santo Domingo, doing well in business administration then hired as the assistant property manager for a gated community in Santo Domingo. And then, like many Dominicans, he had emigrated to New York but, unlike most Dominicans, he came home after a couple years, not only because of the shitty weather but as he put it: "because of all the shitty rules."

I asked him why he hadn't returned to Santo Domingo and instead had picked Las Terrenas. That's when his previously detailed history got a little fuzzy.

"This seemed like the best place for me," he said.

And, indeed, LT appeared as though it was a good place for him to be. He told me he was branching out into construction projects and already had a twelve-unit condo construction gig on the go not too far from my place.

"I know all the tradesmen anyway, so why not make some real money?"

And if his 24/7 on-call status wasn't enough to keep him busy, in his spare time, he had a sort of one-man telecommunications consulting firm that set up and operated the Claro or Orange wireless accounts for most, if not all the expats. Except me.

He seemed to have a ball cajoling and haranguing me about becoming a wireless customer of his. Even in the DR, I was a dinosaur, using only a land line in the apartment I was rarely in, whereas young and old, native or expat here had all apparently succumbed to the global notion that you had to be staring at a little blinking device every fucking minute of every fucking day.

Frank was a pleasant antidote to Mad Tim, a stocky little Irish expat who had operated a car and bike rental place in town for the last eight years. In the briefest of conversations with him, it was abundantly clear that Mad Tim had earned his nickname, not because he was insane but because he was angry about a lot of things. To listen to him tell it, Tim apparently hated absolutely everything about the DR. With or without Presidente (which he of course hated when compared to Guinness), Tim railed against everything—the state of the roads, the schools, the littering problem, the electricity problem, the corruption—everything. He once described the DR—and I'm quoting here—as "hell on earth." I had to ask him if he had ever been to *Cite de Soleil* next door in Haiti to do some comparison shopping about possible rings of hell.

"Well, ya know, it's feckin' honest there, isn't it?" he said in that rising lilt that got louder and angrier with each additional word. "It's a feckin' cock-up from the start and no one thinks different so that's the rules ya play by. Here, they feckin' pretend they're all civilized and progressive, but it's a feckin' nation of thieves and liars and whores!"

You learned to locate yourself some distance from Mad Tim when he was delivering one of his angry sermons with Bill Cowher-like intensity. Otherwise you'd wind up damp from the spit.

Eventually, after a few of these volcanic tirades—just like everybody else—I had to ask him precisely why he continued to live in hell. His answer to me—and to everybody else—was that hippie-esque "everybody's gotta be somewhere" line that meant fuck-all back in the 60s and even less today, what with the decline of psychotropic drug use and all.

Mad Tim—as with most LT residents, native or foreign—would do just about anything for a buck. Last winter, partly to explore my winter country and partly because I often love listening to a good rant, I had hired him and one of his rental cars, an SUV "because the feckin' roads here are a feckin' national disgrace!" as Tim put it. We went to the spectacular El Limon waterfall. "See the feckin' horses they rent out? They don't feed them enough and expect them to carry all those bloody fat tourists." To the remote village of Las Galeras "look how they're feckin' ruining the beach with those bloody dune buggies!" and over the mountains to Samana Bay which we boated across to Los Haitises national park "where they allow feckin' poachers to fish. Protected, my Irish ass!"

The thing about Mad Tim was that he had an absolute heart of gold and would help anybody who needed it. Plus, he amused the shit out of us and didn't seem to mind the question somebody asked him every time he showed up at Big Dave's:

"So, Tim, care tell us what's feckin' pissing you off today?"

Then there was Vlad whom we, of course, called the Impaler. He was a burly bear of a Pole who had escaped the Soviet Republic on a black market passport to work illegally in Germany before getting to Canada where he proved to the authorities that he'd be pretty well fucked if he ever went back to home to Mother Poland. Even after the Soviet death star imploded.

Vlad did nothing quietly and his deep laughter boomed around the quasi-courtyard of Big Dave's.

I made quite the faux pas by asking him if he had been to the diner newly established in LT to serve the growing population of Russian émigrés. I had checked it out. They didn't appear interested in expanding their market niche. I couldn't tell you the name of the place because its small street sign—and menu—were only in Cyrillic and no one welcomed me or even smiled, much less spoke to me when I walked in. They just stopped talking and waited for me to turn around and walk out. There was a small grocery store attached to the restaurant where, presumably, Russians could buy all manner of dough- and root vegetable-related products, just like at home.

Vlad was pretty emphatic in his explanation for his avoidance of the grocery store/restaurant.

"I geeve no money to fuck-keeng Russians."

Somebody—it could've been me—pointed out that he shared his

first name with the current and likely permanent President of Russia, although not Putin's fitness level.

"He's Vladi*mir*; I am Vladi*slov*!" he angrily sputtered before realizing his chain was being yanked and he boomed out a laugh and punched me in the shoulder. Hard.

Representing the aforementioned evil empire was Sergei. Maybe forty, Sergei operated the only bookstore in Las Terrenas. He was in great shape. I know this because he'd whizz by me on the beach from time to time, jogging at a fair clip while he swung hand weights. Sergei and I got along just fine. He loved to discuss literature with me and geopolitics even though he could count on me to take a "they're all childish fucks pissing up a tree" stance. His English was way better than Vlad's although he told me he hadn't been outside Russia before turning up in LT four years ago whereas Vlad had lived in Toronto for fifteen years.

In the multi-lingual universe of Las Terrenas, it's hard to get real cute or punny in just one language. Business-like Sergei had put a sign up over his book store simply saying "Books*Livres*Libros*книгами" and true to his word, he sold English, French, Italian, Spanish, and Russian books. Mostly dog-eared paperbacks that had been consigned to him by departing tourists not keen to pay outrageous excess baggage fees again to lug them back home.

I was a regular at Sergei's store. No telling when a particularly literate vacationer had dumped enough reading material to fill a steamer trunk.

Sergei amused the fuck out of me. Not just because he was wittier in his second language than most people are in their first, but because he was passionate about his books, tending to them like a conscientious shepherd, carefully placing them by genre, fussing with them as he ordered them on his shelves, by language, by alphabet.

"I notice you don't seem to have a lot of the Russian classics," I mentioned.

"Jake, when you're on the beach in the sun, how often have you been seized by the desire to re-read *War and Peace* or *Crime and Punishment* or *The Gulag Archipelago*? No? It's the same for Russians. And by the way, you barbarian, Grisham goes *after* James Lee Burke. Is the alphabet a problem for you?"

"Naw, just fuckin' with you," I admitted. "I'm the same way as you with my books. Otherwise 'Things fall apart; the centre cannot hold'..."

"...Mere anarchy is loosed upon the world," Sergei concluded. "Yeats could have been Russian."

For a brief while last winter, I was caught in a personal DMZ between the Russian—whom I liked because he was studious, funny, and articulate—and the Pole—whom I also liked but because he was chock full of amplified zest, with no room for nuance.

Full disclosure: Lydon, my family name, had been changed from Lysiak a couple of generations ago by my grandfather who had either wanted to fit into his new country or erase any connection to his old one. I'm half-Ukrainian, although not a practising one. Fact is, ethnic background still exerts a tug, like the moon acting on ocean tides. I had an unreasonable reason to be mistrustful of Poles as they had owned my notional fatherland for about five hundred years. On the other hand, Russia's attempted genocide under Stalin and then Putin's continual fucking with Ukraine also pissed me off.

Oddly, that made them both a little suspicious of me which was the only thing they had in common other than their animosity towards each other. This suspicion did not prevent them from sharing their assessment of each other with me.

"Fuck-keeng Russian sqvarehead," Vlad would hiss every time Sergei rolled into Big Dave's.

"Sometimes I miss the good old Soviet days," Sergei had mused, "when we owned their peasant asses."

But towards the end of last winter Vlad and Sergei made peace with each other and we were all glad. Both are sterling fellows and good guys can always put aside old wounds when they just stop picking at the scabs and realize that neither has ever deliberately caused the other any grief. They drowned their differences with shot after shot of Big Dave's bottom shelf vodka one night last winter that I was privileged to witness. It all could've gone horribly awry as these booze-soaked encounters often can, but they overcame it with the underlying warmth of brawling Irish brothers.

I use this national stereotype with complete authority because I saw Mad Tim's County Cork eyes mist up watching the make-up session.

By the end of the evening, Vlad and Sergei were cheek-smooching in that endearing but manly and manful Slavic way.

"Perestroika?" I called out.

"Fuck off!" they had shouted back in unison and we all laughed like hell and had another round.

Another regular was Pietro, like me a six-monther, who would return to his family's ten thousand-acre estate/winery/dairy farm outside Venice for the Italian summer. He was a relatively small, relatively quiet, gentle guy in his mid-thirties who had an easy smile and a swell allowance from his *padre*.

I had asked him about the acquisition of his excellent English. He attributed it to his five years in America.

"Where?" I had asked.

"Oklahoma."

While trying to picture this shy heir to a 10-generation-long Italian legacy fortune wandering around the buckle of the American Bible Belt, he filled in the blanks.

"They have wonderful evangelicals there."

Pietro never pushed his born again-ness, never really even mentioned it, but he did like his beer and apparently the company of sinners and reprobates.

Whenever he was around, we made the effort to yell "For Pete's sake!" instead of "For Christ's sakes!" as loud as we could. And Pietro would smile his goofy smile.

Pietro was an easy guy to talk to and he was usually keen to talk. He liked anything to do with America—starting with the vastness and the variety of things.

"In America, you can make yourself what you want," he explained. "Everything is big and new. In *Italia*, everything is small and old. There is not much room to grow, to flower."

I pointed out there probably was enough room for things to grow on his father's 10,000-acre estate, surely one of the largest in the country. For a man given to horticultural references, Pietro didn't appear to have a fucking clue about farming. I had spent some early teen summers on an uncle's farm south of Ottawa. That was hard work and it showed with some added muscle and many added calluses. Pietro, he of the soft pink hands and slight but doughy frame, allowed that his duties were largely supervisory but even that didn't wash. This was not a leader of men.

But he was pretty keen on being a follower. "This year," he told me "I will be ordained soon by my church and will have the duty to preach wherever I go."

"Just a hint, Pete," I had advised him. "You might want to make Big Dave's a sermon-free zone. It's probably safer that way."

A not-quite regular at Big Dave's was Jose Ignacio Maria Gonzalez, Attorney-at-law. Using his initials, we called him Jim or Yim which soon devolved into Jimmy and sometimes Yimmy. Patrician and dapper as hell, Jose was a prince of a guy. Proud of his lineage, he explained that his particular branch of the Spanish Gonzalez family had had its roots in the Dominican for about 500 years as prosperous landowners. Mad Tim offered an alternate theory, that Yim's ancestor had more likely been a stowaway on the Pinta and a former grave robber.

Jim personally or through one of his eight lawyers in his firm handled pretty well all the legal matters—criminal or civil—for our particular tribe of expats, which is perhaps why he put up with our abuse. I imagined that his appearance at Dave's was much like wandering into his office waiting room—only with beer and drunken arseholes.

Another semi-regular—who wasn't there on this night, I noticed—was Bruce, a real estate agent from St. Louis. When I had decided to buy towards the end of my third winter of long-term renting, I picked his name off a website and hired him as my agent. On the job, he was always crisp, immaculately dressed, and as smooth-talking as *cremosa* peanut butter.

Off the job, he was a strange guy. You couldn't tell at first but he was the most dyed-in-the-wool conspiracy theorist I had ever met.

Long-time paranoid that he was, he had obviously become accustomed to ridicule over all the global Byzantine plans that he and apparently he alone could see. He was especially mocked around the tables at Big Dave's—but the more jeers he took, the more unshakeable he became in his general belief that some combination of corporations and government and religion were consciously responsible for everything bad that had ever happened to mankind over the last two thousand or so years.

Actually, I more or less agreed with him. It's just that I didn't think any of it was co-ordinated, covert, and globally deliberate. Rather, I thought they haphazardly fucked things up pretty much in the open because all these institutions are big, slow and dumb, which, almost by definition, did big, slow, and dumb things. They did not however resort to planting explosives in the corners of the Twin Towers, did not cause every major war in history so they could make money off banking fees, and they did not fluoridate tap water to render us all docile, dumb bunnies—we did that all on our own.

But give Bruce enough time and beer and he'd likely make the case that Adam planted the assassination bug in Cain's ear. To be honest, you didn't ever want to give him enough time and beer. He became more insistent, louder, and less humorous the more he drank and the deeper he got into the wheels within wheels of his maze of plotters down through the ages.

That was pretty well it for the regulars at Big Dave's with me being one of the most recent full-fledged inductees. In this current year, I saw there were a few newbies trying to work their way into the line-up: Henrik, a soft-spoken Swede (I apologize for the redundancy) who, despite having been rolled by a hooker in Punta Cana, loved the country and Klaus, a really funny German (I apologize for the contradiction) who was about my age and hair-length.

Lest anyone get the idea I was just a wobbly by-stander, I was not spared the gang's good-natured mockery. Not unlike a high school football coach or a boxing instructor I once had, these people would zero in on obvious things and then ride the piss out of you. My long hair, my seemingly endless wardrobe of Hawaiian shirts, my Canadian-ness were all fair game. (and I don't give a shit what you say, I've never heard a fellow citizen of the Great White North say "a-boot" for "about", and although we do say "eh?," it's the same kind of sentence-ender the Yanks use when they say "huh?" and the Brits say "yeah?" So piss off, will ya!)

And lest anyone get the idea that we were permanently anchored to Big Dave's, we occasionally took our collective embodiment of the clinical definition of alcoholism to Mojito's on Playa Popy beach east of the town centre. A great setting, good food, and beer that was 50% more expensive than at Big Dave's—which most of us had to seriously consider when drawing up the ol' monthly budget. The place was run by two delightful Cuban brothers—Juan Carlos and Ivan (I swear!).

Because I'd been to Cuba a bunch of times, we talked about their homeland at length. When I asked them why and how they'd left, they clammed up instantly and I had to apologize. There was a pile o' pain and unpleasantness there that I'd blundered upon and I had felt bad for messing up their usual sunniness. If they harbored any resentment for my intrusion, they hid it and we always got along famously after that, even when I bitched about their two-for-one Happy Hour not including Tanqueray.

"We are poor, not stupid," Ivan had memorably remarked as he reached for the house brand gin.

And lest anyone also get the idea that Big Dave's and Mojito's were the only two bars in Las Terrenas, they're not. There are at least thirty candidates. We could've just as easily been group-ensconced at The Drunken Octopus but that place skewed young, with loud 90s music—if you can call it music—tourist-aimed prices, and altogether too many cutesy names like 'Goody-goody Mahi-mahi' on the plastic-coated menu.

West of my place—making it too far to stumble for most of my friends—was Michel's and a couple of other beach bars that I visit alone sometimes, chiefly because I'm normally not very sociable or even friendly. Days go by—here and up in Canada—when the only conversations I have are with myself. A lot of these unspoken chats aren't at all interesting to anybody—including me.

But I like to hold these roundtable discussions for one on the beach that is so unlike Florida's. For one thing, there's an endearing building code which dictates that the height of any building here can't be any greater than the height of the swooping, 40-foot palms. Look left or right, up and down most Florida beaches and you see: A) a ten-story unbroken palisade of condos and B) not a single fucking tree.

The other big distinction is the amount of rules. In Florida, they'll fine your ass for all sorts of infractions. That winter I spent there I watched over-zealous beach patrols emptying onto the sand all the booze and beer they'd confiscated from pissed-off vacationers. Here in the DR, I think you're penalized if you *don't* drink on the beach. The single inviolate law is: you don't get to use the loungers under the *palapa* umbrellas unless you're buying from the bar that provided them.

Our gang could also have invaded the bar area of L'Angosta's in Fishermen's Village. We never discussed it amongst ourselves but I'm pretty sure it was implicitly agreed that our rowdy horde's presence in the quasi-elegant piano lounge would not have gone over well with the owner.

On this particular night, I stayed much longer than usual at Big Dave's. Actually, I shut the fucker down, the motley crew having dissipated at various points in the evening until there was just Big Dave and me, shooting the shit about writing for what seemed like hours. At this time of the night, well, morning really, Dave allowed himself a beer so we sat sipping and talking about books. He knew I had written an international non-seller a few years ago, had actually bought a copy online, and had me autograph it which was real sweet of him. And he seemed happy that I encouraged him to start scribbling. His 35 years in the bar business across the States and now here would, I contended, give him enough material for a whole series of tell-alls.

I finished my beer while he turned off the lights and locked the place up. I helped him stack the chairs and tables, then move their symmetric piles under the awning, to what purpose I never understood.

He was going one way, I the other, so we split up on the sidewalk.

Wandering back down the main street and onto the beach, I had a head full of beer and a heart full of contentment.

CHAPTER FOUR

Even though I have lived a hermetic life for years, I like being around vacation spots. Anywhere south of Florida—and I claim personal vacation knowledge of Barbados, Jamaica, the Caymans, the Bahamas, Bermuda, St Maarten's, three different beach towns in Cuba, five different beach towns in the DR and six in Mexico, as well as living for extended periods in Freeport and Las Terrenas. In every one of those places there is an expansiveness, a fuck-the-way-you-normally-live attitude. After a few days, maybe only hours, in any of these places you can't avoid imagining what it'd be like living there. I can't, anyway.

Heat matters to me. Not manufactured, furnace heat, just the heat of the air for hundreds of cubic miles around you. The kind of heat that makes putting on flip-flops seem like overdressing. The kind of heat that comforts me because it's the same indoors and out, so unlike the dread I used to feel up north when I'd step outside those 8-inch thick insulated walls in January with the understanding that my exposed flesh could freeze in under a minute. I'd spent more than a half-century in Canada circling the thermal wagons for six months every year. Enough is fucking enough. Time for a new plan. I don't have and will never have much money but I do have the burning goal of not ever seeing snow again. My low-grade dose of Aspergers helps with obsessive cheapness.

You always pay more for consumables in these places, but in return, you get surrounded by people who are usually in a good mood. Even the people who have to work. And you're surrounded by the pleasant surroundings that made it a vacation spot to begin with. I got a taste for it when I taught high school in Freeport in the late 70s. During tourist season, the bars were open until 7 or 8 in the morning. I have much first-hand experience that they stayed closed only long enough to sweep out the drunks and cigarette butts before they re-opened again at the crack of 10 a.m.

It's sorta like that where I do my summertime living—in and around a three-season log home on a small lake in cottage country about two hours north-east of Toronto. Once you get past all the government prohibitions designed to take away fun in exchange for a civil and safe society, it's a good life in the middle of all sorts of green stuff and water and loons and, thank Jeebus, a nearby bar.

Jake, you ask, why such an emphasis on drinking? And if you have to ask that question about Caribbean life (or cottage life), you've probably never spent much time in these kind of places. And if you have, you wasted your fucking money.

Now the National Institute of Health says that drinking five or more drinks on the same occasion on each of five or more days in the past 30 makes you a heavy drinker. You're a binge drinker if you have five or more alcoholic drinks on the same occasion on at least one day in the past 30. Down here, that's called Tuesday.

Jake, you continue—and quite judgmentally, may I add—you're a booze addict! Yeah, so? You can *have to* have something and still like it. Take oxygen. I like oxygen.

Mark Twain's delightful defence of his daily scotch drinking is on point.

Mr. Clemens famously observed: "I do it as a preventative of toothache (insert stand-up comedian's dramatic pause). I've never had a toothache, (repeat pause). "I don't ever intend to have a toothache."

There are other health benefits. Hydration is a good thing we are told. I mean, that's why you see nattily dressed morons on a city street clutching their water bottles—no doubt fearful of collapsing and dying of thirst on their three-block walk to the bus stop.

Turns out, there's a fuck of a lot of water in beer. But it's a diuretic you tell me; it actually removes not adds water. Horseshit, I reply. I've done the math. And not just once. We're talking a forty-five-year test period. I know that I usually have to pee after four beers (or 2½ *grandes*), forty-eight ounces of liquid. No way I piss that much. The next whiz usually happens after two more beer. Another twenty-four ounces. Again, I haven't got rid of two and a half quarts so I'm in a water surplus situation as I tuck into my next two. It may very well eventually catch up to me but in the meantime I am fully hydrated. And either feeling great or sleeping.

But Jake, you weigh in—and, frankly, you're starting to bore me—what about all the ugly and messy things you do when you're loaded?

I can see you're dealing in vague generalities. Nastiness happens to some drunks all of the time and some drunks some of the time. But it doesn't happen to all drunks; I'm one of those drunks.

Well, aren't you just superhuman special? you sarcastically comment.

No, Mr. Smartass. I just had the good fortune of having the chicken soup beaten out of me as a teenager by a patron of a seedy bar who was in no mood to tolerate an ignorant, belligerent asshole (that would be me). After the bruises cleared up and the cuts closed, I understood that I'd been given a providential life-lesson, a sort of drinking version of a child touching that hot stove element for the first and last time. Since then, I'm a goddamned sweetheart when I drink.

And speaking of excess—and oxygen—I occasionally examine my fierce addiction to smoking. Smoking takes ten years off your life, we are told. Dr. Denis Leary has it right: "Well it's the ten worst years, isn't it folks? It's the ones at the end! It's the wheelchair-kidney dialysis-adult diaper-fucking years." I have to listen to him; he's a friggin' doctor!

I'm banking heavily on ol' Billy Blake's observation that "the road of excess leads to the palace of wisdom." Although to be honest, I don't much care if I either acquire wisdom or live in a palace. Those would be happy by-products but the road trip's the thing because, as someone not William Blake said: "Getting there isn't half the fun, it's all the fun." As it turns out, I like fun and at a very basic level. Same as I like oxygen.

Jake, you seem awfully defensive, what with your half-assed math and quoting famous people.

Yeah, well you started it! Now fuck off and leave me alone.

It was a little after 2 a.m. when I made it home. I want to say it was a quiet, albeit a somewhat unsteady stroll but it wasn't. The Galaxy Nightclub across the street from Fishermen's Village was just getting cranked up as I passed it, their techno-*bachata* music boom-boom-booming into the street crowded with mostly Dominicans all decked out in their post-disco finery.

By the time I reached Casa del Mar, the air had quietened again. Really the only sound, the eternal sound, was the ocean rolling in, rolling out.

At the gate I checked in with Né-Né, one of four rotating night watchmen who usually could be found fighting off sleep at the barrier he raised for incoming and outgoing vehicles when he wasn't patrolling the lush grounds with his pistol-grip Mossberg 12-gauge shotgun favoured in our community.

I know it's a Mossberg because I looked it up on the Interweb. I do that kinda shit all the time.

The shotgun was for show as you could plainly see the empty breach chamber. I was pretty happy that his employer hadn't seen fit to equip it with shells, which was probably just as well. Né-Né liked to swing it around like he was a teen-aged Iowa baton-twirler practising for the state finals.

I didn't pay particular attention to the police sirens as I drifted off to sleep—or into a temporary coma, if you want to get all nit-picky. That wasn't a rare sound in Las Terrenas, particularly at this time of night.

"Somewhere there's somebody ain't treatin' somebody right," I thought. Well, Bob Seger thought.

# CHAPTER FIVE

The news spread quickly the next morning. A frightened, terrible, angry wave swept over our town, reached me at the grocery store.

A *gringa* had died.

Who, where, when, how, and why were not yet answered, but the what had been.

Murder.

The hushed conversations in English, Spanish, and French down the aisles of the *supermercado* agreed on that.

With no daily local news source, the way you collected and confirmed news in Las Terrenas was by triangulation. Talk to enough people and quite quickly the facts will emerge, the story will build.

By mid-afternoon at the Banco Popular, I had learned the who, the where, and approximately the when.

Sally Bartlett had been killed in her home sometime late last night or early this morning.

I was completely shocked and deeply saddened. Who gets used to hearing that someone you knew has been murdered?

Immediately, I pictured my former landlady.

DR was going to be home—actually, probably already was her true home—and she would involve herself in everything because she viewed the whole country as one giant humanitarian opportunity. She was the tireless epicentre and she could send shock waves out by sheer force of will.

I recalled her gratitude to me for a bit of PR advice I had given her after she returned from a pre-Christmas trip to Santo Domingo to buy dolls to hand out as presents for the Haitian kids. She was mightily pissed off that she could only find Caucasian ones. Call the newspapers, I had told her. It might lead to some purchasing changes at DR Wal-Mart and Costco while racking up some bonus points for expats. She did and got a bunch of stories out of it. Which of course emboldened her to call the media whenever she wanted to address whatever was outraging her at the time.

And now that voice was stilled. Forever.

I left the bank, not knowing what to do or where to do it. Stunned, I started walking and without really thinking headed away from my place east along the Playa Popy road. Just past the police station and Dot and Margaret's Mariposa Inn I stopped at the road's intersection with a narrow, unpaved, winding, and potholy road.

328 yards up that road lay Sally and Paul Bartlett's two houses. I knew the distance because I had walked that road almost every day for four months last winter occasionally counting the number of paces as my particular brand of OCD dictates.

Aw, fuck it, I thought as I started walking up the sandy/gravelly lane.

I didn't have much to do with her last winter when I rented there. I was there to write a book, a follow-up to my first which no one bought and she was preoccupied with her small construction crew putting the place up on the empty lot next door to me. During the whole process, Sally would hover around, shouting comments and instructions in her terrible Spanish to her project manager and chief labourer, Tico, a powerful Haitian who would smile and acknowledge them politely and return to doing what he was doing. Near as I could tell, they would laugh about it at the end of each day.

He kept up his good nature when she would have him undo something he had just finished because it didn't strike her as perfect, and she wanted the place, she told me, to be perfect. For example, she had decided that the plastered walls inside and out were too rough, even though she had asked Tico to make them look Mexican *rustico* as hell. So he spent whole days sanding them down by hand. Then, when the loft apartment was almost finished, she determined, long after they had been installed—we're talking months—that the granite countertops were too dark for the airy look she was going for. So Tico ripped them out and put in new lighter beige replacements.

And once construction was over, she spent maybe a day or day and a half relaxing before throwing herself into the next project: decorating the place to magazine-quality perfection.

She rented Mad Tim and a truck and off they went to Santo Domingo, returning with an apartment-sized stacked washer and dryer, various and sundry small kitchen appliances, a 40-inch flat screen TV, a Bose sound system, a few lamps, and tons of cushions, all in some combination of mid-blue, white and lime green. The rest of the furniture she sourced locally, finding craftspeople to build bookcases, tables, a bed platform out of the same dark-stained wood—mahogany I think—that trimmed the doorways and windows.

Both houses bordered on a large swampy area maybe 50 acres square which Sally in her glass half-full kinda way had christened "protected wetlands" but really was just a grassy watery plain into which all the houses on three sides emptied their sewage systems. On the fourth side to the south, the land rose quickly to steep hills upon which were perched some pretty spectacular villas.

Despite the occasional whiff of human secretions, the plus of having this natural no man's land was that no man with larceny in his heart would cross it. On the minus side, it was a super-incubator for clouds of mosquitoes. Occasionally, the government would spray the area, but mostly you had to get used to defeating the blood-thirsty little fuckers by yourself. Sleeping under nets, spraying the window screens with Off! every night. There was a good reason all the grocery stores featured shelves of sprays, candles, and devices aimed at eradicating nature's most nearly useless creation.

It wasn't just the mosquitoes you had to contend with, but the smaller no see-ums which had migrated inland from the beach areas. These bastardly sand flies were the reason that window screens here were a tighter weave than their North American counterparts. But still some of these microscopic sons of bitches got through.

Sally had just laughed at my collection of red welts and showed me hers. Something else you had to get used to here which, she contended, was a whole lot simpler than bitching about it. And she was right; you did get used to it.

I rounded a bend and saw the cop cars, a van, and a multi-racial crowd milling around. Big Dave was there, so was Nick. Margaret and Dot too.

Usually, I have just about zero empathy. I don't know exactly why this is true but it is. With adults anyway. Kids always make me smile and break my heart but then they grow to adults who, mostly, can go fuck themselves. But I hugged my friends. None of us said a word.

I could see Tico sitting by the side of the road in the brush across from the houses. He was alone and weeping inconsolably. I walked towards him but he shook his arms violently to keep me away.

So there I was standing out front of Sally's—a place that had been cruelly transformed from her tropical fantasy to a crime scene—with Dave, the ladies, and Nick who was so obviously bullshit angry that I feared for the safety of the two policemen assigned to keep people away from the house now girdled in yellow police tape.

I stared up at the new house, at the ornate white burglar bars on the windows through which I could see various figures moving around and the occasional flash of a camera.

Then I recognized someone in the front yard talking to other cops.

"Arty!" I called out to Chief inspector Arturo Diaz. He raised his head, quit his conversation, and walked out of the yard and over to me.

"You should not be here, *Ingles*," the head cop of our region said.

"You kidding me? The sun, the beaches, the friendly people? Where else should I be?"

"You know what I mean. This is not your affair."

"Fuckin' right it's my affair. She was a friend of mine."

That was stretching it a bit. But still.

"You can do nothing," he said gently but firmly.

"I know, but you can," I said. "You can tell us what the fuck happened."

Arturo stiffened up. I should have known that this was not a man who was going to let himself be publicly put on the spot by some foreigner.

"Please. Leave now. All of you," he said with a whole lot of something that smelled like a threat. "And *Ingles*?"

"Yes?"

"You will be in the town for the next several days?"

"Of course."

"Good. I will need to speak to you. And your friends here."

I could see Nick working himself up to a possible outrage, so I pushed against his barrel chest and said: "Cool it, Nick. Let's get out of here."

He backed down and we all turned and trooped back towards the shore road. No one said a word except Nick who uttered one bitter and very loud "Fuck!" All of us likely were dumbstruck by the pointlessness of Sally's death and the helplessness we felt in response.

On the coast road, Dot and Margaret wordlessly peeled off to return to their inn. Dave, Nick, and I trudged back towards the centre of town and straight into the late afternoon sunlight occasionally breaking through the palm trees with near-blinding intensity.

"Beer's on me," Dave finally said which seemed like a good thing to say.

When the three of us reached the bar, we found that it was nearly packed even though Dave hadn't yet opened the place. The full complement of regulars had unstacked the chairs and tables and were now all seated and smoking as though they were quietly waiting for an after-dinner club act to take the stage.

Not surprisingly, the mood at Big Dave's was somber. The regulars who had gravitated there drank in silence. They—we—were uncharacteristically polite, thanking Dave as he delivered the sweating Presidentes. I'm sure I had the same expression as everyone else. Grief for certain, but something else, something like sad astonishment that vicious reality had intruded and stole something, that the perpetual party was, at least for now, over, when it seemed as though it would last unabated forever.

And under it all was a layer of something that had never been a factor before: mistrust. It wasn't just me; I could see the others quickly looking around at their co-mourners. Everyone, I bet, wondering if the guy or the gal next to them was capable of this monstrosity. However brief, it was there. And once there, I remember thinking that no speech, no amount of private conversation, no act could dissolve this suspicion cloud until we actually found out who did this evil.

After a couple of beer, I left. At about the same time, most of the other expats did likewise.

I made it home just as Alejandro, the world's best bartender™, was closing up his pool-side bar for the day. Seeing me, he unlocked his cabinets and freezer.

"*Hola, Senor* Yake," he said in our mutual Spanglish but without his customary smile. "Gin *y tonica*?"

Without waiting for an answer, he mixed the drink—at least a double—and slid it across the stone counter to me.

"Is on the *casa*," he indicated.

"*Mucho gracias.*"

"The *gringa* was your *amiga*?" he asked as I sipped.

"*Si*. She was."

"I am *mucho* sorry, *amigo*. I will leave you now. *Por favor*, lock and put this key here when you are *finito*," he said indicating the stack of napkins.

He briefly rested his hand on my shoulder before he left.

The drink did not refresh, tasted only bitter. So too did the next one. And the one after that.

## CHAPTER SIX

For completely mysterious reasons, I went on a binge the day after we'd learned of Sally's murder. Not drinking but cleaning. I swept, caused toilets and sinks and even the goddamned shower to sparkle, did laundry—sheets and all my clothes—whether they passed the sniff test or not—dusted everything dustable and actual-ly emptied my fridge of everything I could no longer identify. I even took buckets of water to the tiled balcony, sloshing the dirt, cigarette ashes, and dead insects down the drain at one end of the open area before I squeegee-mopped the floors indoors and out.

By the time I was done, I had 1200 square feet of spic n' span. But to be honest, my cleaning jag wasn't one long, ammonia-fuelled frenzy. As I've been doing all my life, I paced myself. In the heat down here, you almost had no choice but to pace yourself. During my imagi-nary union-mandated smoke breaks, I considered Chief Inspector Arturo Diaz.

I had just met him this past November, shortly after I arrived for the winter and Alejandro, the world's best bartender™, had informed me that there was a new head cop in Las Terrenas. Not the head cop for the tourist police. The *policia de turismo* or Cestur was different from the regular police. They were in places like Puerto Plata, Punta Cana, Caberete, and here in Las Terrenas to look concerned and helpful and speak some English—or French, or German—to the short- and long-term renters or owners. They were universally young and smiley and unarmed. They drove colourfully-painted 4X4s that made them look more like they were riding in the company car for a zip lining attraction.

The real policing was done by the regular force, the *policia nacional dominicana*. They had the guns. Their new boss in Las Terrenas was Chief Inspector Arturo Diaz.

In early November, I was sitting at Mojito's drinking alone—which I've never had any problem doing—and watching the sun set over the giant palms lining Punta Popy, the point of land that separated crescent-shaped Popy beach from Ballenas beach in front of my place.

He just sat down across from me with one of those said mojitos in hand and introduced himself. I was a little startled because most expatriates and Dominicans hold this distance between each other and most everyone holds this distance from the police, even cops in civvies as he was. It was only much later when he confessed to me that he was on the job that night, getting familiar with all the characters staying in his town.

He was a little shorter than my 6'0", a good deal lighter than my 220 and some years younger than my 60. Whereas I'm in a constant state of dishevelment, he was casually but impeccably dressed and groomed. And whereas I am almost freakishly clumsy, he moved with an assurance that gave him a graceful, even feline aspect. He was not a big talker—a sort of taciturn Latino Gary Cooper. It finally hit me; he's Lieutenant Castillo from *Miami Vice*, only without the moustache or Olomos' undertaker wardrobe.

Turns out, he has the same trait I either am blessed or cursed with: making snap judgements about people. He decided quickly that I was both harmless and a pretty fair drinking companion. I determined the same about him. So with that out of the way, we drank and talked for hours. By inclination and profession, Arturo asked a lot questions. So do I. For a while there, we were duelling Alex Trebeks.

"You ask a lot of questions, *Ingles*?" he finally said.

"I'm Canadian, not English," I insisted.

He shrugged and then smiled as though he knew it'd piss me off a bit.

That's when I christened him Arty.

At any rate, as the mojitos kept coming, we kept talking.

The fact that we were yakking at length intrigued me. Like his appearance, Arty's English was impeccable.

"I like to read," he said. "I have done so since I was a child. I decided that when I read British or American authors, it should be in their language. Translations are OK, but I trust the true voice of the writer more. So I studied."

He wanted to know how I came to be in Las Terrenas. The question stopped me a bit and he noticed that.

I could have given the long-form answer, telling him about how my late wife, Beth, and I had frequently holidayed in the DR—sometimes renting houses, sometimes pigging out at an all-inclusive. Puerto Plata, Sosua, Caberete, Punta Cana, La Romana. For different reasons, we had enjoyed them all. I particularly liked the north shore because it didn't then and perhaps never would have the hotel development of Punta Cana or La Romana, that were essentially small artificial towns created in the service of the mega-resorts now claiming miles of beachfront.

While staying in Caberete on Kite Beach, Beth and I had gone on a whale-watching trip to Samana Bay. Just before the coast highway turns into the peninsula and down to the bay full of frolicking whales, we could see miles of enchanting, wide, and completely empty beaches, with uniformly tall and graceful palms lining them, the land impossibly green, the sea impossibly blue. We vowed to return one day.

But then she went and died.

Fucking cancer.

So now here I was alone, wintering in the closest town to those endless beaches, sticking to our pledge, in some way a sad echo of the dream we had. I could've told Arty all that and maybe, if we became better friends, I might.

"Internet search," was what I said instead. "This looked like the right-sized town with really good beaches."

In return, I asked him how he became a cop and how he had wound up in LT.

He told me about a teacher of his in Santo Domingo who got him interested in first the Spanish then the English versions of the Sherlock Holmes mysteries. He was nine or ten and he read them all. It's what made him want to be a cop.

"Arty, you must be relieved that it wasn't *The Happy Hooker* you were reading."

Turns out, he was a purist. He thought that the Robert Downey movies were crap. "So little thinking, so much fighting," he pronounced. I agreed although did not admit that I get fascinated when things blow up real good. And things blow up real good in those films.

A silence descended and I realized he hadn't answered my question about why Las Terrenas. Instead he just looked out at the ocean and I shut the fuck up. I wasn't going to ask again.

For a lot of guys who are strangers, sports can serve as a decent icebreaker, so I asked him about his athletic interests.

Arturo told me that he had never played and did not even like baseball. That sort of endeared him to me. Not just because we shared the same pure boredom with the game, but for his rarity on this island. Everyone else seemed to play or watch. Kids with a ball and a stick on the beach, on precisely-measured diamonds, in the deep grass of empty lots, on any sort of flat ground. And all the kids dreaming of becoming the next Sosa or Bautista or Colon. In a form of tradesies, I confessed to having spent my childhood in Canada avoiding the hockey rink.

He smiled.

"So what do you watch in sports?" he asked, looking pointedly at my paunch which led him—elementarily—to conclude that I sure the fuck didn't participate in anything athletic.

"Football not *futbol*. NFL."

"It is likewise with me."

"Raiders, by any chance?"

"No, no. Evil team. I am a fan of the Packers of Green Bay."

"Well, imagine that! You a *cabasa de queso*."

He had actually laughed out loud.

"The season's half over," I said. "You should come over and watch a game."

He paused, got all serious, and thought a while. I was to discover that he did that a lot.

"Perhaps," he had very deliberately answered.

Arty intrigued me and intriguing people usually leave some kind of e-trail on the web so I went tracking.

While most of the articles were in Spanish, and somewhat difficult for me to decipher—even with the alleged automatic translation—it was pretty easy to piece together most of Arty's career.

Ten years ago as a young sergeant in the National District, he was credited with cracking a drug smuggling case that saw the seizure of 100 kilos of "a white substance believed to be narcotics" and the arrest of five sea-going smugglers, a Belgian who owned the yacht and four Dominicans, one of whom was a captain in the national police. During the chase out of Santo Domingo harbour, Arty had been shot in the leg and apparently had almost died from blood loss.

Less than a year later, Arturo, himself now a captain, was gone from Santo Domingo and turned up in Punta Cana according to an article on *DR One* which named him as the lead investigator of the team that was credited with unmasking a shady land developer who, in concert with a corrupt Senator, had fleeced millions out of a host of international investors in a bogus subdivision scheme in Cap Cana.

Three years after that, a Sergeant Arturo brought down a child prostitution ring in Santiago. Owing to his much lower rank, I thought maybe it was a different cop as Arturo Diaz might be a pretty common name, but the article's accompanying picture was of a slightly younger version of Las Terrenas' very own Chief Inspector.

There was a five-year gap in the news stream before Arty turned up in a few small news items, ending with his appointment last summer as the new top cop in LT.

Days had passed since our initial encounter. I had seen him a couple of times. We'd acknowledged each other with a smile, a slight wave. One day on the street, we had briefly spoken and I had volunteered my address in case he was interested in watching a game.

"That is not required," he said.

But that Sunday, he'd showed up at my place, with a six-pack of Stella no less, and we spent a swell afternoon watching his Packers beat the shit out of my Raiders.

You can learn a lot about people by watching them watch sports. I tend to yell at the TV a lot, because something somewhere inside me apparently believes that: A) coaches can hear me, and B) they'll agree with my innovative scheme to prevent the fucking safety blitz that's killing us. On the other hand, Arty never betrayed much in the way of emotion. He'd acknowledge a spectacular, scrambly, off-balance 60-yard Rodgers completed pass on a broken play by leaning slightly towards the big screen and giving an even slighter fist pump.

At halftime, it occurred to me that I hadn't told him where I lived.

"It is my business to know things such as this," he replied.

"What else do you know?"

"You were very generous with your gift of a fire truck to this town."

"I'm not a hero. I just don't want *Pueblo Pescadores* to burn down again. Plus, I sometimes smoke in bed."

"Can you explain where the money came from for your donation?"

Although I knew I didn't have to, I told him about my reporter buddy's turning over 200K from his book deal arising from the international kerfuffle I caused a few months back. Arty interrupted me.

"Ah, yes, you have experienced an active year so far this year."

"So what did you deduce from that, *Senor* Sherlock?" I asked.

"That maybe you are an intelligent man, maybe a good man and, for certain, you are a lucky man."

"Funny, that's what I understand about you."

He had arched an eyebrow and smiled. Then he rolled up his pant leg to show me his bullet wound, a purple, nasty-looking through-and-through.

"I am grateful that Belgian was not very good with a gun," he noted.

"Like I said, you're a lucky man."

In another typical male form of tradesies, I pulled up my Hawaiian shirt to show him the 3-inch scar where a bullet had ploughed through my Buddha belly about four months ago.

"And as *I* said, you are a lucky man," he said.

But Arty didn't offer up anything further on his checkered career in law enforcement. I was dying to ask what he had done to get himself relegated to the sleepy north-east corner of the island but he quickly pointed out that the second half kick-off was about to happen.

Of course, Oakland's 10-point loss had me grumbling.

"We out-passed you, out-rushed you," I complained. "We deserved better."

"The scoreboard says what you deserved, *Ingles*."

We finished our beers and he got up to leave.

"I enjoyed myself, *Ingles*. Thank you."

"I did too, Arty. Do you mind me asking why you came here today?"

"It is possible to learn a lot about a person by watching him watch sports."

CHAPTER SEVEN

On most mornings down here, there is a time when there are moments of magic, a very specific time. These moments happen for me while sitting on the balcony, waiting for the sun to rise, drinking the dark roast native coffee that is nothing if not ambrosial. The sun nibbles at the wall of green and the roosters and the dogs start up and cigarette smoke drifts slowly like three-dimensional batik, its lazy swirls shot through with light. The mourning doves—not a pair but a squadron—start cooing their little heads off and the knobby grass is littered with morning glory flowers that have wilted and dropped unseen in the dark and then, as the sun hits the bougainvillea trees below me in a particular way, they light up like Christmas trees of pink and orange and lavender.

And then it's gone. All the elements are still there but not affected that certain way anymore by those few minutes of first light.

Over my second coffee of the next morning on the balcony, I stared at the blue ribbon of ocean waves visible across the road and thought about Sally. It was disturbing to say to myself the sentence beginning with "The last time I saw her alive..." But the last time I had seen her alive was at Big Dave's a few days earlier. I was drinking and talking with her, Nick, and Margaret and Dot. Actually, we were doing less talking and more listening as Sally was expressing her disappointment that her husband was not going to be making it down to join her for Yuletide in the DR. She bitched and moaned about his work, about him being hell-bent on making money and so on, before getting all sad.

"I miss the big lug. He hasn't been down here for more than a year."

"We're still going ahead with dinner on the beach, aren't we?" Nick asked.

Apparently Nick was like a big kid about Christmas. It had been Sally's idea but Nick took over the logistics of getting shit out to the deserted and spectacular Playa Coson about a 15-minute drive west of town. He had arranged transport for BBQs and propane and fish and lobsters and chairs and tables, plates and cutlery, and even a fake Christmas tree. He was going to buy the fresh shrimp, lobsters, and fish the day after tomorrow, I remembered. Dave's job was to source the turkeys and he was kicking in a keg of Budweiser but told us he wouldn't be going. We were all contributing side dishes. I got olives, buns, and cranberry dressing—you try to find real cranberries in the Caribbean and good fucking luck with that! They don't grow anywhere near here, I found out. By a majority vote, we passed on the turkey, upped the seafood order, and decided instead to stuff the grouper with crab meat.

While she took some advice, Sally was in charge of the guest list that had grown to over 30.

I assumed the dinner on the beach would be cancelled. Atheist or not, I was disappointed. They're a good bunch of people. I'm not related to the Pilgrims but I had enjoyed a real turkey dinner on American Thanksgiving with the same gang at Big Dave's. A high-light was Dave explaining to the Mexican ladies in the cantina how to make candied yams.

None of it would—ever again—be the same without Sally.

I also thought about Chief Inspector Arturo Diaz's impending visit. He was not a man to make appointments but rather, I guessed, would just show up expecting to find me. I also knew by his tone the day before yesterday at the crime scene that he would not be making a social call.

I was headed inside for another cup of coffee when there was a knock at my door.

There was Arty and, rather ominously, a uniformed cop of considerable size.

"May I come in?" he asked.

"Of course! Of course! Coffee?"

"Please, *negro*," he said, indicating to his man that he should remain outside.

We settled down in my rattan tub chairs on the balcony.

"So, what do you have so far?" I asked.

"A very little of patience for an *Ingles* first thing in the morning."

Instantly, he made me feel presumptuous for asking a question that made me sound like a colleague wanting to share notes on a case.

"C'mon, Arty. Give me something."

"What about a month in La Victoria?"

The thing about Chief Inspector Arturo Diaz is that he's a pretty funny guy. At least I assumed he was joking about thirty days in the country's largest, oldest, and likely least fun prison. You wouldn't know about Arty's comedic talents right off the bat. But then again, because he's so stoic and serene and proper, you really wouldn't know much of anything about him.

"Please, Arturo."

"First, you will answer my questions and then after, perhaps...," he said, drawing out a notepad which instantly rattled me.

He wanted to know where I was the night Sally was killed. But, because he didn't write anything down, it was evident that he had already found out where I had been and was just looking for confirmation.

His pen sprung into action when he asked about my relation to her, how we'd met, and so on.

So I gave him the facts, then rambled on—way too long—about her construction supervision, my book writing.

I was nervous, OK? You get quizzed in a foreign country by a chief inspector conducting a murder investigation and tell me just how fucking cool, calm, and collected you'd be.

Arty's pen lifted during my shaky filibuster.

"Any other relations you might have had with her?" he asked, his dark eyes staring intently at me.

"NO!" I had instantly answered. "God, no."

Sally was a big flirt with no apparently serious intentions. I had none either—for more than a decade and a half between my Beth dying and Alexandra.

That out of the way, Arty was really interested in the crowd at Big Dave's that night—who was there, when had they arrived, when had they left. He made brief notes as I ran down the list of attendees I could recall through my beer-induced haze. And of course, I appeared completely evasive when I couldn't supply any last names or any indication of their arrival and departure times.

By this time, I could see myself trembling and feel the sweat starting to come as surely as any Mike Wallace interview subject.

I then made the situation more hopeless by launching into a long-winded explanation of how informal everybody was, how we routinely switched tables, how drunk I was, and how there was no clock, and I don't wear a watch.

"See," I said holding up a bare wrist, as if that would prove anything.

To my great relief, he had stopped writing again.

"One last question, *Ingles*."

"Which is?"

"Who was not there?"

That led to some painful moments of silence as I wracked my wee brain trying to picture all the expats I knew, building a list of who was at Big Dave's that night. After Sally, I could only come up with one other name.

"Bruce Anderson."

His last name I did know, owing to our business dealings.

"The real estate man?"

"Yes, the real estate man."

My real estate man.

I didn't say anything else to Arty about Bruce and couldn't tell him where Bruce was that night.

He closed his pad and I breathed a sigh of relief. I guessed that Arty had already cleared me as either a murder suspect or a useful witness.

"That would seem to be all for now," he said.

"Whoa. It's your turn."

"Are you sure you want to hear?"

"Yes.

"We do not have all the tests back but we know she died between midnight and one. Two slashes to her neck. From a long blade, probably a machete. One, starting here," he said, indicating the right side of his neck, "Across the vocal cords. Not too deep. She grabbed her throat. Then second one went the other way. Much, much stronger. Cut off some fingers, went very deep, to her spinal cord. It almost removed her head."

The image sunk in, stunned and horrified me.

"Would the first one have killed her?" I finally asked.

"It would be eventual. From losing blood. Not in the instant."

"You have DNA?"

"No. That is troubling. No DNA."

"Any fingerprints?"

"What an excellent idea! We *should* get fingerprints. I will see to it immediately," he said sarcastically.

"Are you finished?"

"There were six sets that we have identified. Hers, of course. Her husband's—he had an assault record as a teenager in Denver. Dorothy Walden from Mariposa. Also Tico and his worker, Ricky, we have checked."

"That's five."

"And yours."

Of course he could find my records. After last summer's brouha-ha, my prints were on file with the RCMP, the Boston Police, the Toronto police, the FBI and, for all I know, the fucking Audubon Society.

"Yes, I was in the new apartment. She asked me up to see the finished construction job."

"Do not worry; you are not able to do what was done. And there were five other sets we do not know who."

"One of them may be the killer's?"

"What is it you *Ingles* say? No shit, Sherlock."

Like I said, Arty could be quite the comedian.

"So you think it was a crime of passion?"

"Perhaps."

"Or a robbery gone wrong?"

"Perhaps."

"That's it? Perhaps?"

"Sadly, *Ingles*," Arturo said with a look of polite impatience, "I have done this many times. It is early. We must start with the possible things and, because many, many things are possible, we must throw them away one at a time until we are left with the likely things."

"Tico sometimes had a third worker on his crew last year," I volun-teered. "He would've known Sally."

"You know this to be true?" Arty asked, re-opening his notepad.

"Yeah, it's true. I met him last winter when Tico had the big job of building the house and the swimming pool for Sally. He was a younger kid. Quiet. Big like Tico. A Haitian too. I didn't get his name. He was there off and on until the house was finished."

"Tico did not relate that fact to me. We must question him again."

"Go easy, Arty," I said, remembering Tico sitting by the side of the road crying his heart out.

Arturo rose to leave. At that moment, I realized I was tired of saying and doing absolutely nothing of value.

"I could help, Arturo," I blurted out. "You know, like the Baker Street Irregulars," I added.

He smiled a bit at the Holmes reference.

"Look, Arty, none of the expatriates will tell you much," I continued, pressing my case, "and I speak enough French to get by with the Haitians. I can actually do a lot more than you can."

"You believe the Haitians will talk to you?"

"Are you kidding me? With this smile?"

Arturo, as per usual, thought for a bit before answering.

"Do not get in the way, Senor Wiggins, and tell me *everything* you learn."

At the door I asked: "What's with Mr. Muscolo outside?"

"I have learned to be careful around you foreigners. Some of you are quite violent,"

## CHAPTER EIGHT

The first thing I did after Arty left was confirm that Wiggins was the unelected leader of Arthur Conan Doyle's Baker Street Irregulars, Sherlock's gang of street urchins/informants. Damn, Arty *had* read the books.

I then felt pretty bad because I hadn't intended to get Tico in shit; I knew him to be a good guy.

There were—are—a lot of Haitians in Las Terrenas. It's as if by migrating to the north-east corner of the DR they wanted to get as far away from their homeland as they could without actually leaving the island that the two countries uneasily shared.

As everywhere in the Caribbean, for sure in the Bahamas when I was a high school teacher there, the Haitians did all the shit jobs no one else wanted to do and, as everywhere, they were resented for it.

Tico was the perfect example. He was attached to Sally as every expatriate homeowner had at least one Haitian or Dominican attached to them. We furiners couldn't function without them. For not a lot of money they become the house manager/contractor/security patrol/gardener/pool maintenance guy/and general all-round fixer. They ensured the *aqua purificado* got delivered on time, that your vehicle got fixed, that you weren't overcharged for top soil, and on and on.

Last winter, when I wasn't massacring pixels in pursuit of another international non-seller, I used to hang around the delightfully private pool that came with the place and Tico would show up to do various property management things—water the garden, check my fresh water supply, hack away at the relentless giant bamboos, clean the pool—and we'd shoot the shit.

With our odd mixture of English and French and a bunch of good will we could communicate.

"*Lentamente por favor*"—"Slowly, please"—is one of the first Spanish phrases you learn in the DR—right after "*cerveza y Marlboro blancos, por favor*"—because Dominicans speak their language at an astonishing speed. So do Haitians with theirs. Or at least it seems that way to a largely unilingual arsehole such as myself. Get them arguing—which they're often inclined to do—and you hear only a machine gun blur of sounds.

I already knew the French equivalent—"*lentement s'il vous plait*"—which made me good to go with Haitians like Tico who broke out his dazzling smile in genuine warmth when I first spoke to him in my high school French.

I got some of his story, a story whose only conclusion could be: "Jake, you don't know jackshit about the hard times people can go through."

Tico's smile went away when he talked about the earthquake.

He was at school in Port-au-Prince when the quake hit without any warning. He described how the whole visible world just shimmied back and forth, demonstrating with his big hands shaking liking an umpire permanently signalling "Safe!" In panic, the students fled the crumbling building. He made it out just as a concrete piece over the doorway broke off, crushing the back of one leg as he ran. He rolled up his pants legs to show me the horrible shiny scars.

"My sister was not lucky," he added.

He had recovered in a Red Cross hospital, the doctors having been

able to repair the breaks. After months in a bed then painful rehabil-
itation, he started looking for his family amid the rubble.

"Papa, dead. Sister, dead," he said. "Brother *disparu*. But I find
*maman*!"

"What happened?"

"We could not stay in the city. There was no food or water. It was not
safe. There was no police. The prison fell down and many, many bad
men ran away. All the white people had men with guns to protect
them. We did not. We left, my mother and me, and went north into
the hills but there was nothing there for us. We could not cross the
border so we tried to swim Dajabon."

Here Tico choked up, but he did continue, describing their moments
on the river that divides the two countries.

"She sank in the river. I floated on wood for a long time and reached
the far side, the Dominican side. Then it was just me in the world. I
cried. I walked here. I am here five years and Miss Sally hire me. And
I am happy. But now..."

When Sally and Paul bought the small parcel of land next door to
their house I was renting from them and started construction of a
new house, Tico took over the whole project and there didn't seem
to be anything he couldn't do. Not that building codes are all that
rigorous here, but still, there was some nifty engineering on his part
to create the large one-bedroom loft sitting on eight ten-foot high
concrete piers. When he poured the steps, he implanted lengths of
bamboo into the wet cement then sawed them at a 45-degree angle
and fastened another piece as the railing. Clever as hell.

At the same time as he was building the house, Tico also installed a
swimming pool. Sally must've figured her Olympic diving days were
over and she wanted just a splash pool. Maybe 10 X 16, five feet deep,
with built-in steps.

Tico had a crew of one, sometimes two more Haitians. Ricky was his right hand man. Reserved and mostly expressionless, Ricky was smaller, older and as hard a worker as Tico. We didn't have a whole lot to do with each other beyond saluting each other or asking "*Ce va?*" The other guy, I never really met beyond him saying "bonjour" to me.

For the excavation, Tico brought in an operator running an ancient backhoe and a battered Mercedes dump truck belching diesel exhaust to haul away the excavated earth. The truck was as beat-up as the backhoe, with wobbly wooden sides and a steel bed; it had no discernible colour I could tell, light blue perhaps at one time. It looked as though it could've seen service with Rommel supplying the Afrika Corps.

The backhoe was out of commission most of the time, so Tico and Ricky pretty well hand-dug the hole, shaped its sides dead smooth, cut in steps, built the forms and hand-mixed and hauled the cement.

Tico wasn't just a bull worker; he had the touch of an artist. As he was painting the pool's inside walls and floor, he painstakingly worked in a subtle butterfly design—maybe four feet across—on the bottom using different shades of blue paint that he mixed to match the multi-hued tiles he inset just below the lip.

"*Et maintenant des plantes,*" he announced and set right to work borrowing cuttings and small shrubs and flowers from my place—oleander, bougainvillea, bamboo shoots, elephant ears, a dwarf palm—then carefully planting and watering them all.

Given that basically the whole project was built by hand, I was astonished that from start to finish it had taken just four months.

We stood, admiring his handiwork.

"Worried about earthquakes?" I asked.

"*Ami,* if God wants to break the pool, He will break the pool."

Overall, I most remembered Tico's child-like kindness and fatalism that existed in him despite of—or perhaps because of—all the shit he had endured.

In all my dealings with him the one incident that really stood out was last Valentine's Day. Tico showed up for chores around the place all dressed up in red—pants, red billowy shirt, even goddamned red shoes. Valentine's is apparently a big deal among the Haitians here.

I asked him why the Hallmark-generated holiday was so important to him.

"*Beaucoup chocolat; beaucoup d'amour,*" Tico had said with his patented toothsome grin.

"And just where are you going in such a *très chic* outfit?"

"Pétionville"

Named after Haiti's first democratic president, Pétionville is the place outside of town the Haitians had group-built for themselves, across the swampland from Sally and Paul's. It was over a mile inland from the sea, down a narrow road that was little more than a worn path. Pétionville was a sort of a social club, a drop-in centre for people who were not ever invited to drop in any other place.

Last winter, Sally had been quite proud to tell me that she would go there sometimes, the only non-Haitian allowed, with Tico acting as her passport.

Sometimes last year, late at night, I could hear their joint was jumping. Drums and amplified guitar from at least a mile away.

I had asked Tico if any of the voo-doo that they do was going on out there. He allowed that the older folks were still into it but that club rules, such as they were, let the seniors have the place only for specific holidays or important ceremonies but that for the rest of the time, "*les jeunes dansent.*"

Another thing that stuck in my mind was Tico's odd affection for Sally's dog. I say odd because Bruno was one of those high-strung, yappy as hell border collie-type dogs which I thought would require more effort to love than was humanly possible.

Somehow, Tico had convinced Bruno to be quiet and the animal with a brain the size of a frozen pea would follow the Haitian around as though it were a week-old baby duck.

I also say odd because I couldn't help but notice—I think all expats noticed—that dogs avoided Dominicans and Haitians like the plague.

No way a sweet, dog-loving guy like that murders a person he adores in a bloody rage.

# CHAPTER NINE

A nd speaking of odd, I also thought about Bruce Anderson.

Mercifully, I didn't have that much to do with him, once he figured out I wasn't a big player. He didn't spend a lot of time trying to sell me real estate. But then again, he didn't have to. I didn't want to own a car down here and for sure wasn't going to join the motorcycle set that crowded and buzzed the streets like amplified mosquitoes. Also, I don't like challenging myself by walking up anything with a steeper grade than a shopping mall's accessibility ramps, so that ruled out all the villas either for rent or sale in the hills encircling the town. Not to mention that when the heavy rains came in the late summer and early fall the dirt roads winding up into those hills could become a slurry and all but impassable. All in all, it meant that Bruce had to find me a place within flat walking distance of everything in town.

For a while, he kept on pushing me towards a larger villa in the hills but I wouldn't budge. Later, of course, I figured out his real motivation. At any one time, upwards of half these lofty homes are on the market; some had been listed for more than a year. You don't talk to guys like Bruce about why this is so, but it's not hard to guess. It's a more expensive version of why tourists buy timeshares. Come down here on vacation, fall in love with the postcard beauty, and buy your piece of it. But as soon as you spend any time here, reality sets in for many. The act of getting your car fixed consumes days. Replacing a fridge or air conditioner or water tank, hell, even a blender often meant a three-hour drive across the whole country to

Santo Domingo on the south shore where you could get anything you wanted—and lots of things you didn't.

I remember Big Dave providing a great one-line summary of LT, really of every place in the world: "If it was paradise, everybody would live here. And then it wouldn't be paradise anymore."

On the plus side, nature's inexorable too. You can almost watch the bamboo grow. A clump planted in the spring might be ten feet high by fall, twenty-five feet a year later. All the other plants you recognize from the indoor tropical section of The Home Depot back home. Down here, they grow outside and to a Brobdingnagian scale. I had originally rented based partly on the exterior photos on Sally's website. I was pleasantly surprised to see that Tico and nature had turned the yard into an ordered jungle, its surrounding compound walls completely hidden by green. Sally told me she had taken the much sparser website pictures just a year and half earlier.

For me then, that left all of five places for sale at the time as candidates that fit my particular bill. About $150K, in town, less than 10 minutes from the beach. Either with a pool or enough room for a pool. Because little Jakey doesn't play well with others, I thought I'd rather get a house.

But then I realized the tropics feature quick decay, especially near the ocean. Metal of any kind rusts, paint fades, wood rots. All that happens in the north but much more slowly because it's all flash frozen for months every year. Here, with the heat and humidity, it happens triple-time. And that means the bigger your place, the more shit you have to maintain.

So what I bought was this 2-bedroom, 2-bath condo in a small complex. It was all rather Spartan but it had a massive covered balcony facing the ocean and for 40 bucks a month in fees somebody else would maintain all the grounds, spray for bugs, take away my garbage, provide security, and give me propane, decent cablevision and Internet while bringing me great bottles of drinking water.

I realized that what I got wasn't much of a place but I didn't need much of a place. That's the thing about the south. You're outside. A lot of northerners don't understand that and look for homes that are, well, just like back home where you spend five or six months imprisoned after you give up trying to bullshit yourself into believing that cross-country skiing is fun.

Because I'm not normally a big fan of neighbours, I was a little leery of people living on the other side of my walls. The 50 units in Casa del Mar were mostly rented out to short-termers. Consequently, I had only occasional and completely superficial contact with vacationers. And in return, I had to put up with a bit of party ruckus but only during the peak holiday period in February and March.

Bruce wasn't exactly thrilled with my purchase, presumably because his commission was less than half of what he would've picked up if I'd bought a house in the hills. He sorta acted the way cabbies act all huffy when they get a short haul fare. But Bruce was smart enough to remain pleasant with his customers after the fact because you just never know when he/she might want to either upgrade or leave.

If I was sitting with Sally, Bruce'd have nothing to do with me. She had been the most vocal opponent of his conspiracy theories. Sometimes I'd pitch in, largely with the media angle—that mathematically, it wasn't possible that every journalist in every country since the invention of the Gutenberg press had been either a lazy sonofabitch or bought off.

But then I had stopped, faced with the futility of arguing with a man of unassailable conviction. There's a great scene in *True Believers* when James Woods' weary lawyer looks at Robert Downey, his idealistic protégé, who's been pointlessly arguing with a mental patient about whether or not the phone company had been broken up. "Are you kidding me?" Woods asks in disbelief as he walks away.

One night last year, Sally and Bruce had words. It wasn't over Obama's secret birthplace. It was what she had said to a couple from Philadelphia who had been on the verge of buying a house from

Bruce, a house Sally believed was both overpriced and too far from the town to be anything but inconvenient and impractical. Sally had talked them out of it. Right there in front of Bruce.

Bruce had tried to put on a stoic face but as he was leaving empty-handed, he leaned over to her and I heard him whisper "Bitch!"

I debated when and how to tell Arty about this. Or even if I should.

But first, I wanted to find Tico and give him a heads up.

Small town that Las Terrenas is, it turned out it wasn't all that hard to locate Tico. I ran into Frank having lunch at the French bakery. He told me that, after months of listening to Sally extol Tico's abilities and after he had tried to hire the Haitian several times, he had finally succeeded, what with the Haitian no longer having an employer and all.

Tico was now working as a general labourer for Frank who was G. C. on a small condo complex being built back behind mine.

The first thing Tico did was apologize for the way he had been in front of Sally's and then apologize again for working just days after the tragedy.

"*Ma famille* must eat," he said.

"What family?" I asked.

"*Tantes et oncles* in Haiti," he said. "I send money."

"Of course, *bien sur*, Tico. But we must talk."

"What is wrong?"

"Nothing is wrong."

"*Quoi?*"

"Did the police talk to you?"

"*Oui.* Yesterday. They took my machete."

"But today?"

"*Non.*"

"They will."

"Why?"

"Tico, where is the other guy from your work crew last year?"

"There is only *moi et* Ricky."

"Tico, *c'est pas vrai,* not true. You had someone else. I saw him. Very young."

"Him? Oh, him," he said way too casually. "That was Xavier. Work one day only. He is gone *longtemps.*"

"Did you tell the police?"

"No. They would send him back. Or do something *très mal.*"

"Where is he?"

"I don't know. Just gone. *Disparu.*"

"The police need to talk to him."

"He does not need to talk to the police."

We went quiet for a bit.

"*Tu pense un Haitian* did this?" he finally said.

"You don't know everybody."

"No! *Non! Pas possible!*" he said suddenly getting real upset.

"The police are not agreeing right now," I said.

Tico went silent, the way a lot of the locals went silent when the topic of the police came up.

"*Non, pas Haitian,*" he finally said, softly, firmly, his eyes fixed on mine.

"How can you be sure?"

"Because we all know she is *bonita, une belle dame.* No one touch her. Ever."

"Someone did."

"There are bad men here."

"Where?"

"There," he said, waving his hand over his shoulder but not looking back.

"Tico, do you mean in the hills?"

"*Oui.*"

"What bad men? Dominicans? Foreigners?"

"*Oui, je pense.*"

"Do you *pense* or do know who did this?"

He stopped himself.

"...it is time to work," he announced.

He got up and grabbed his shovel. I found that odd because I'd never heard him volunteer to work. He could bull labour like a madman but, following a sort of Caribbean protocol, you always had to suggest it first.

I walked home, thinking about "the bad men" Tico had alluded to. Sucker for stereotypes that I am, the first bunch of bad men that sprang to mind were the Russian mobsters that apparently lived in the DR pretty much as an open secret. But there was nothing and nobody concrete to consider so I dropped the vague notion.

At home, I worked the Internet, easily finding the kind of stories about the Sally's murder that I had expected to see.

*"US Tourist Hacked to Death in Caribbean"*; *"American Citizen slain in Dominican Republic"*; *"Murder in Paradise";* Et cetera. Et cetera. Et fucking cetera.

Light on detail and quick to blame the Dominican authorities for their inaction, the news items were followed by the usual trail of ignorant comments about what a hellhole the DR was, oh, and Mexico too while we're on the subject. Which we weren't, but what the fuck? Toss in the same comment you've added to all sorts of forums. "Why would anybody even visit [Insert foreign country here]? It's a nation of liars, murderers, and thieves. Vacation in your own country."

You probably don't even have to type out the whole fucking thing. No doubt you have it filed for quick copying and pasting. There. It takes you ten seconds to pass along your pearl of wisdom and feel real swell for doing so.

# CHAPTER TEN

They held Sally's funeral procession on the main street ending at the cemetery. Her hearse was a white Toyota pick-up truck with her coffin in the bed, surrounded by flowers. The coffin didn't quite fit so the tailgate was down and Tico sat on the edge, his feet barely clearing the pavement. With one hand he steadied the coffin; with the other he wiped away his more or less continuous tears. Following behind was a battalion of scooters and cars and trucks and people walking among them. Some were part of the procession as they were carrying flowers or had blossoms fixed to their hoods or handlebars. Sally was well-liked. Others were just stuck in another impromptu Las Terrenas traffic jam.

A handful of exceedingly white people walked behind the truck. I assumed they were Sally's friends and family from the States who'd been able to scramble up a flight, likely to Santo Domingo, then rent a van for the three-hour drive north.

I spotted Arturo on the sidewalk and joined him without acknowledgement. We stood there in silence as the procession passed.

I was aware of a few "what-the-fuck?" stares directed at me by locals and expats alike. Some people down here say that just about the last thing you want is the attention of a Dominican cop, but that's horseshit. Mostly. Some of the lads are, to be sure, a little too enamoured with carrying a gun. They have that swagger that a sidearm bestows, not unlike the swagger you see from a guitar player. And these guys—the younger ones mainly—will apply the little bite for all sorts of things. For these *morditas*, there's never any paperwork and the pesos just disappear into their khaki pockets for broken tail-lights, jay walking, dirty license plates, and such.

Well, so what? No one getting beaten, no one's getting busted for serious shit. It's really something like a surtax. In our little corner of the country, that seems to be just the way it is. I couldn't swear to Santo Domingo because I know some pretty bad things happen there, as they do in any city with millions of poor people.

And besides, getting along with a chief of police anywhere is not a bad thing.

"What's wrong, my friend?" I finally asked, seeing his glum expression.

"It has not been an easy time," Arturo confessed. "Many people in Santo Domingo want to see this go away. Murder of expatriates is not good for tourism. All the newspapers in America are talking of how a US citizen was killed. You know that."

"Yes, I do."

"So, we are told to arrest someone soon."

"Even if they didn't do it?" I asked.

"That would be helpful. But right now, my superiors do not think it is mandatory."

"And even better if you can find a Haitian who did it?"

"Sadly, yes. That will cause the cries to be rid of them to grow louder. Which is always a good way to get votes."

"Did you talk to Tico again?"

"Yes. He told me about...Xavier," he said, taking out then flipping through his notepad. "He said he worked one day only. But you said more than one day."

"Maybe I was wrong," I lied. "Maybe, from a distance, I mistook Tico for him. They're both big."

"As you say."

"Are you going to arrest Tico?"

"No. I will not arrest an innocent man. He did nothing except love her."

"And you tested his machete?"

"Yes. No results as of now. But it will be a waste of time."

"What about your bosses in Santo Domingo?"

"How do you say it—they can come fuck their hats."

"So now what?"

"We look for someone else."

Arty went back to staring at the procession, the main body of which had already passed.

"Do you see anybody missing?" I asked him, motioning to the tail end of the mourning parade.

"Who do you mean?"

"The husband. His name is Paul."

"*Madre de dios*! I should have checked the husband!"

"Alright, alright."

"He was in Denver."

"How do you know?"

"His Skype account, her Skype account. She talked to him on the morning of her death. As she did almost every morning. She had a big voice. The neighbours heard her."

"So why isn't he here?"

"The Denver police were told. They left messages. They went to their house, his work. That was two days ago."

"Don't you find that a little strange?"

"Yes...and no. It is because of us we must bury her. We could not keep her any longer at the coroner. I called his work myself and told them. They said that after Paul talked to her, he was taking tourists into the hills to make tents in the snow. I do not understand it, but that's where they said he was. Gone for five days. No telephone, no Internet. But with eight witnesses we will question when they return."

"How can they take people into the mountains in winter with no communication?"

"A very good question. One I asked them. It is for the *authentico* experience, they said. They have flares and a marked plan so they know where they are supposed to be."

"Alright then, why didn't you send her home?"

"In her house we found her papers. She had arranged a place in the cemetery here. We thought we should honour her wish."

I didn't go to the graveyard. I had walked through it once. Rows of crypts—some centuries old—all above-ground, sealed concrete boxes with crosses. The cement was grey and streaked black from the residue of the fir or tamarack or some weird type of pine or whatever the fuck those wispy-needled trees were.

There was something like a spontaneous wake at Big Dave's that I went to. The full gang was there as near as I could tell plus a few dates—either long-term spouses who didn't normally accompany their mates to the bar or much shorter-term accompaniment. We all acknowledged each other with slight waves and a look that said "we all lost something here."

The beer flowed and, leave it to the Brits, so did the memories of Sally. "Miguel" and Mad Tim first gave voice to the outsized member of the troupe no longer with us. They were joined by Vlad and Sergei and soon everyone was serving up Sally stories in a sort of profane and pretty funny group eulogy session. Tales of her social activism, her yappy dog, her fearless negotiating, her single-minded effort to fit in and love the place where she was, the place where her life had been taken. Each story ended with a toast.

I offered my own experience of Sally mercilessly and to no avail riding Tico's ass during construction and was met with not quite stony silence but close. Only Nick, Margaret, and Dot seemed to appreciate my recollection.

I then realized that, for the rest, they didn't believe what we believed: that Tico was completely incapable of murdering our friend. And nobody but me knew that he had been unequivocally cleared by the police.

While unaccustomed as I am to public speaking, I told them.

"Tico's innocent! The cops think so too!" I announced.

Nick pounded the table and threw in a couple of "Hear, hears!"

When Nick pounds a table, people tend to listen so I was glad for that.

And then I went home.

## CHAPTER ELEVEN

From time to time, I drop by Sergei's book shop under the pretense of looking for something to read. What I'm really looking for is conversation that goes beyond the beer-fuelled sarcasm and mockery of Big Dave's bar. Sergei always seemed to be happy to oblige and we'd sit out front yakking about pretty well everything. History and politics mostly. We both had spent quite a bit of time looking into the DR's history and as outsiders—me more than him—we had a little bit of distance.

Our chats always get lively, especially if they're fueled by espressos from the French Bakery across the street, as they were on this day. I'll admit that those dark beauties when added to the five or six cups of coffee I'd already had at home might have made me a little jittery.

Because he's Russian and I'm part-Ukrainian—the family name change to Lydon from Lysiak happened a couple of generations back—it wasn't long before we ruled out Moscow's current belligerent relationship with Kiev as an unwise topic. Right or wrong, the pull of ethnic origin is pretty much insurmountable when things get heated. We cheer for nationalistic shit even if our ties to it are faint. I could only get so far with my repetitive KGB thug accusations, about the same distance he'd get with his counter claims of the CIA clumsily fucking around.

But normally I much prefer discussions that degenerate into passionate arguments rather than just sitting around in mutual agreement. I already know what I think. Show me what you got and, more importantly, why? Maybe it's because I have a pathological need to argue, maybe it's because you can actually learn things this way.

On this morning, I was hungry for one of our chats. Something abstract, something involving, something that didn't have to do with the pall on our town.

It didn't start out that way.

"What you said last night about the police clearing Tico, you know this to be true?" Sergei asked as we settled into our painfully uncomfortable black metal bistro chairs.

"Yeah, I got it from the top guy," I said.

"That is not the popular opinion at the moment."

"Look, I'm a big fan of democracy, but I'm happy that we don't hold town-wide votes on guilt or innocence."

"It would seem that everybody not a Haitian wants it to be a Haitian."

That touched off a more general discussion as Sergei traced the history of the animosity between the island's two neighbours. He believed that originally—we're talking 300 years ago—it was the traditional Spanish-French dust-up that got picked up by the people whom the Spanish and French owned.

That simmered for a long time.

"We're better than you! No, we're better than you! Like sports fans," I said.

"But then the DR went and broke away from Spain by joining Haiti in 1822."

"I did not know that," I admitted. "Must have made sense at the time. Two countries, one island. Why not make it one country?"

"It didn't work out. And the DR spent the next twenty years trying to get a divorce from Haiti. Did you know that the DR independence day of February 27 marks the break from Haiti not Spain?"

"Didn't know that either," I said. "But it's not like they can ignore each other. Like after the earthquake, the DR sent tons of help even if they didn't have much to begin with. All the foreign aid came through here as well. And—no big surprise—a lot of Haitians escaped the ruins and made it across the border."

"That wasn't a first. The DR has been importing Haitian labourers since the 1940s, mainly to work in the sugar cane fields."

"And now there's that new fucking immigration law," I said. "Even though the constitution automatically grants citizenship to all children born here, the new law has revoked that citizenship to all Haitians born after 1929 who can't prove they were born here. But the government knows that Haitians never have a lot of paperwork, so if you've got no proof, you can be deported—"

"—repatriated they call it," Sergei interrupted.

"Repatriated. Fucked is what I call it. Can you imagine what it's like living under that threat? That at any minute there could be a knock at the door."

"Yes, Jake. I can imagine..."

Here, Sergei's voice trailed off. I'm such a fucking idiot. Of course he knew what that was like. He'd have been a teenager when the USSR went away, so he'd know first-hand what the surveillance, the intimidation, the arrests did to a family, a neighbourhood. Everybody knew somebody who was taken away. And nobody could do anything.

"Sergei, you know I'm a big fan of this country..."

"As am I."

"But when they pull shit like this…"

"Agreed. What's interesting to me is that, even with the new law, the Haitians keep coming."

"But not really surprising, is it? The DR's GDP is—what?—eight times higher than Haiti's. Right next door. Within walking distance."

"Like Mexico is to America," Sergei said.

"Exactly. And if we're not surprised by those two situations, how can we possibly get exercised by the flood of immigrants that want to come to Europe or North America because we got all sorts of stuff (and brag about having all sorts of stuff) they don't?"

"They don't want to come to Russia," Sergei noted. "And that may be a good thing. All our problems we made."

"What's your birth rate?"

"Mine? Zero."

"I meant Russia's."

"I have no idea."

"Less than one and a half babies for every family, among the lowest in the world. It means that without immigration, according to my calculations, you might live long enough to be one of the last Russians on the planet."

"Hmmm…." Sergei said. "Real estate prices will become much more affordable back home. Traffic will not be too bad either."

"You—the Kremlin—will soon have no choice but to bring people in."

Sergei was unconvinced.

"Ask the Arawak and Taino Indians all over the Caribbean how they feel about immigration," he said. "Oh, wait, you can't. The Spanish immigrants killed them all five hundred years ago."

"Got anything a little more recent to justify your xenophobia?"

"OK, what about the English and French treatment of Indians in North America?"

"Touché."

"You in North America liked it fine when the immigrants were white and from Europe. Look, you even took Ukrainians and Poles!" he said with a smile.

"Arsehole!"

"No, Canada and the US were just wonderful to all the Europeans. If you ignore their crazy hate for Jews, the Irish, Slavs, Italians, Catholics. Oh, wait, let's not ignore that. And now the immigrants are brown or worship another type of god, so fuck them. Build a wall."

"Bullshit! Canada brings them in. And in two generations, it's mostly fine. If you make sure they can get jobs and don't stick them in ghettoes."

"Canada will never take enough to make a difference."

"No, the difference will be when America or Russia take more in."

"Like Europe now? They seem happy, don't they? No problems, right?"

"Think about it, Sergei: You guys—and all of Europe—are used to people wanting to get *out*. You don't have much of a history of taking people *in*. You're shitty at it. But Canada and America only exist *because* of immigrants. So now you have to learn what took us centuries or you will just disappear."

"*They* will disappear," Sergei pointed out. "And we, my friend, will still be getting drunk in Las Terrenas."

"But solving the world's problems while we do it."

I gotta admit, I get jacked after a lively discussion. I always know when it's been a good one when I think of all the things I should've said but lack the wit or on-the-spot smarts to say them.

All you ever need to know about a country comes from the people living there who decide they don't want to live there anymore. It's math. The greater the number of people who want to get out, the shittier the country is they want to get out of. Then you find out what they are willing to do to not live there anymore. To my knowledge, there has never been a flotilla of rafts and leaky boats leaving from Tampa and trying to sneak Michigan retirees into Cuba or Haiti, never a fleet of airless transport trucks abandoning scores of Vermonters in the high Sierra outside Juarez, never a West Berliner who took a bullet in the back trying to climb the Wall into East Berlin. And coincident with that, think about what kind of government has to pen up its own citizens, forbidding them to leave. The kind that's scared shitless that the ensuing mass exodus would lead to "last one out, turn off the lights!" Well, if they had lights.

So that tells me why people want to leave but, of course, not what to do about them arriving.

And for all our chatter, what I thought about on the way home was Tico's situation. And finally the single image of him struggling to hold onto a piece of drifting wood as he crossed the river into the DR.

And a close-up of his eyes as he watched his mother lost to the current.

CHAPTER TWELVE

I'm not interested much in any form of self-examination, maybe because I'm scared shitless at what the results might be but more than likely because, if I take a step—or two—back, it really doesn't matter at all to me what I might find.

I had my head read just after Beth died, more as a favour to Dr. Dan, my kind and concerned GP. He was worried about my increased drinking that had led to my renewed interest in punching. The shrink he sent me to concluded that I "suffered" from low-grade Aspergers, coupled with a dash of OCD. But there were drugs I could take. As I don't view it as "suffering", I declined. To quote Popeye: "I yam what I yam."

And a major part of what I yam is a person who loves a routine. Not that I know anything about physics but it's the fucking law. Newton's Law: Every object in a state of uniform motion tends to remain in that state of motion unless an external force is applied to it.

For example: Other than my sorties to Big Dave's or Mojitos, I'm rarely at large after dark. Being a life-long early riser is a factor. So is my awareness of the pathetic factor of dining alone. After that, what's to see anyway? It's dark.

More than a little ironically, the DR is not the place for lovers of routine. There doesn't appear to be anything like a fucking schedule in Las Terrenas. For anything. Garbage collection or restaurant hours or the delivery of the *agua purificado* that you go through like, well, water unless you want a sure fire weight loss program courtesy of the local tap water.

But for all my bitching and whining, it takes me about ten minutes to acclimate myself to doing things this way and not spending my time being pissed off. Which is a routine of its own, if you think about it.

I most welcome the irregular appearances of Nelio, the fruit and vegetable guy. How he decides what day to appear is a mystery to me, but it adds an element of suspense to my life. He shows up from time to time in his battered flat bed outside the parking lot gate manned 24 hours by our rotating security force of Né-Né, Esteban, Jose, and Oswaldo.

Nelio stands on his horn for a bit to let everyone know he's there and we all troop out like a flock of hungry chickens to walk around his truck and pick over all the produce mounded up in colourful piles, atop which usually sits a kid or two presumably learning their old man's business. Nelio is this short, powerfully-built Haitian with a permanent smile that makes the Cheshire Cat look like the fucking Grim Reaper.

I love a guy who loves and knows his job and Nelio loves and knows his job. In some weird combination of French, English and Spanish, we reach understanding about the state of his avocados. Do I want one for today, *manana* or *le prochain jour*? *Les trios*, I say and his huge hands deftly pluck three football-sized avocados at precisely different stages of ripeness. Into the plastic bag they go along with limes, potatoes, tomatoes, mangos and carambolas, a bittersweet, citrusy star-shaped fruit the bastard got me hooked on with a few free samples a while back. The bastard.

*"Combien?"* I ask.

He stares into the bags of mixed fruits and vegetables and names a price. I have no idea if he's clipping me or not. But 300 pesos? Nine bucks, Canadian, for two bulging bags of fresh things is a good deal with me, even if I know I'm going to be tossing at least half of out when I tire of grazing no matter how fucking good it's supposed to be for me.

But this afternoon, a day after Sally's funeral, Nelio wasn't smiling.

"*La bonita?*" I asked.

"*Oui...qui faites ca?*"

"*Un animal.*"

"*Animal mal,*" he agrees because what other kind of person could have done this to Sally?

Asking that question got me think, think, thinking again.

That's when the accumulated months of watching *Law & Order* re-runs kicked in. Woman dies; you gotta look at the husband. It bothered me that Sally's husband had what turned out to be a very convenient story. Talk to her in morning then disappear into the snowy high country for days. Could Paul have made it to the DR in time to kill her? I had no beef with the guy; nor was it as if he stood out as the most likely murder candidate. But it'd be handy to know if it was even possible.

If he talked to her early morning Mountain time, with the three hour-time difference, he would have had to leave Denver by 10 a.m. his time at the latest to get to the Dominican. On-line, I went through the airline schedules for Tuesday, the same day of week as the murder. It took a while to enter the four international airports from which he could've made it to LT. El Catey near us, then Punta Cana, Puerto Plata, and Santo Domingo were all possible landing destinations from Denver. After all that, only two flights seemed possible. One 9 a.m. local time Delta flight direct to Santo Domingo. Seven and a half hours in the air to the capital. l factored in the customs and immigration hassle and then the baggage-claiming hassle then the car rental hassle before the three—OK, if he really motored, the two and a half hour drive. Which means that he could've made it to Las Terrenas in the dark at around 11. It could be done. Same for an earlier American flight through Houston. I checked and re-checked.

Early the next morning, I went to see Arty with the results of my search. With no phone number for him, I figured I'd walk to the police station. If Arty wasn't in, I could at least leave a message. He wasn't and I did. I told the desk sergeant I'd be on the beach.

I strolled across the road and sat down in one of Mojito's loungers. It was low tide and the sea was calm and normally I'd be occupying my time by just staring. But on this morning, I was building a movie, a horrific short, of Paul convincing a friend to handle the happy snow campers, of Paul boarding the flight to Santo Domingo, of Paul driving north to Las Terrenas. Of Paul brutally murdering his wife.

During my debate over whether he would have driven the rental up the laneway to the house or stashed the car farther away and walked undetected in the darkness, I realized someone was sitting in the lounger beside mine.

Arty.

"Did you know that Paul Bartlett could've made the trip from Denver to Las Terrenas after he talked to her, killed her, and left again?" I quickly asked him.

"Good morning, *Ingles*."

"Yeah, yeah, good morning. Paul could've—"

"No," Arty said interrupting.

"No, what? No, you didn't know that or no, he couldn't have done it?"

"No, he could not have done it."

"Yes he could. I checked the available flights. There was a direct flight from Denver and another one through Houston that would have given him enough time."

Arty was getting that impatient look again which pissed me off because it likely meant a policing lesson was coming my way.

"First, we do have a computer to scan passports," he said. "There is no record of him coming and going into this country at that time. And second, if the agent did not scan, as sometimes happens, Bartlett still could not have come here because, *Ingles*, there is a difference between theory and reality."

"What the fuck are you talking about?"

"In theory, you are correct. There were two possible flights. According to schedules, yes, he could fly here in time. But in practice, on that day, December 12th, there was a big snow storm in Denver. The flight to Houston was cancelled and the direct flight to Santo Domingo was delayed nine hours. So not possible, much less likely."

"But..."

"There is no 'but'. It is a...a...*callejón sin salida*."

"A dead end?" I ventured, translating 'alley without exit'.

"Yes, a dead end," Arty said, looking pleased to have acquired another English expression.

He stood up, clapped me on the shoulder, and said—not unkindly— "You are making progress as an investigator, *Ingles*."

After he'd gone, I smoked and thought some more before picking myself up and wandering over to the cop shop.

The lads at the station were getting used to me being there and Arty had obviously left instructions. I was waved into his office.

"What about the real estate guy?" I asked.

"Bruce Anderson? Likewise a...dead end."

"How do you know?"

"I interviewed him. In this very room."

"And?"

"And I showed him photographs of the murder scene. Not Sally, but all the blood on the floor, on the walls."

"What'd he say?"

"Nothing. He vomited in that garbage can," he said indicating the trash can at the side of his desk.

"And that means he's innocent?"

"It means he is *likely* innocent. If he could kill her with a machete, without a panic, why would a picture cause his reaction? Automatically. No one can decide to vomit."

Leaving the police station defeated, I walked east, back to Sally's, and stared at the home.

Sally's two houses—pretty well everybody's houses—had burglar bars on all the windows and doors. Often there'd be no glass, just screens and those ornate bars and hurricane-proof shutters. There was a business in town, probably several of them, where welders fashioned bars into vines or clouds or flowers, then spray-painted them something other than black, so as not to appear prison-like but do the same job.

There's a fair amount of B&Es in town which isn't really surprising given the amount of poverty. And it's not really practical to begin a discourse with a thief on the job  about the economic theory of supply and fucking demand, that the more expatriates who visit and stay cause more houses and condos get built, and more stuff to get bought, the more stuff has to be maintained, all of which creates more jobs. And it's likely to fall on deaf ears anyway, especially when said thief and likely his family are trying to live on less than 1/20$^{th}$ of what you are.

Security wasn't just in the form of window bars. Many houses were in compounds surrounded by six to eight-foot high walls. Some of these fortifications had coiled razor wire or bits of glass embedded in the concrete along the top. Sally's did not. She had a walled yard and a car-sized gate with a heavy lock but when I was her temporary neighbour, she didn't seem to fasten it that often.

What worked best with intruders or, at least, what everyone thought worked best, was ownership of a dog. Any dog. The noisier the better.

It hit me. Sally had a dog. Well, not really a dog, just a quivering bundle of furry neuroses named Bruno. For the winter I spent beside the construction, Sally and the dog were there every day. Bruno and I had reached somewhat of a detente. After an initial fusillade of barking, he'd spend the rest of the day just growling a bit whenever he'd see me, but he wouldn't bark at me and, in return, I wouldn't swat him. A fair deal. We had to repeat this dance every day because, apparently, Bruno had the memory of a fucking goldfish.

Finding out what became of Bruno was not likely to engage me very long, but I did wonder.

Sadly, what happened when some foreign home owners got overwhelmed by their Caribbean fantasies gone sour and sold their places, they'd just let their dogs go. This *Born Free* act led to the formation of packs of abandoned and roaming dogs up in the hills or in town.

There were dogs everywhere but mainly on the beach. Judging by their plumpness they were expert at cadging food from the tourists and restaurant owners. Harmless and relentlessly hopeful, they had become part of the eco-system, scrounging for scraps, playing with each other, and generally hanging out, doing doggie things in the sand.

Maybe Bruno was now among them, although I did doubt the little shit would be welcomed into their wandering fold.

Have you ever had those moments when you get so deep in thought that you don't actually see what's in front of you? I get them a lot. It's something of a wonder to me that I haven't been turned to road kill yet. Wrapping up my tangents on burglar bars and dogs, I realized that the police tape was down and the gate was slightly open—which I found odd.

Looking inside the compound, I saw a figure through the maze of concrete piers. He was standing by the pool out back. I approached the man, shouting out an exploratory "Hey!"

## CHAPTER THIRTEEN

Paul Bartlett turned around as I drew up to him. He had a look of faint recognition.

"Jack?" he said.

"Jake. How are you, Paul?"

Without answering my idiotic question, he turned and went back to staring at the pool and surrounding walkway and gardens, the high white walls now mostly obscured by climbing plants.

I stood stupidly, uselessly, beside him until he began slowly walking around the patio, examining the potted plants, the outdoor furniture tastefully arranged in the shade created by the apartment above it.

"She did such a good job, didn't she?" he turned and said.

Suddenly, he swept his arm across a side table, clearing pottery and candles and a lamp off its surface, sending them crashing onto the tile.

What do you say, what do you do in that situation? Fucked if I knew. I steered him towards a red-cushioned chair and sat him down.

"I'll get you something. Gimme your keys. Hang on, bud."

I ran up the stairs, unlocked the front door, and took a deep breath.

And still I wasn't prepared for what I saw.

Dominating the first view of the large, airy, open-concept apartment was a massive ugly rust brown blood stain, reaching across the white-tiled floor from one wall almost to the other. The interior wall had large splashes of the same colour.

I avoided it as best I could as I picked my way along the place's perimeter, staring at it just once. It was dry and shiny, like the skin on a pudding. I tore my eyes away, tried to concentrate on the various colour-co-ordinated knick-knacks and toss cushions and native paintings as I made my way to the kitchen at the back. Retrieving two Presidentes from the fridge, I opened them at the kitchen counter, glancing quickly out the window over the sink at the view overlooking the small pool, the wall, and the "protected wetlands" beyond. A slight breeze rippled the grass plain in waves. The hills were as green as ever.

I then retraced my steps, focused solely on the island vibe of lime green, mid-blue, and white that Sally had produced. And still I could not block out the evil dark stain.

Paul seemed grateful for the beer as I sat down beside him.

'For once, Jake, just once, shut the fuck up,' I told myself. 'And for Christ's sake, don't stare'.

"She loved it here," he finally said, his voice cracking. "Her heart was here, this was her home. I was never here long enough to get that attached. I don't know what I'll do."

Silence.

"I can't go up there," he said. "I just can't. I tried. I got halfway up the stairs but I can't."

I was glad he hadn't. If he was catatonic now, it would have been a whole lot worse for him if he had seen what I'd just seen.

"Two years," he said. "That's all we had to wait until I was done with my job. Now what?"

More silence.

Like I had a goddamned clue about the wisest life choice for him right now.

"You'll figure it out, Paul. Give it some time," was the only weak-ass bromide I could come up with.

"I told her it wasn't safe here," he continued. "I told her she had to be careful. I told her to relax and just enjoy the place. But no. She just had to get involved, didn't she?"

"Involved in what?" I asked quietly.

"Involved in the lives of these people, and all the shit that's around them!"

He fought back the urge to anger and lapsed into silence again.

I stared at the pool, focused on Tico's butterfly design.

"Have you seen Bruno?" he finally asked.

"No."

"God, I hate that fucking dog!"

"Not on the top of my list of favourite pets either," I replied.

He smiled quickly.

"It took two years before the fucking thing stopped barking at me."

Then he went back to staring.

"What am I going to do? What am I going to do?" he said.

"Look, don't decide anything right now. How long are you going to be here?"

"I don't know. A few days."

"If you can't stay here, you're welcome to bunk with me. And I can help you get things in order."

"Thanks. Dot said she'd put me up."

"Well, if you need anything or just to shoot the shit...call me, OK? And if you're up to it, maybe meet at Big Dave's later?"

He didn't reply. I got up, briefly rested my hand on his shoulder, then left him in his grief.

## CHAPTER FOURTEEN

I stopped at the cop shop and asked to see Chief Inspector Diaz again.

Once in his office, I closed the door.

"Should I be looking into finding you a permanent desk here?" Arty asked.

"Sally's husband is in town," I said.

"We know."

"Have you talked to him?"

"We will. For now, we must leave him alone in his sadness, no?"

"But you've ruled him out as a suspect?"

"Yes."

"What if he hired somebody?"

"Possible. We know he has not been in this country for more than a year. So how? Telephone or e-mail, only. We are getting his records. It will take time."

"Or he found someone in the US and sent him here."

"Or that. All possible. But all not likely. Tell me, you saw him?"

"Yes. Just now."

"And....?"

"He seems pretty fucked up."

"So? What of your murder plot?"

"So not likely. Have you found Bruno?"

"Who?"

"Her dog."

"There is no dog."

"Well, there was."

"Maybe he became frightened and ran away."

That did make sense. Bruno always struck me as completely self-serving—more like a cat than a dog—and for sure not one of those faithful canines in old Disney films that sleeps on his master's grave for years.

Arturo was writing again in his pad.

"Would the dog bite?" he asked.

"Fucking right he would."

He wrote some more.

"Perhaps this is only useful if we find him and then find someone with bite marks," Arty said studying his notes.

"Who found Sally?" I asked.

"A neighbour out for a walk because he could not sleep. He saw her gate and then her front door open. He went to see. It was—here it is—2:45 when we were called."

"And the neighbour's clean?"

"78-year old American from Louisville. I do not think he could lift a big machete let alone use it the way it was used."

"Did you find the murder weapon?"

"No. There was a machete in the shed but it was completely clean when we tested it. We think the killer brought his own."

I asked Arturo about the way Sally's death blow had been administered.

"First, we think it was a back way."

"Backhand?"

"*Si.* Backhand, to measure the distance perhaps and then a full swing from the normal way."

"The forehand?"

"*Si. Rapido.*"

He demonstrated, making first a softer then a louder whistling sound that startled me as he swung.

"Unless he was left-handed," I pointed out.

"Yes. Unless he was a left. But left makes no sense to use the back-hand on the big swing. "

"Nothing makes much sense."

"We know only some of the people—you included—who did not do this. We are back to looking at robbery as likely."

"Were there signs of a break-in?"

"No."

"So it was someone she knew, someone she let in."

"Possibly. But..."

"But what?"

"It is also possible she did not lock her door or the thief was waiting outside and caught her as she was unlocking."

I remembered an incident last February just after Sally finished her project and I was house hunting. Sally and I had walked back together to our side-by-side homes late after a session at Big Dave's. It must have been about midnight when I was unlocking my gate and she was unlocking hers. A fair-sized local lad had stepped out of the darkness near her. He surprised the shit out of me but he was talking to and approaching Sally.

 "*Agua?*" the stranger had improbably asked, as if his late night stroll had forced the need for hydration.

"*No agua aqui,*" Sally had instantly and firmly answered as I was making my way towards them. "*Lo siento. No agua.*"

Some combination of my presence and her forcefulness caused the guy to wander away down the road towards the beach.

But what if?

How easy was it to just write Sally's murder off to a botched burglary?

Pretty easy. The pre-conditions existed. In this country of more than ten million mostly poor people, there had been several other cases over the years of expats killed resisting thieves. All tragic, all sad and all with screaming headlines. While the actual yearly number was small—the annual tally that would mark a slow *day* for violent death in Chicago—the effect was not, judging by the volume of uninformed and hysterical comment trails following the articles as they always did about anything to do with the DR or Mexico.

"Did anyone hear anything? The neighbours?" I asked.

"Not a sound. She died without a sound," Arturo answered, slightly gesturing to his throat.

"But the dog. It would've barked. A lot."

That stopped Arty. He wrote in his notepad again.

"Unless it was somebody she knew," he said.

"So a crime of passion?"

"Perhaps."

"Or a cold-blooded murder made to look like a crime of passion."

"Again, perhaps."

"Anything missing from her place?"

"We do not know for sure. But not much, I think. Drawers in the bedroom had been taken out, things were on the bed, so maybe some jewelry. But the TV was there. It was new. Same for the music. A Bose. We have the receipts."

"Computer?"

"No computer. We know it is missing. She had a work place with printer, router, but no computer."

"She used it all the time. I don't recall the make but there was a butterfly sticker on the cover, if that helps."

Arty wrote some more.

"So it *is* possible she interrupted a robbery," I said.

"Perhaps. But she died without a sound, as I have said. No one heard anything. So why not take the TV and Bose? She was not alive to stop them and the *electronica* are the most costly things she had."

"Or the *bandito* only wanted the computer."

"Perhaps."

"Maybe he panicked?"

"Perhaps."

"Would a thief bring his own machete to a crime?"

"Perhaps. To deal with a dog maybe. To defend himself if he was caught."

"You keep saying 'he'? Could it be a woman?"

"Possible. But from the cut, a tall woman, at least 5 foot nine inches."

I left Arturo shaking his head. He wasn't anywhere with this and it was really pissing him off. All the possibles and perhaps-es were annoying the hell out of me too.

In my twenty-minute walk back home I thought mostly of the murder weapon, could see the humming blade, its horrible impact. And in that maybe one-mile walk, I saw six machetes, either in use or idly hanging down at someone's side.

Dominicans and Haitians who work outside—and that's a lot of them—handle machetes the way most Canadian kids handle hockey sticks. There's a practised ease, a casual grace in the way they swing the deadly blade, whether they're decapitating a coconut for a fancy drink that the tourists buy from beach vendors or cutting sugar cane or brush, cleaning fish, or felling and stripping bamboo to make things.

Lots of people walk around LT with machetes and you don't really take notice. On the streets of Toronto or New York, they'd attract attention. Down here, it'd be like getting upset by seeing a guy with a briefcase on Wall Street.

I had my own personal near-encounter with a machete that I remembered vividly as I passed the stretch of Playa Popy where the fishing boats came in, next to the cemetery.

Sometimes—not a lot of the times, but sometimes—you have no idea how badly you've pissed someone off. Looking back, it wasn't a big deal but it was memorable. I was down on the beach looking to buy something fresh-caught. What I caught was the fisherman I was bargaining with holding his thumb on the spring of the communal scale weighing the red snapper I was about to buy. I had called other fishermen on it from time to time as it's a pretty standard tactic. There usually was a sort of sheepish grin and a shrug and we'd go back to weighing and negotiating. But this guy was mad. Maybe not because I'd called him on it but because I had cancelled the deal and turned to buy shrimp from another who commandeered the scale. Eight bucks for two pounds of *camarones gigantico*, the very definition of fresh as their spindly legs were still twitching over the edge of the scale's dish. As I was paying, I heard a very loud 'thwack!' behind me. I turned to see Cheating Red Snapper Guy standing at the sheet-metal clad cleaning table. He had just decapitated one of his fish with a single clean stroke of his machete. He was looking right at me.

It bothered me, not because I feared I was in for a public hacking—and not in a computer way—but because it was a spoiler. In some form or other, this kind of peripheral exchange is the same sort of angry incidental contact you see in Toronto or Chicago or Paris. But here in LT, the land of laid-back and happy, it was a damper.

So I went back the next day to buy some red snapper from him, I swear, but he wasn't there.

I did find him a couple of weeks later and bought two lobsters from him. Our bargaining, however, was not pleasant and I folded early in the negotiations. Having paid too much, I watched him dress the crustaceans, taking a mallet to the edge of his machete to loudly split the things down the middle.

Today, it took a while to banish the single image of a whistling blade. I could picture it so clearly. Not the identity of its wielder. Just a hand and a long thin machete blade, mostly blackened by age and weather but with a thin gleaming strip of silver on its edge where it had been sharpened and sharpened again.

Get rid of the visceral, the emotional, and use your fucking brain, I told myself. I reminded myself that I really did have a talent for think-think-thinking. It's the reason why several police forces in Canada hired me from time to time to cast my odd eye on particularly puzzling cases. The same talent that I'd used—along with some pure dumb luck—to figure out just what the Christ was going on with the international hacking scheme I had uncovered this past summer.

It didn't take me long realize that I'd better get my ass in gear. I was frustrated. Arturo was nowhere with the case. He was frustrated. I hadn't kicked in anything of value, and instead had more or less been wasting the Chief Inspector's time.

And there was still a murderer on the loose.

## CHAPTER FIFTEEN

The mood at Big Dave's had lightened over the days since the funeral. You could tell by the elevated noise level. Although some people might not like the fact that the impact of Sally's death was already starting to lessen, I didn't see a problem with it. Who gets to proscribe the correct length of a mourning period? How the fuck does anyone know how long a death should affect anyone else? And when? And in what way?

Wounds close. And that's good. How long it takes, how deep the cut rests only on the one with the scar. Everybody else, together with their opinions and judgments and tsk-tsk-tsking, can just go fuck themselves.

A bigger problem is not letting go, wallowing around in the grief until it's not mourning any longer; it's the habit of mourning. I knew something of that from Beth's passing. A simple concept that took years for me to accept. She's gone and she ain't comin' back. Except she would. Unbidden and at the strangest times . She'd just appear in my mind, doing simple things around the house, lying beside me in the night, giving me shit for smoking, staring at me in connection, in love.

I was and am unable to bullshit myself into believing she's waiting for me to die so we could be together again in some celestial cottage country for all of eternity. It's one reason we agreed to cremation for the other. That way we would never have to imagine our respective corpses moldering in the ground.

I suppose, as a chain-smoking, alcoholic diabetic, there was the general assumption that I'd be croaking before her. But it didn't work out that way. And that was the big lesson for me—me, who *never* seeks lessons. Shit really does just happen. Randomly. For no particular rhyme or reason. The obvious corollary, one I lived by: have a bunch of fun before it does.

Her ashes were scattered onto the lake in front of what was supposed to be our retirement place. I did the scattering, so did my daughter Halley who was eleven at the time and Carl, my good friend who lives on an island across from my place. We silently watched her ashes dissolve. That was a truly shitty day.

And for the last fifteen years, I think of her often. Unlike some people who claim they consider, say, their dead parents at least 365 times a year even though they've been gone for 20 years, I don't think of her every day. But often. The lasting smack-down has been the gap, the hole, the missing element in my life.

And Paul will likely have that hole. But no one else will.

So the crowd at Big Dave's was getting on with the business of living. Good for them.

I sat with Vlad for a time. His usual exuberance may have been blunted a bit but not by much.

I asked him about the Russians that Tico sort of hinted at.

"Oh, I see, you ask me because I am Slav, just like a Mexican you ask about what go on in Peru?"

"Oh, fuck off. I asked because it's a small town and an even smaller foreign population."

"I jerk chain. Here ees truth: wheech Russians are gangsters? Every fuckeeng one of them. It ees their way."

"Even Sergei?"

"Maybe not him," he allowed.

"So 150 million Russians but not him?"

"Your turn to fuck off," Vlad said, looking up. "Sergei! Tell him fuck off!"

His newfound buddy had just arrived at Dave's.

"Fuck off," Sergei said to me as a greeting. "Why exactly am I telling him to fuck off?" he asked Vlad.

"He theenks all Russians mobsters. Tell him."

"We're not all mobsters."

"See? What I tell you?" Vlad said and got up, laughing heartily as he headed off to relieve himself.

"You know, Jake, all Russians really are not gangsters," Sergei said, getting serious.

"I know, Sergei, I know."

"It angers me. I hear this all the time. Some of us were poor so we left to open businesses somewhere else, usually with Russian customers who have also left. Some of us had businesses back home that made money and, at the same time, made enemies too. So, just as Stephen Miller sings, we take the money and run. Under Tsar Putin, we cannot go home. So we must live somewhere. Why not here?"

He waved his arm towards the beach.

"But there are gangsters here too," I said.

"Of course, there are. Some Russian, some Italian, some American or French, why even some Canadian. But most—maybe all—of them in this town are retired."

I'm sure not a lot of people consider the life of a retired gangster but it made sense. Not all bad guys get killed or caught doing bad guy things. They have to retire somewhere. So, indeed, why not Las Terrenas? Or a thousand other such towns in a bunch of Caribbean countries with warm weather and lax immigration and tax laws that will let them play out their lives in sunny anonymity.

"Besides being retired gangsters," Sergei continued, "they have another thing in common."

"What's that?"

"They are alive and they wish to remain so. That makes them careful."

And that made sense too. They had to be fully aware that their past lives could catch up with them at any moment. This healthy fear of vendettas required a certain vigilance that, say, a 30-year employee of the water commission or school board didn't need. OK, bad example.

I had noticed a common reaction when you were approaching the older European guys on the beach. You knew they were European because they were universally thin and darkly tanned and wearing nut sack Speedos. Some would have a Dominican woman at least 30 years younger on their arm, some didn't. They'd approach you with their gaze fixed dead ahead, but you could tell they weren't staring at anything in particular, just avoiding looking at you. As they'd walk by you'd get a quick sidelong glance. Maybe to see if they recognized you. Maybe to see if you had a switch blade hidden in your shorts.

"You know these guys?" I asked.

"Some, yes. So do you."

"Who?"

"You make a joke, right?"

Vlad returned, clapped us both on our backs and asked: "Weech son of a beetch will buy me beer?"

We traded insults for a while until Vlad decided to call it a night but not before punching both of us on the shoulder.

"I think I liked it better when we were not talking to each other," said Sergei as he rubbed his upper arm. "It didn't hurt as much."

By tacit agreement, we returned to our gangster discussion.

"You seemed shocked by the very idea that there are mobsters here... or anywhere for that matter," Sergei offered.

"And you seem perfectly fine with it."

It was pretty clear that Sergei had thought long and hard about this.

"You are right. I am not outraged. Any more than I am angry at the sun because it rises each day. Like the poor, the criminals you always have with you. They cannot be criminals unless they supply things that people want. If you want to stop bad guys from being bad, it is us—not them—who must change because we create the demand. We cannot be angry about the narco-wars in Mexico and South America —or meth labs or killer new drugs like fentanyl— because they only exist so bored North American or European teen-agers can get high. And we cannot be all prudish about the legalized prostitution and the amount of hookers on the beaches and street corners in the DR because most of them are not making money from the locals; they are there because the tourists want them to be there. So we sure cannot be surprised that we get gangs—some old, some brand new—who can see there's a dollar—or several billion of them—to be made."

"But you're only talking about the retail criminals," I pointed out. "The ones who supply a product. There is a different class—the wholesale thieves—who just steal from their countries by either buying the government or being the government. They don't deliver anything; they just rip off people, like fuckin' pirates."

"And just like the pirates they hide their treasure—trillions— around the Caribbean."

"Well, that was a pretty goddamned witty allusion."

"Thank you. And, thanks to the Panama Papers, also true."

Sergei thought for a while.

"Let me build on my goddamned witty allusion," he said. "Today's gangsters—the ones here anyway—are like pirates in other ways. They do not like to fight. That is not their business; stealing is. Usually, the Spanish had more men, bigger ships, better cannons. But the pirates—the successful ones—had brains. They knew their best weapon was fear. They built their reputations as crazy killers so they'd scare the shit out of people who would then surrender a ship or a town without a fight."

"Ah, public relations," I said.

"Your former job, was it not?"

"The second oldest profession," I said. "But what about the French guy? l'Olonnais. He actually did cut into a guy's chest and tear out his heart. He got off on doing shit like that all the time."

"Until the Kuna Indians in Panama barbecued him at a very young age. Look, if you are a murderous sociopath, piracy was a good line of work to get into. But he was the exception."

The beer was cold; the night was warm and cloudless and a sea breeze found its way uptown and swirled around Big Dave's courtyard and everything seemed just right again, until the crowd, table by table, went silent as they looked towards the street. There on the sidewalk under the light post that also held about a hundred electric power wires, were Paul Bartlett and Bruce Anderson chatting up a storm before they entered.

They sat down together and an impromptu receiving line formed as we all got up, some us rather unsteadily, to offer our condolences. Bruce was respectfully quiet throughout the bar wake, studying papers he'd brought while Paul was gracious as hell. When it was my turn, Paul asked me to join them.

"Jake," he said, "I've decided to sell both places. There's a bunch of good people here but I just can't see myself spending any more time in this...this place."

"I understand. I'm sure we all do," I told him.

"At any rate, I'm going to list with Bruce here."

I bit my tongue. The fact that Sally hadn't liked Bruce was coolly academic now.

"We'll try to sell the two together, you know: live in one, rent the other," Bruce added, winding up his sales pitch.

"Jake, you stayed there most of last winter," Paul said. "You know the older place. I want to hear what you'd do to fix it up."

"Selling turnkey?" I asked.

"Yeah. Everything."

I thought back.

"Outside, not much. There was only one lounger which was fine for me but maybe not to a buyer. And the old charcoal barbecue with the rusted grill, that was a pain in the ass."

"And inside?"

"Not a lot to do there either. The wood trim could probably use a re-staining. A few more pots and pans wouldn't hurt in the kitchen. Maybe a set of steak knives. And a water dispenser instead of always having to tip those big bottles over to fill the coffee pot. Oh, and I'd get a better router. The one that's there sucks."

"The new owners can do all that," Bruce said.

"Why fuck them from the get-go?" I asked. "If they know the Las Terrenas situation, they'd know right away that doing all the things that needed to get done would be a real hassle. And that'd affect price. It ain't a sellers' market, is it? And if they were newbies, they wouldn't be too happy to find out later. And that'd affect your reputation, wouldn't it, Bruce? I mean, Paul could give a shit; he'd be long gone."

Paul turned to Bruce and said "Just make it happen."

Bruce was a little pissed. Owing to some combination of the heat down here and the logistical challenge of getting stuff, the first reaction of most people to *any* request is "Nope. Sorry. Can't be done."

"But I think the big issue will be upkeep while you're trying to sell," I continued. "Tico was a fucking artist, the way he looked after the gardens. But with him gone...."

"Tico's not there?" Paul asked in surprise, directing his question to Bruce.

"No. I thought you knew," I said but Bruce cut me off.

"Not a problem. We use Frank. He's got lawn guys. It'll be fine. I'll look after the house stuff. Let's get this paperwork out of the way, shall we, so we can enjoy a drink? Jake, will you witness?"

As we were autographing the listing agreements and other such documents, I couldn't help but notice that all three of us were left-handed, the odd kind of thing that lefties—or maybe just me—recognize.

"All southpaws," I said.

The other two stopped and noticed it too.

"Aren't we just so special?" Paul said.

Paul had a beer, a *pecuena* while the rest of us drank *grandes*. He was pretty quiet but then again, he had always been pretty quiet.

He left, followed soon by Bruce. I sat alone, ordered another beer, and was pleasantly surprised when Margaret and Dot joined me. They were subdued, almost proper, but then, they were hardly salacious boozehounds like the rest of us.

"So whaddya think, ladies?" I asked.

"About Paul?"

"Yup."

"He seems in a very bad way," said Dot.

"He showed up at the Mariposa two nights ago," Margaret added. "Said he had been to the house but couldn't go in."

"He told me the same," I said.

"Not too surprising that he's selling."

"Nope," I said. "If it were me, I'd be long gone too."

"Well, he will be, day after tomorrow, he told us."

I relayed my offer to help clean up or out because Paul was likely going to steer clear of the place. There had to be some heavy lifting involved, boxes and such. We arranged that I'd be there at nine the next morning.

Despite a decent beer hum, augmented at home by a couple—well, more than a couple—sips of Cazadores *Reposada*, sleep didn't come easily that night.

Wait a minute. Sleep never comes easily to me. Getting my chatty wee brain to shut the fuck up was a nightly ritual. Has been all my life. When I was kid, I used to rock myself to sleep. I don't mean gently. I mean violently, on my hands and knees, until I raised a sweat and tired myself out. Now that I've become terminally lazy, the most strenuous activity I can undertake is playing endless games of solitaire on my shitty laptop until I start making rookie mistakes which is my signal for lights out. And even then, I usually have to lie down on my most excellent sleeping couch in front of the TV, flicking from channel to channel until I find a movie I've seen before. That'll put me under.

But lately, it was the murder keeping me up. Obsessed? You bet. Why, you ask? I don't have a fucking clue and, like many, many other things, I'm long past caring about finding a reason.

The killing could have been—and very likely was—completely random, in which case, it would be solved or it wouldn't. A break might come if a piece of Sally's jewellery or her computer surfaced or somebody ratted somebody else out and a confession came, maybe with some police encouragement.

Las Terrenas' population had gone nuts over the last 15 or so years, more than tripling to about 35,000 in town and along the nearby beaches. Toss out the kids, toss out the elderly, toss out the women—nary a female charged with murder around these parts and not that many who were five foot nine—and you still have about 7,000 possible suspects and that doesn't even begin to consider out-of-towners.

On the other hand, most murderers know their victims so maybe the killer was much closer to home, someone Sally knew.

So who?

All we knew for sure it was either an *hombre malo, un homme mal,* or a bad man.

That description didn't exactly fit anyone I knew down here. Certainly not anyone in our drinking crowd who were the people closest to Sally. I'd like to think that the whole *in vino veritas* thing is generally accurate. And I had had enough drinking time with them that they only confirmed the snap judgements I had made from the beginning. Everyone can be an asshole from time to time (I should know), but over the long haul, they are who they are.

But—and it was a Trumpian yuge BUT—I can't say I'd ever hung out a lot with calculating murderers so I don't truly know what they're like when they aren't busy murdering.

Leonard Cohen, before he used his "gift of a golden voice," wrote a poem called "All there is to know about Adolf Eichmann." In it, he catalogues the mass killer/bureaucrat's physical and mental characteristics as all being "medium" and his distinguishing features as "none." Cohen concludes with: "What did you expect? Talons? Oversize incisors? Green saliva? Madness?"

While Lenny —I think—was talking about the sheer human ordinariness of extraordinary murderers, it could also serve as a description of the normalcy of monsters *after* the killing's done.

Another Lenny—Briscoe from *Law & Order*—came to mind along with his mantra: motive, means, and opportunity. Get those three things lined up and, voila! You should find the killer.

I thought of Arty's process of elimination—move from the possible to the likely, discarding along the way.

I sat down with a writing pad I was using less and less as I relied more and more on my shitty laptop. Down the left-hand side, I wrote all the names of the people I knew Sally knew and then made three columns, respectively titled Opportunity, Means, and Motive.

I stared at the names and the empty columns and it struck me that Lenny Briscoe's recipe for finding murderers wasn't complete. Conceivably, you could have all three elements going for you but what if you were morally, spiritually, psychologically incapable of taking a life? Was there even such a thing? That you could have a character that made you absolutely unable to kill another human. I realized that, so far, Arty placed a whole lot of significance—and so did I—on this missing fourth ingredient.

Everybody, except Big Dave and I, had the opportunity. Unless I have a Jekyll/Hyde thing going on that I don't know about, I was with Dave until well after the time of the murder so we alibied each other. I came to Paul and reluctantly added his name as having had no opportunity to kill his wife. Arty had been pretty persuasive about the impossibility of that happening owing to flight schedules from Denver during snowstorms.

As for means, everybody could get their hands on a machete; they're as common here as drunken pink tourists on the beach yelling "Woo-woo!" for no apparent reason. But means also had to include the physical ability to swing the blade with such destructive force. The fact is: if it's properly sharpened, there doesn't have to a lot of muscle behind it.

When I was renting, I tried to use one just to see what it felt like. I borrowed one from Sally's shed and took a few swings at a stand of bamboo to little effect. But Tico came by. He took Sally's machete from me, claiming it was *"pour le bebe"* and gave me his. After a few practice swings under his tutelage, he set me back to work on the bamboo thicket. I was quite surprised at how deeply his heavier, sharper tool sliced into the trunks.

But still, according to Arturo, Sally had been nearly decapitated by a single blow so some effort had been required.

Here again, pretty well everybody got ticked for having the means. No question, Nick, Sergei, Bruce, Yimmy, Trevor, Frank, Mad Tim, and Vlad, were physically able to have done it. For sure, Henrik and Klaus, the newbies, were too. Automatically, Tico, Ricky and Xavier, the occasional worker from last winter, were on the list as all three both knew her and how to swing a blade. Miguel, the eccentric Brit, and Pietro, the slight Italian evangelist, also had to be considered for the list but they were close calls; the former because of his age and continual drunkenness and the latter for his apparent piety and insubstantial size. Pietro, I guessed, was maybe five foot, six so he'd be under Arty's you-must-be-so-high-to-kill height requirement. Maybe Arty's forensics were a bit off. In a straight up or down vote, they had to be included.

I hesitated over Margaret and Dot and Nick's wife, Yafrete. Even if Arty's calculations had a range, I doubted they could that wrong. Dot was maybe 5-2, Yafrete even shorter. They had to be disqualified. But Margaret was a possible, so let's set aside the chauvinism, shall we? Yes, she had the means too.

On to motive. Money and love are the big ones. There are exceptions, bug-fuck craziness being one. And here we had a big fat fucking zero. I could check Bruce as having a possible reason for killing Sally but even that was slender. Last winter, Sally had screwed up a sale for Bruce, costing him some thousands in commission. For sure, it had pissed him off; I had witnessed it. But, think harder. Does it make a whole lotta sense that Bruce lets a year go by, stewing over it the whole time, until he decides to borrow a machete, savagely kill her, make it look like a burglary, and then puke as soon as he saw photos of his handiwork? I'm thinkin' that even Bruce, the conspiracy nut, himself would say you were *muy loco*. But still, he had to be a possible.

The rest? All question marks. Why people do the things they do is decipherable only if you know something of their back-story, know their interactions with others and, even then, you're usually not there at night with them as they lie awake, staring at the ceiling and thinking odd things.

And you had to consider the victim. What could Sally have possibly done to get anyone in her circle so enraged as to kill and kill so brutally? Not a chance that an expat did her in because he or she was so fed up with having Sally put the financial bite on them for one of her many causes. So maybe she *had* become romantically involved with someone and broke it off. Possible. But would any of her potential lovers—all likely middle-aged, all likely having already experienced every sort of human relationship mess—get that fucked up over their dissolution? Doubtful.

But, then again, what did I expect? "Talons? Oversize incisors? Green saliva? Madness?"

# CHAPTER SIXTEEN

OK, OK, I told myself, so far, after really considering each name in each category, I had the square root of fuck-all. Now let's see if I could narrow it down on the basis of some half-assed character assessment.

I had made judgements on the crowd at Big Dave's but there was no pretending that they were founded on any kind of deep and lengthy analysis. People strike you one way or the other or not at all. And you stick with that perception until something else happens to disprove it.

Vlad—On the surface, he was the most opened-faced one of our bunch. On the surface. I had never, not once, seen him be anything but loud and cheery. Judging by his background, his menial work history in Germany while separated—for five years—from his wife, the illegal intrigue that had brought him to Canada where he prospered, I had one conclusion: Here's a guy who'd busted his ass all his life and who was now determined to wring every ounce of fun out of his remaining time on the planet.

Pietro—Don't think anyone really knew him well but there didn't seem to be much to know. I suppose we could explore daddy issues, and growing up in privilege issues and more successful brother issues but he had every indication of having reached peace with himself through our living Lord, sweet bleeding Jesus as well as wide-eyed of love for everything American—excepting presumably the Sodom and Gomorrah-like bits. He was friendly and soft-spoken and would stand you for a beer.

I couldn't give a shit what route he had taken to get there. But maybe, his apparently deep faith had been deeply offended by Sally's infrequent but evident irreverence. Could her irrelegiosity piss him off enough to make an atheist martyr of her? You only saw it when she'd been drinking at least a bit. I can't remember if he was around last Easter Good Friday when she had stood up at Big Dave's and wished everyone "Happy dead guy on a stick day!" which I thought was pretty funny but not a lot of other people did.

Or could Sally have been in the process of calling Pietro and his church out? Was she working on some researched exposé? That might be a swell reason to steal her computer. A quick Internet search of my own revealed that the First Assembly of Christ the Bloody Redeemer was one of those new superchurches that could draw enough Sunday worshippers to fill the stadiums of those attending that other Sunday ritual, the NFL. Based in Tulsa and headed by Reverend Harvey Wheaton, the First Assembly of etc., etc., etc. seemed largely devoted to collecting money—sorry—offerings. So maybe Sally was spending her spare time nailing them for misappropriation of funds. But, judging by the unabashed photos of Reverend Harve's cars, houses, and Lear jet, the whole outfit was set up, as far as I could see, to misappropriate funds from its donors and apply them to the lavish lifestyles of the rich and righteous.

Was she accusing them of tax evasion? Churches here and in the US don't pay taxes, so that didn't wash.

What about the dark side of organized religion? Pedophilia. Ding! Ding! Ding! Why not? Pietro had an androgynous Peter Pan-ish vibe. That, of course, doesn't automatically translate to molesting kids but if you were a piece of shit child predator, this country could accommodate you at least a little bit more easily than many others. It was possible.

Moving on: let's stick with money as a motive. Could Sally have been an unofficial informant for the tax department? She could've reasoned that if everybody paid their full share of taxes the government would have more money to do more good. There were more than a couple of businesses she was well acquainted with. Sergei's book store, Mad Tim's car rental, Margaret and Dot's B&B, and Big Dave's bar were all largely cash on the dash operations.

Nah! This was all penny ante stuff and it'd mean that she was dropping a dime on the people she partied with. And if she was sending e-mails to the government, why would anybody be dumb enough to take her computer? The e-mails had already been sent and received.

And besides, Sally—just like everyone else here—worked at least part time, off the books. Her tenants—and I was one—brought US cash to pay the balance of their rent. I couldn't see her screaming down the road to the bank to report her haul to the government so she could pay up to 28% of it in sales and service tax, which was a big source of government revenue. She was a lot of things, but a flaming hypocrite wasn't one of them.

It also meant that it's unlikely she deposited it at all, to avoid possible questions because the government here is pretty wired into the banking system. And that meant there might be a sizeable amount of cash on hand at her place. So maybe somebody told somebody she was hoarding greenbacks. She'd be an easier target than say, Nick, who I know did exactly the same thing with his renters. Nobody in their right mind would think about breaking into Nick's for the world of hurt that awaited them. But Sally's? For maybe a few thousand US bucks? It was possible.

Well then, there's Ricky. I had overlooked Ricky, maybe because, after Tico, he would have had the most exposure to Sally, and therefore I assumed he had seen first-hand that she was a *belle dame*, a *bonita*. I had no idea what he was like among his friends and family—or even if he had either—but he always struck me as reserved, almost stoic with not much emotion as he worked, steady, quiet, almost enduring. He might steal cash because he's oppressively poor but why would he take the computer? He'd only do so because he had been hired to, not because it had any intrinsic value to his life and not because he could fence it for much—which he'd know. iPads maybe or smart phones, but not laptops.

But would Ricky—perpetually poor like every other member of the Haitian community—hire himself out as a first-time robber and contract killer? I couldn't see it.

Same went for Tico's temporary help from last year. If—what was the guy's name?—Xavier needed the cash—and he did—why would he wait for more than a year and how could he not have known that she was a *bonita*?

Sergei —He was a physical fitness dude. He was also smart, even-tempered, and thoughtful. And, he seemed to like to keep things orderly, wouldn't ever be accused of being a disruptor. Maybe that was something. Sally was a shit disturber.

Big Dave—of all of us—with the possible exception of me—was the hardest to get to know. His years as a barman or perhaps something that got fixed when he was five years old kept him on the periphery, a watcher. His observer status meant that he had picked up tidbits on pretty well everybody that came into his place more than once. But he had something like quiet dignity, and more importantly, he had a rock solid alibi: me.

Miguel—He was poor and always bitching about it. Maybe he had talked himself into improving his finances if he had heard that Sally had cash. In his very brief non-drinking hours, he did hang with the locals. Maybe he heard a rumour that Sally had money lying around and he acted on it. Maybe he hired a Dominican for the job? Maybe.

Nick—had a temper but not a chance. Not a fucking chance in the world.

Same for Mad Tim. His pissed-off tirades couldn't hide his big heart.

But what about Frank's wheeler-dealing or Jimmy's sizeable law firm or Trevor's "development work" or Bruce's profitable real estating?

Frank—I imagine that anybody who spent much time with Frank would find themselves exhausted in the face of his perpetual optimism and enthusiasm. No laconic islander, he was in constant motion. But maybe all his dreams were costing him more than he had.

Jimmy—What possible beef could he have with Sally? He didn't need the money. Maybe pride. An unpaid bill might have enraged him? Nah. He was a friggin' lawyer and if he sued, he had home field advantage of always pleading in court before fellow Dominicans. Any revenge he wanted could have been extracted through legal means. Rule him out.

Trevor—He was the epitome of the 'Stay Calm, Carry On' Brit. No question his "development" work was shadowy as the only developing he seemed to be doing was his beer gut. He once told me there was "millions to be made" here—and maybe there is—but he had no apparent crispness, no energy, no steady stream of bullshit that any developer I'd ever met routinely oozes. It's as if his years in the tropics had just worn him down and bleached him out. He seemed at least as inert as I was and it was likely he hadn't been ert in a very long time. Out.

Bruce—the paranoid real estate guy wasn't at the top of my favourites list. He was too self-contained in his crazy conspiracy world to be any kind of fun to be around after his first or second beer. But annoying didn't mean dangerous.

The newbies—Henrik and Klaus? I had had a few pints with both, together and separately. There was much more to learn but Henrik was one of them gentle good-natured Scandinavian types. He had said nothing critical about anything or anybody since getting here this past fall, even about the hooker who had rolled him.

On to Klaus whose English was as atrocious as his Spanish. I couldn't imagine how he'd ever be able to understand anything well enough to either become outraged or arrange a hit. Plus, he was wearing a Rolex when he first arrived until I told him to hide it, so money probably couldn't be a factor.

At that time of the night, I was getting pretty loopy. It occurred to me there might be some combination, a joining of the two oldest and overwhelmingly prevalent motives. What about love *and* money? As in: someone was loving someone they ought not to and Sally found out and was blackmailing them. A stretch. A really, really long stretch. Like the Acme rubber bands Wile E. Coyote used to string across the road kinda stretch.

'Pack it in, Jake,' I finally told myself. 'You ain't gettin' anywhere.'

After spending a lot of time amateurishly wandering through the ephemeral contents of the human psyche, I had to face the fact that we had only one cold hard fact. Sally's missing computer. Any motive was likely tied to that. Discard the theft-for-profit motive. The re-sale value on her laptop couldn't have been much. The TV was worth a whole lot more, so was the Bose sound system and both those would've been more attractive on the black market.

Barring a stupidly simple explanation like the laptop was in a repair shop, Sally Bartlett had died because of what was on that machine.

## CHAPTER SEVENTEEN

I didn't sleep for long, maybe four hours. When I got up, I realized I actually had somewhere to be at a certain time. I had promised to help Margaret and Dot with cleaning out Sally's place. It was 8:50. Pitter-patter, let's get at 'er.

In the real world, I used to be manically punctual. Down here, and in semi-retirement, that compulsion has faded. I wasn't alone. Island time is a very real phenomenon.

I had my first hint of it in the Bahamas when I taught school there. It's not like I had a day-timer full of appointments but occasionally I actually did have people to see at a specific time—government officials, dinner dates, that sort of thing. So you'd be sitting there, on time with your thumb up your ass and you might get a call explaining why it was absolutely impossible to keep the scheduled promise to appear. They had a wonderful expression—"Soon reach"—which translated from the Bahamian is: "I'll be there when I'm fuckin' there." I figured then and figure now: if you can't beat 'em, join 'em in not ever showing up on time except for airplanes.

In the DR, there's "*manana*", which is the nudge-nudge, wink-wink way of defining as exact a time as, for example, a repairman was prepared to promise.

In other words, I had time for a coffee and a butt before I headed out. I made it Sally's by 9:45 which I reckoned was pretty good. Their car was there and Margaret was there. Dot was not.

Margaret was in the grim process of mopping up the blood. It was chilling to watch her swoosh the big stain around, then rinse, then mop some more then rinse, then empty the bucket of brownish-red water and start over again. For several repetitions, it looked like she had made no progress beyond just spreading it around a bit. But then, gradually, the swirls of colour, the darkness, began to fade.

"Dot can't see this," Margaret said.

I went back downstairs and opened the storage shed/pool pump house and started cleaning out all the various tools and such when Dot appeared.

"May as well leave most of it for the new owners, dear," she said. "I don't think Paul wants to ship hoes and shovels back home."

We both were silent when I brought out a machete. Newer and shorter than Tico's blade, I held it like a venomous snake.

"Especially leave that," she said. "Maybe someone else could use the tools. Tico or Frank?"

"Maybe Tico'd like the rest of the tools but he's got his own machete. He thought this one was a kid's toy."

"We'll ask Frank too," Dot said. "Leave them for now."

Instead, we watered the plants and flowers and collected a few knick-knacks that had been busy accessorizing the patio furniture. We then trooped upstairs with them to find the tile floor a sparkling white.

"Thank you, thank you, sweetheart," said Dot as she hugged Margaret. "I just couldn't face it."

"I know, dear," Margaret said. "It had to be done and it had to be done first."

The ladies starting cleaning out closets and drawers in the bedroom while I began with the living room and kitchen. I left all the stuff in the kitchen except the contents of the junk drawer that everybody has. I emptied it onto the dining table. It was, as advertised, mostly junk—the detritus of living. Rubber bands, piles of business cards, scotch tape, coasters from bars, a few brochures for tourist attractions, the odd screwdriver, scraps of paper with recipes, restaurant menus.

Her computer work area was real tidy. The peripherals Arty had mentioned. The computer had sat on what was essentially a small table, not a desk. It had one shallow drawer that was nearly empty. Pens, a few software CDs, a couple of obsolete cables that nobody can ever bear to throw out. Ditto for the mouse with a cord.

There were pens but no writing pad. I did find a notebook with one page of writing—a list of about 20 names and telephone numbers. The names were all Spanish or French, the numbers all with the 809 local code.

I could hear the women talking.

"Paul said to donate the clothes to a charity. Bag them up separately."

"Make-up, hair dryer and such should go to the girls from the school."

I looked around the living room, picked up the few framed photos she had displayed. A wedding picture, a striking sunset. Her shelves held a lot of books. Mostly self-help guides and thrillers by writers I didn't know. But I did recognize one tome. Mine.

"Books going next door for the rental house's library?" I asked out loud.

"Sure," said Margaret.

I hefted my novel. Great cover that no one had judged the book by. 638 pages I remembered. I idly thumbed through the pages. That's when money began fluttering out. A lot of it. All in US denominations.

I did the same with the other books. Mostly hundreds floated down to a growing pile.

"Ladies!" I yelled.

They dropped what they were doing in the bedroom and watched in amazement as I scooped up the bills and began counting.

"Twenty-one thousand, six hundred dollars," I announced when I was finally done.

"Holy shit!" Dot said.

"That's a lot of rental money," Margaret said.

"Bullshit," I said. "There's no way she collected that much. Do the math. That's about every penny she would've got for 50% of her rental charges for four years. And besides, she had to live down here, and she had to spend a lot on this place, pay Tico, utilities, and on and on."

"Well, it doesn't really matter where it came from, does it?" Margaret said. "By rights, it's all Paul's."

"Of course it is," I said. "But the police should be told. If Sally's killer knew about the money, then perhaps we've got a motive."

"Are they calling it a robbery?" Margaret asked.

"That's what they're leaning towards."

"So whether they were after a TV or this cash, it's still a robbery. What's the harm in just giving it to Paul? We turn this in as evidence and it will disappear."

I was about to start a spirited defence of the police under Chief

Inspector Diaz but bit my tongue. Practical Margaret was right.

"Then it's decided?" she asked.

We agreed and she took control of the great pile of dead presidents to return to Paul that night.

"Let's finish up," Dot said and we went back at it.

All in, it took most of the day to pack or throw out all the personal things. Time is always lost with a task like this. Each item has got to be considered. I went into the bedroom to find Margaret and Dot sitting side by side on the bed, slowly turning the pages of a large scrapbook. I joined them, Dot in the middle.

"Sally was making this to keep at the library where she ran her school," Dot said.

Group photos of the girls and boys, individual shots, all having in common the broad, dazzling smiles of her students. I knew some of them from my occasional English classes. These were good kids who had hope and enthusiasm. Ribbons and dried flowers had been glued on as decoration. Poems the girls had beautifully hand-written, some in Spanish, some in French.

Dot started to cry. We both put our arms around her.

"What happens to the school?" I asked.

"We've been talking," Margaret said. "We owe it to her—and to the kids—to keep it going."

"Count me in," I said.

"Good. We'll wait a couple of weeks and start contacting the students somehow."

"Wait just a minute," I said. I got up went to the living room and fished the notebook out of a box. "This list should make it easier. It's gotta be the kids' contact info."

My last job was to empty the refrigerator and freezer. Margaret wanted to give it all to her maids and the groundskeeper at the inn. But she insisted I take the opened bottles of rum, gin, and Grand Marnier.

"I'm *sure* Sally would've wanted you to have the booze," Dot said and we had our first and only chuckle of the otherwise sad day.

By 4 o'clock, we stood around in the driveway beside their small SUV packed to the gunwales. It was a somber moment, I think because we realized we had just erased Sally's presence from the house she built and loved.

"And the rental?" I finally said, pointing next door.

"Nothing to pack up there, but it's a problem. The people who were renting left the day after. I don't blame them, what with the police and the gawkers and all. The very idea that right next door a...that *that* happened."

"But Sally was proud she was fully booked until the end of April," Margaret said. "So there's going to be a lot more people coming down. And soon."

"I didn't find any records, reservation forms, anything like that," I said. "All the e-mails and such would've been on her missing computer."

"Well, Paul and Bruce will just have to figure it out. Maybe a sign on the gate with Bruce's number."

I tore a page out of the notebook, found some tape and scrawled Bruce's name and number from the For Sale sign on the compound wall, titled the thing "Attention Renters!" and pinned it to the gate. I resisted the temptation to write "For a scary time, call Bruce

Anderson at 809...."

Margaret and Dot declined my offer to help unload and I declined their offer for a lift home.

"You gonna strap me to the roof?" I said, looking at their vehicle so full that one of them was walking.

So Dot and I headed down the road the quarter of a mile to the Mariposa. She was still pretty shook up.

"I don't know why," she said between sniffles. "I just felt that something like this might happen."

"How come?"

"I don't know why," she repeated.

The walk back to my place was slow, the semi-bequeathed liquor bottles clinking noisily in the bag I hugged to my chest like a clumsy school kid with a load of books.

The first thing I did at home was mix a *gigantico* tequila sunrise, substituting Grand Marnier for grenadine. Lots of ice, lots of lime juice, and lots of sorry, Sally, for what truly had been a shitty day.

I awoke early Sunday morning, like real early. 4:30 in fact. Unable to get back to sleep, I made up a 10-cup pot of coffee, had three and then was overcome by a rare and inexplicable desire to walk. Rather than stumble around in the dark, I waited for the beginnings of a sunrise. It was quiet sitting in the dark on the balcony waiting for dawn to light up the gardens.

Quiet except for the fucking roosters. One of many, many new things to become accustomed to down here are roosters. I've talked to tourists who express their intense dislike for being awakened at 5 a.m. by the insistent and suddenly piercing crowing. You never know where and how loud it will be because chickens here are of the true free range variety. They wander in their loose packs or flocks or whatever the fuck as willy-nilly as the stray dogs. And it's not as though the roosters limit themselves to early morning vocalizing. Any time of the day you can hear them, as if they're pretty well pleased with themselves 24/7.

By dawn's early light, I headed to the shore, hung a left, and walked west, along Playa Ballenas, away from the town, past Michel's and around the point and onto the less populated Playa Bonita. Must have been three miles one way.

This was not a march-or-die speed slog that you see the tourists grimly put themselves through. More a meander, pacing myself again, stopping to have a cigarette from time to time and stare at the water. Looking for what? A shark fin, a passing whale pod maybe. Or for nothing at all.

Standing on a beach, any ol' beach down here but particularly the spectacularly vacant Bonita, you get some amazing skyscapes. Clouds don't seem to hover down here; they honk along at a very noticeable clip. Early morning, just as the sun's coming up over the hills is the best time for a sort of art history slide show. One moment, the sky's all Turner with giant fuzzy blue-grey thunderheads shot through with yellows and soft whites, a gentle blurring. Wait a few minutes and the celestial movie set gets torn down and up pops some of Vinnie Van Gogh's crazy swirls. Turn your head north and there's a squadron of Monet's vague and puffed cotton ballsy clouds floating in formation.

It is a time for thought to vanish and a sense of complete insignificance to prevail.

This feeling of fuck-allness didn't last too long, but long enough to temporarily wipe the brain slate clean.

Out of proverbial left field came a quote from my boss in another life when I was a corporate PR slut. This boss—a hard-nosed billionaire whose murder I had helped solved last year—once said: "Sometimes you have to stop thinking and actually do something."

I had spent an ordinate—for me—amount of time looking shit up.
It had helped complete the picture but a computer screen was, is,
and will always be a crappy substitute for reality. Time to get my ass
in gear and get out there to talk to actual real, live humans.

I just had to be sure what I was talking to them about first.

I was back at the condo before ten where I micro-waved a cup of
burnt coffee and returned to the balcony and my shitty laptop. I
skipped my normal global news sweep and instead idly flipped back
and forth again over five or six US articles on Sally's murder.

The only person who had even hinted at some shred of hard knowledge about the case had been Tico when I talked to him briefly at his
new job, and even then, all he had vaguely indicated was there were
"bad men" in the hills around the town, meaning the ritzy villas.
And that wasn't exactly a solid lead or even news. But I didn't doubt
he had more to give. I just had to get him to give it.

It was a good day for another walk I decided —wait, what am I saying? It's *never* a good day for two walks. But it was a good day to find
Tico again. Sunday was the only day most Dominicans and Haitians
get off and, even then, a lot of them work that day because, however
paltry, it means another day's pay.

Frank's construction site was closed down when I got there. It was
still early on Sunday so I reckoned that Tico hadn't yet struck off
for Pétionville. The only other place he was likely to be at was the
Haitian barrio at the south end of town off the main street.

Ours is a small town and theirs is a small barrio. Even at that, I had
been warned that it wasn't the swellest of places to be after dark. I
had taken this piece of advice on faith but now, as I left the main
street and entered the two-square block 'hood, I had to ask myself
why I had automatically assumed it was dangerous.

While the barrio may have been bounded by more or less perpendicular streets, nothing inside the square was at right angles. A collection of dusty trodden paths threaded their way among shanty houses, some cinder block, many just bits of wood and metal or plastic sheets lashed and nailed to narrow poles. Laundry lines were strung between the few hydro lines. Diaperless kids screeched and laughed and ran while the adults hung out in small groups dressed in their finest Sunday clothes, the men aggressively playing dominos, slapping the tiles down with a loud clack.

Want to be appalled at the abject poverty? Go ahead and be appalled. This place and tens of thousands like it shelter more than half the planet's population. I've actually had people tell me they wouldn't return to the DR—or Jamaica or Mexico or a bunch of other southern countries—because the poverty was so terrible. Smart decision. The sight of poor people hurts your eyes so much. Makes sense. You shouldn't have to look at it. And wouldn't it be just great if everybody felt that way, right? Then you could shut down almost every hotel and restaurant, thereby crippling the economies of about thirty countries that rely on tourism. That'd be a good thing, wouldn't it? Oh, except for all the even poorer people it would create. But that's OK; you wouldn't be around to see them.

Now I'm not saying the barrio citizens fell over themselves trying to welcome me to the neighbourhood. I was met with stares, not angry or contemptuous, just brief curious, why-the-fuck-was-I-where-I-was stares.

*"Tico est un ami de moi,"* I said to a group of teenagers. *"Il est ici?"*

One waved in a general direction that I then followed, repeating my question to an old woman who narrowed his location down for me.

I found him sitting on a plastic chair in front of a one-room shack, maybe 12 by 15. He was flicking through his cell-phone, his one connection to the world. He looked up only when a small dog came charging out of the house at me, barking his tiny head off. Just the way he always did.

"Bruno!" I said, reaching down to him in, I swear, a friendly way. And just the way he always did, the dog danced around growling and yapping fiercely until his new master took over.

"Bruno," Tico said quietly and the dog shut the hell up and lay down at Tico's feet. The wretched dog looked at me as if to say: "You are so fucking lucky he's here. Otherwise, I'd rip your trachea out. And you know I'd do it too, don't you, buddy?"

We—that'd be Tico and I—exchanged pleasantries, using the furry bark machine as a prop.

"I come home one day and he is here," Tico explained. "He find me."

"How is that possible?" I asked and saw Tico instantly stiffen up, not particularly enjoying being doubted.

"I take him before sometimes when Miss Sally go to America so maybe he knows the house."

"He came far," I said, imagining the trek across the swamp and into town.

"*Oui.*"

"The police want to know where he is."

"They cannot have him! He is my friend," he said, reaching down with his long arm to gently scratch under Bruno's pointed little chin.

"Tico, I know you loved Miss Sally. You must help find out who did this thing to her."

"*Je ne peut pas!*" he protested. I can't, I am not able.

"*Pourquoi pas?*"

He looked away, his dusty feet suddenly tapping nervously.

"Tico?"

He turned on me, furious.

"I am afraid!"

"The police can help."

"Police help Haitian?!"

"Yes. You have my word," I said, knowing I could guarantee nothing beyond the fact that Inspector Diaz was a decent guy. Tico settled down. "Tico, you said there was a bad man in the hills."

"*Non.*"

"What do you mean *non*? Tell me who."

Silence from Tico.

"Who is it?" I prodded.

"El Gordo."

"Who?"

"El Gordo. All I know."

"Good. We have a name. Good. The police will handle him."

"I should handle him! I am a man. I should cut him," he said, looking at his three-foot long machete leaning against the doorway.

"*Pas un bonne idée, mon ami,*" I said. "You will suffer for no reason."

"I am frightened."

"Why?"

"He has bad friends."

"Who?"

"*Les Russes.*"

"Russians?"

Tico nodded.

"Sergei, the book seller?"

"*Non! Non!* Other Russians. From the south."

"For fuck's sake, Tico. The whole country is south of Las Terrenas. Who?"

"I cannot say," he said, returning to his phone.

This was, I realized, the point in the conversation when conversation had to stop. Tico wasn't going to give anything more than he already had. And maybe he never would.

# CHAPTER EIGHTEEN

First things first. I got home before noon and immediately tore up and threw away all my meandering notes and observations on the expat community of drunkards. I had pretty well pulled everything I wrote about them out of my ass. Tico had supplied the first real lead and it didn't point to any of my drinking buddies.

But now I had a name, or rather a Spanish nickname as I presumed that no Dominican mother looking at her newborn son, no matter how chubby, would decide that he obviously had to be called El Gordo—The Fat One—for the rest of his life.

I was more than relieved that my associates now seemed beyond suspicion. None of them were grossly overweight. In fact, now that I thought about it, except for Trevor, I was the porkiest of the lot and I knew I hadn't done anything bad—unless you count serially walking under the influence.

And Tico had given me the pretty strong hint of a conspiracy involving Russians. Russians who weren't from Las Terrenas. And judging from the fear in Tico's eyes, Russians who could excite dread.

In total, it amounted to not much, but it was something. I started another little debate with myself about whether or not I should go directly to Arty with what Tico had told me.

It didn't much matter how convinced I was, I'd bet Arty would need more than my earnest expression to work with.

Terry, Howie, and the FOX gang were on and I happily settled into my usual seven-hour Sunday NFL viewing habit. Second last Sunday of the regular season, four or five play-off appearances yet to be decided, a fridge full of Presidente *giganticos,* and a big bag of Cheez Doodles. All the fixings for my idea of a swell Sunday. Short of hanging out stupefied in an opium den, I can't think of any better way to pass the time and clear the brain than watching flying pigskin and large men fall down go boom, as my daughter once described the game.

When I used to spend all year in Canada, I'd feel bad about missing a sunny fall day by hiding inside in a darkened room. Down here, because almost every fucking day is sunny, I convince myself that I'm actually taking care of myself by taking one day off a week from cultivating a grade-3 melanoma.

Don't misunderstand: I don't watch football as background pictures while I drift off. I am fully engaged, as they say. In yet another character quirk—or flaw, if you insist—I do not ever combine two of my favourite things, bars and the NFL. I want to watch the game, not other people watching the game.

And at Big Dave's, one of his two big screens had to be devoted to fucking English Premier League soccer. Try as I might, I can't talk myself into giving a good goddamn about whether or not West Bromwich Albion beats Swansea City—which they probably didn't because all the matches end in 0-0 with a total of 9 shots at a net the size of a fucking drive-in movie screen. And don't get me started about the smaller men who—although untouched—fall down go boom as if they've been shot, writhing in mortal agony but, who, thanks to the miracle-working trainers trotting onto the pitch to tend to invariably a mid-shin injury, make a complete recovery the second after the sight-challenged referee awards a penalty and plays flash cards with the protesting villain. Shakespearean as hell perhaps, but the kind of antics that would get you beat up by your own teammates in football or hockey.

At any rate, just me and my remote, beer, and Cheez Doodles are all I need on most Sundays. By week 16, I'm in fine form, flicking (alliteratively) back and forth between the games, timing my channel jumps just before the truck and boner commercials start to get me to live action somewhere else, so the afternoon is spent watching almost continuous play, only with many different coloured uniforms.

I love that simultaneity, the ability to in real time (fuck PVRing games, they've already happened; tough titties if you missed them) to leapfrog around the country. Snowy and cold in Green Bay, sunny in Miami, and drizzly in Seattle. Think about it—but for not too long lest you descend into the arcane musings of my wee brain—you can't do that with anything else. Not baseball, OK? If you're watching baseball games—for what reason I can't discern—then the weather's good. Maybe soccer but I've already dealt with that alleged sport a little earlier.

Sated, and with the pleasant dynamo hum of eight pints in seven hours, I fed myself a perfunctory egg-based meal and emerged all squinty-eyed into the great outdoors of my balcony.

Firing up my shitty laptop, I think about how I might better understand the murder of Sally Bartlett by finding out more about her beyond our casual conversations.

What I decided might be useful was to discover if there was some hint from Sally herself as to just what the fuck was going on. I could go back and interview people who knew her and maybe I could get something. But whatever that might be, it would also be hearsay, your honour. What they said she said.

Her apartment hadn't told me much; at least nothing out of the ordinary, except for the wads of cash I found. I didn't have her computer to run through anything she might've jotted down but there was one possible source.

I e-dusted off my Facebook account. I set it up having been led to believe that it would be essential to selling my book. It might've been, had I actually had any friends. I hadn't looked at for close to a year.

I wracked my wee brain for my password. Oh, yeah. 111111.

And there I was.

I was diverted a bit—as I was meant to be—by scrolling down and looking at all the things that had been sent my way. If you've got time on your hands, Mr. Zuckerberg wants it. All of it. And then some.

My, my, things had changed in just a year. Not that Facebook—or my tiny corner of it—had ever been a non-stop forum of original thought and lively discussion about all manner of cultural, social, and political topics but this was just a rolling parade of postings and re-postings from somewhere else. And fucking lists. Longer and longer lists to keep them ads coming while reminding us just how stupid we all apparently are because almost every hysterical headline implied or stated that I don't know or can't do jackshit. "208 of the most fascinating bones you didn't know you had", "Making toast: you're doing it wrong," that sort of thing. Or "Whatever happened to...?" click-throughs of casts of TV shows that had been cancelled a couple of months earlier. Like I had stayed up nights wondering.

There was a steady stream of those mini-posters which strive to look more authoritative than ordinary sentences by gussying themselves in fancy typestyles and dreamy background photos. (Why hadn't Deep Thoughts by Jack Handey or even Stuart Smiley ended this pretentious shit 20 years ago?) You know what? Uploading posters with big text of some inane, completely inarguable statement made by some psycho-babbler who makes his or her living writing inane, completely inarguable statements about how we're all supposed to be nicer to ourselves, our friends, and our dogs or how fucking grand and strong we are for "enduring" all the tough things in our first-world lives—when we're the crown of fucking creation—like the deaths of parents or friends or parakeets as if somehow we just found out that living things sooner or later stop living is not a philosophical proposition. It's life by bumper sticker.

This bumper sticker mentality is, of course, astoundingly lame-brained when you're addressing a particular issue as you must reduce yourself to pitting your bumper stickers against someone else's with an opposing view. "An armed society is a civil society" was a popular slogan plastered on the bumpers of almost exclusively pick-up trucks in the parking lots around The Ralph when I used to attend Bills games. "Rid the piece, keep the peace" was the answer given by people who favour sane gun laws.

This is how nuanced arguments have become.

I started to enter 'Sally Bartlett Las Terrenas' and up she popped. Turns out, she was a friend of mine, one of 37 in total and one of only eight whom I hadn't gone to high school with. I had forgotten that we had become friends in cyberspace a few weeks after we became friends in real life three winters ago during the last gasp of trying to hawk my dying quail of a book.

I ran through her home page which was pretty standard stuff. Her postings and re-postings offered a lot of comment on US politics—a lot of articles critical of Trump or memes about him or comedian takes on him—all of the sort that get shared by middle-class white people who grew up in the 70s with SNL, *Rolling Stone,* The Far Side, and *National Lampoon.*

On the personal front, there were lots of pictures of her original LT house and lots of pictures of before, during, and after construction of her new house/murder scene. There were pictures of sunsets, pictures of meals in LT restaurants, birthday parties at Big Dave's, group shots from her unofficial school, stuff like that, together with pictures of her and Paul alone or with their friends doing mountainous things back in Denver. There were also some pretty funny anti-Trump posters and a few articles on the sheer madness of US gun laws.

In my books, there aren't a lot of things more impressive and beautiful than palm trees in silhouette. And it's not because I've got an unhealthy thing for postcards, but just that at the beginning and ending of a day, I'd rather see rows of those feathery leaves backlit by blazing oranges, reds, and yellows than just about anything else.

Judging from Sally's Facebook page, she was a big fan of those trees too. I dug a little deeper and found she had a photo album—must have been a hundred pictures of them. As pretty as they are, they have in bulk numbers the appearance of 'seen one, seen them all' sameness. Except one picture that really stood out.

This particular photo caught my attention because of a rare timing thing. On the left, a full palm tree in silhouette. The yellow/white setting sun dead centre against the flaming orange sky. And on the right, three pelicans in flight. That was unusual, mostly because you normally didn't see three pelicans in the DR or really that many birds of any kind compared to other islands I've been to.

An old Dominican shopkeeper once claimed to me that this was so because the American army had carpet-bombed the DR with DDT when they invaded the country in 1965. As planned, it killed the malaria-carrying mosquitoes, but it also wiped out all the other insects which in turn starved or drove away all the birds. Some 50 years after the fact, they were returning.

After the photos came her words. Sally's comments were all grammatically perfect, although she clearly believed the exclamation point was the most essential punctuation mark you could use. Even better when you use two of them in a row as she tended to do. I smiled. That fit her exuberance, whether it was over a *cabrese* salad at Don Pio's, the overwhelming cuteness of Bruno, or the beauty of yet another postcard sunset.

I e-rooted around some more. There's no question it felt weird crawling around the life of a dead person, a dead person I had known. I've got no idea how this works. Someone dies. How long to do they live on in Facebook? Who takes them off? Relatives sending a copy of a death certificate? A vote among her friends?

Background: Born in Fort Worth, Texas, which I knew.

Worked at: Retired. Previous employer: Excel Energy, Colorado's largest utility. I knew that too. She'd met Paul at Texas A&M then moved to Denver and spent 35 years in Human Relations at Excel before drawing her pay and fucking off with a nice defined benefits pension and a perfectly sensible desire to not see snow again.

Birth date: May 9. No year given which, I guessed, was pretty standard for a southern girl who simply didn't talk about certain things, like age and weight.

She had friends, lots of them, 1,068 in all. I started rolling through them. I found several, five at least, with the last name of Stephenson which I assumed was her family name as three of the five were also from Fort Worth.

Mixed in with what looked like a homogenous group of middle-aged American friends and the odd Canadian were quite a lot of Dominicans and Haitians. That made sense too because of her local involvement.

I went back to the scores of pictures from charitable events that came into being because of her tireless energy. She wasn't being braggy, for she described each civic undertaking as the kind of thing all expats *should* do to make life in their town, in their adopted country better.

There was one incident not recorded which to me summed up Sally's no-nonsense, let's make things better attitude. A bunch of us had gone out for dinner at not Dave's, not Mojito's, but a Dominican place with cheap but great fried fish and chicken. A few ladies had ordered a bottle of wine. When the glasses came, Sally got into a heated discussion with the server about their cleanliness, sending all three back for re-washing. We were all kinda dumbstruck, especially us bachelors who live like slobs. But she was adamant. "They have to learn. They have to raise the bar," she'd said.

Her Likes were numerous—everything from Springsteen to Adele to Martin Luther King. And then pretty well the entire directory of Las Terrenas restaurants, all of which were glowingly reviewed with liberal exclamation points. Except two which weren't really restaurants: the Galaxy Nightclub and Club Jam. Her only comment for them: "These clubs are a travesty in our town!!"

I passed Galaxy across from Fishermen's Village all the time walking into town and back when I didn't take the less direct beach route. During the day and well into the evening it was shuttered. At 10 o'clock, the self-imposed curfew time for *most* of my excursions to Big Dan's or Mojito's, the club doors were open and the post-disco electronic thudding with a salsa inflection thundered onto the street as intellibeams and lights flashed. There was still nobody around. It was the oddest sight because deafening shitty music like that is slightly more tolerable when you can see that at least some people are enjoying it.

Actually, if Mojito's was my originating point, I also had to also pass the other club, named Jam. It was strategically located at the 'T' junction of Calle Duarte, the main north-south street, and 27 de Febrero, the Playa Popy coast road. Right across from the high and mural-filled wall in front of the cemetery, Jam was the same, same as Galaxy. Near as I could ever tell, it had the identical playlist consisting of one interminable pulsating song whose volume I thought would have the permanent residents of the graveyard tossing and turning.

In another posting she wrote: "El Gordo should be arrested for what goes on in his clubs!! Those poor girls!!"

Cue the proverbial sound of screeching brakes in my wee brain.

The same El Gordo whom Tico had indicted? Well, of course it was. I was, if not angry, at least a little miffed at myself for having taken so long to clue in. If I had popped my head out of my ass and spent more time getting out and about in our small town I would have made the connection sooner.

I'd never met the man Sally named as the owner of the clubs, but there was one guy who fit the bill. I had occasionally seen him around town; he was hard to miss. Usually he was in the back seat of his black chauffeur-driven Crown Vic. I had always found his little display of ostentation kinda funny. The double barrel of numerous pot holes and oil pan-scraping speed bumps meant there was no smooth cruise through LT. With the suspension on his big Ford boat fully active, the car bounced and bobbed up and down like it was being driven by an LA gang banger with OCD who just couldn't stop playing with his custom air shocks.

You got the full measure of the man—as it were—when he wasn't being ferried around. Rare for a Dominican, El Gordo was true to his nickname: fat, over 300 pounds hanging off a medium-sized frame and wrapped up in expensive three-piece linen suits acting like sausage casings. I'd see him sometimes at the upper end restaurants in Fishermen's Village across from the Galaxy Club, always with his accessories: lots of gold on his fingers and around his neck, a large bodyguard, and a wondrously beautiful *chica* who, no doubt, was attracted to his loads of character.

With that link made, I read on, trying to banish El Gordo's image from my mind. Judging by all the organizations and groups she belonged to, Sally was a joiner—which, given her outgoing attitude only made sense. Texas A&M Alumni, Denver Perennial Society, book clubs, yoga groups, environmental charities. In the DR, she belonged to only one outfit: Friends of Paradise Regained/*Amigos de Paraiso Recupero*. I went there, fearing it might be a bilingual fan club for the lesser works of John Milton.

On its landing page were the words: "Dedicated to improving the DR experience for everyone" and a 'Join/*Alistarse*' button. But membership wasn't automatic or open to the public so I had to apply. It was a pretty detailed questionnaire to fill out which normally annoys the shit out of me. Birthplace, town of residence, age, all the way down to level of education. You also had to pick a screen name that, according to the instructions, "would allow our members to comment freely." That also annoys me because I wasn't ever reluctant to publish my real name on any of the Comments sections I occasionally ranted on. Finally—and oddly, I thought—I was advised that any photo icon I chose "should not be an identifying self-portrait." I chose Snake for a name and dropped in the Oakland Raider logo.

It was the least I could do to recognize Mr. Stabler and the hours of pleasure he had provided me back when the silver and black inspired fear and loathing.

For all my snooping on Sally's social media presence, there wasn't much there. She loved her unlovable dog. She loved her adopted town. She was keen on sunsets. She tried to make things better.

Oh, and she was the second person in less than twenty-four hours who had fingered El Gordo, the night club owner, as a very bad guy.

Just a name. But the not much was growing into something.

# CHAPTER NINETEEN

I slept in finally, repaying at least the exorbitant interest on my sleep debt, and I woke up famished and with absolutely zero inclination to make something for myself. A couple of smokes, a couple of coffees and I was taking the noon foot train, on the road towards Mojito's.

Sometimes, I will actually go out for a meal, beyond the most excellent fish tacos at Big Dave's subcontracted *cantina*. Of course I have my rules to consider. It has to be a sunny and calm day. And, if I'm dining alone—as I usually am—it has to be while staring at the ocean. In Las Terrenas, there is nothing between the coast road and the water but palms and sand except for the slightly pricey restaurant row of Fishermen's Village, the cemetery and a few beach bars—Michel's west of me and Mojito's in the east across from the police station. Although it was a little farther to walk, Mojito's had really swell eats in addition to its really swell drinks.

There's no kitchen on the beach side where Mojito's is. You place your order from a small but uniformly good menu and the waiters then have to scurry across the coast road, dodging *motoconchos* and scooters rented to tourists who believe they've become Evel Kneivel's offspring, to get to the kitchen at the small hotel where the cooking gets done. They then have the reverse trip—only with armfuls of food.

There are also no washrooms beach side which, the more shit-faced you become, the more interesting is the challenge of beetling across the road to the hotel *banos*.

Basically, the bar is just a very big tiered deck sitting on nautical-looking posts sunk into the sand. Partially shaded by a roof, partially shaded by giant sea grape trees whose broad waxy leaves keep off a brutal midday sun. The joint has a maybe 12 X 12, eight-sided tiki bar hut, plunked down in the middle of the deck usually housing, depending on the time of day, one or both Cuban brothers who own the place.

Ivan was in the booze house on this day. We chatted a bit as he slid me my first drink of the day over the well-worn countertop. I reckoned that he, as a fellow member of the hospitality sector, would know something about El Gordo.

The normally gregarious Cuban was suddenly not in a talkative mood, thereby making for a clumsy conversation rivalling any of Clouseau's.

"Ivan, what can you tell me about El Gordo?"

"He is fat. Like his name."

"Geez, have you noticed he always has a bodyguard and a pretty girl with him?"

"He is rich."

"Do you ever hang out with him?"

"No."

"He ever come in here?"

"No. Another beer?"

"Yes."

"Excuse me, please."

Ivan turned to the cash register and fucked around with some receipts next to it.

'Alrighty then,' I thought as he ended our chat. I took a table at the far end of the place.

Club sandwiches are the great levellers of millions of restaurants. It's rare to get a bad club sandwich. The differentiator for me is the accompanying dill pickle. And Mojito's had excellent dill pickles. I placed my order, sucked on my beer, and stared at the ocean.

"Talk to me about anything other than this case, *Ingles*!" Arty cheerily announced as he clapped me on the shoulder and sat down to join me. "Unless you can prove who did it and why."

"How did—"

"It was deductive reasoning to make Sherlock proud. I saw your hippie hair, cigarette smoke, and ugly shirt from across the street," he said, pointing at the cop shop about 75 yards away.

"I was going to see you right after lunch," I said.

"Why?"

"I know who's involved in the murder."

"Your problem, *Ingles*—one of your many problems—is that you do not listen."

"Arty, I'm serious."

"So am I. Do not talk to me about this."

Arty did indeed look serious. Maybe because this high-profile case was going nowhere, maybe because I hadn't contributed anything that was even remotely useful to him.

'Well, I tried,' I said to myself. The fact was, I had no facts. Going to Arty now with Tico's hearsay and Sally's general distaste for El Gordo wasn't exactly an ironclad case. I let it go.

Instead, we shot the shit about the Sunday games. He took some glee in mentioning that my Raidahs were again out of the play-offs while his Packers again had a first-round bye.

He was almost as annoying as the Cheeseheads of Florida.

"Talk to me about anything other than Raiders," I said.

The obvious general topic was life in the DR. I was truly interested in what this smart, pragmatic man could tell me.

It must be difficult to be a full-time conscientious cop and a part-time apologist for all the generalizations he had to be aware of, coming from dumb expats like me who didn't know his beloved country nearly as well as he did. What I really liked about Arty was his refusal to just spout the bullshit propaganda of government officials or tourism websites whose only interest is pretending that absolutely everything in the country was totally acey-deucey, hunky-dory, *and* the cat's pyjamas. He could actually explain the why of things, rather than the knee-jerk reaction of some expat jerks or his own government.

Take for example his view on the choking air of every main street in every coastal tourist town around the country. Walls were stained grey from the noxious fumes, sidewalk trees stunted and yellowed by the exhausts coming mainly from the omnipresent *motoconchos* but also from the four-wheeled beaters the locals drove.

On this day, with me dropped into this idyllic setting of ocean, sand, and greenery—including the green Presidente bottles—it's an effort to tune out the sound but at least the offshore breeze kept the smell away.

I made some off-hand comment about the fact that a tourist-y post-card photo of the picturesque main street along the ocean couldn't capture the stink of gas and diesel fumes.

"So, we should bring in your emission rules?" Arty asked.

"It's a thought," I said. "Lots of places have them."

"A bad thought. Those laws would hurt the economy and make poor people poorer. These bikes are like the family cow or horse. They are the only way they get to jobs, the only way they get to school, to church to stores beyond the local *mercado*. How do they carry water?"

And it's true. Pretty much every day I had seen the impressive feats of balancing on these slender bikes. It wasn't uncommon to see three full 5-gallon jugs precariously tied down, or a small washing machine, or cages of chickens. I would often see two or three soldiers, decked out in desert camo and black combat boots reporting for duty astride one of these.

"Take them off the road and people are trapped," Arty continued. "And for many young men, it is not the way to get to their jobs; it *is* their jobs."

"Yeah, but don't you think we've got more than enough *motoconchos* here?" I asked.

"So, *you* will decide this, *Ingles*? Or should we pay for a government department that has the wisdom to say: oh, sorry, there must be only 27 *motoconcho* drivers in Las Terrenas? The rest of you trying to live on the few pesos you might make each day, you must be fucking off now. We wish you good luck."

Seemed to me that was a pretty sturdy defence of free markets. But Arty wasn't done.

"They may come here from 50 miles inland because here we have some stores, a doctor. And if you have a car? *Madre de dios,* no matter its condition, it is worth gold. It is the village's car. The people fix the cars, the bikes themselves. And surely they cannot afford brand new mufflers."

Likewise, he delivered a chastening explanation on the stray dogs which I had noticed—I think every expat had noticed—seemed to, as a general rule, automatically shy away from the locals. "It's horrid the way these people mistreat animals," said one foreigner, a kindly stout Brit named Gladys who hailed from a country where cats and dogs had been elevated to at least human status, if not higher.

"I wish for you people to think longer of things," Arty said. "Of course, the dogs know they will get more pats and above all more food from you foreigners. Why in the *nombre de dios* would most Dominicans not give a kick instead? We keep pigs and goats and chickens so we can, one day, eat them. A dog will beg and keep coming to houses with people so poor they can barely feed their own families. We do not need them or their *mierda* and piss in the yard while they beg for that which they will not get. For protection? What is it that most Dominicans or Haitians have that people want to steal? *Nada!* I have learned to watch the Dominican houses where dogs are kept. It will mean someone has money—and for many— the only way he got that money is against the law."

Similarly Arty would get all cranked up when faced with the accusations—well, the fact—that many members of his police force and the *turistico* police viewed their salaries as supplemental income to their real source of revenue—shaking down foreigners and businesses for *morditas*. The little bites.

"Think again, *Ingles.* Do you know the pay for a new constable?"

I confessed I didn't.

"About 250 US dollars."

"A week?"

"No," he laughed but didn't mean it. "A month!"

"That's not a lot," I said, realizing that was about two weeks of my bar tab at Big Dan's.

"In the small villages you may survive on that," he continued. "Rent is nothing there—although so too are the *casas* to buy. Fruits and vegetables, nothing. And there is nowhere to shop. But in this place or any place the tourists are, it is different. You think the SuperPolo or any other *mercado* here has a different price for Dominican police officers?"

"So it's OK with you. The *morditas?'*

"No!" And it was the first time I had seen Arturo really angry. "It is not OK! And it is not an excuse. But it is an explanation. You should see that!"

I have this tendency to react—not in a good way—when I am told I *should* do something. Anything. For me, 'should' is what they now fashionably call a trigger word; I have no idea why. Childhood sociopathy, maybe. But at my age fixing that automatic response isn't high on my list of things to do. So instead, I just let myself get all amped up with Arty.

"Maybe you could explain to me why six of ten murders are never solved?" I demanded. "Or the fact that 10% of those murders are actually committed by police? Or how about why there has to be more armed security guards than national police?" I asked, citing some alleged web statistics while forgetting for the moment that I was speaking to a man with a gun.

"Bullshit!" he almost shouted, certainly bringing some silence to the crowd at Mojito's just as Ivan was delivering my food and Arty's drink.

The Cuban barkeep looked as though he was about to advise us to calm the fuck down when he saw that Chief Inspector Diaz was one of the shouters. Instead, he gave me a pissed-off look.

"Bullshit," Arty repeated, picking up the thread of our conversation after Ivan left, only this time in a whisper. "What is murder? What is self-defence? The police force meets many desperate young men with guns."

"One reason they are desperate is they know about your prison system and life in La Victoria."

It took us several minutes of silence to really calm the fuck down. It was Arty who spoke first, returning to his soft, deliberate voice.

"The question for this day, *Ingles*, is why you are using these numbers which are not true? What is your motive? Let me suggest one. You want me to agree with the stereotype that Dominican police are either stupid or hired killers."

"That's not what I said."

"That is what you *meant*. And now you want me to answer for it. You want me to defend all the government, all the police, all the people? That is not my profession."

By the way his eyes were darting around, I could see Arty was working himself up to another rant/lecture.

"You Americans, Canadians, all you *Ingles* think that all the world should be at the same place, at the same time as your countries. You think about the good things we should have. I know. I think of them too. I think that journalists should not be jailed or killed for being journalists. That all politicians should live in houses they can afford on their salaries. That...that teachers would make good pay. And the police make good pay. And everybody makes good pay.

"But when *you* are here, you mainly think about fixing the things that anger you. That buses would always be on time, the Internet would always let you watch your stupid videos, the electricity would always be on. That no one threw garbage. That drivers use their signal lights. And you wish that everybody would speak English. And any country which is not as you would like, should not be surprised when the CIA arrives to do those things to make sure a country is not the country it wants to be. As they have done here for 60 years! Invading us, deciding who wins elections."

"Whoa, Arty. It is not my profession to defend the CIA."

"Sorry, *Ingles*. I wish for many things for my country, above all good schools. I wish prostitution was no longer the first and only choice for many of our girls. I wish my people would stay here and not go to New York. Did you know we have ten million people here but there are another two million Dominicans living in America?"

"I didn't," I said, "How do you..."

"Imagine, we have *Senor* Google!"

"So, that means 200,000 in Canada?" I asked, applying the "Canada is 10% of the US" Rule.

Arturo smiled again.

"Are joo keeding me, mang?" he said in a cartoon Spanish accent. "Some of my people may want to leave my country but that does not mean they are crazy enough to go to yours. There are many more Haitians in your Montreal than Dominicans. Your beautiful weather has brought maybe 10,000 of us to Canada and I assume more than half of them are now under a physicians' care. Or planning to ski across your St. Lawrence River to freedom."

"So now who's dealing in stereotypes?"

"It is irritating, no?"

Arty should have been a fucking teacher.

I made one last stab at being an annoying prick.

"So if everyone shuts up about the country, everything will be fine?"

"I did not say that. But things are getting better."

"Better? So how come the news is full of all the protests about corruption, how come you've got all those government officials on trial?"

"That *proves* it is getting better. The people are angry and the government has no choice but to do something about. And the criminals, they are being caught. Twenty years ago, that would not be true."

Game, set, and match to Arturo.

"When I was young..." he began again.

"Arty, I don't think you were ever young."

He smiled.

"When I was young, I wanted to change my country, the world, by myself."

"And now?"

"Here, in Las Terrenas, in this little corner, I can make a difference, do the right things. That is all I can do and that must be enough. Soon, all my men will behave. Soon, I will make it safe—not just for you *gringos*—because it is much more dangerous for the Dominicans and worse still for the Haitians."

Arty was staring out to the water as he spoke. He turned to me, his eyes full of business.

"I *will* find and stop evil," he said.

There could no mistaking his seriousness, his fierce conviction. And he knew his earnestness was showing.

"And now, if you will excuse me, I must return to stopping evil," he said with a smile.

He finished his drink and pulled a bunch of pesos out his pocket. and put them on the table.

"No, I got this," I said, pushing the bills back to him.

"I am shocked, *Ingles!*"

"Why? Because a cheap Canadian bastard tried to pay?"

"No... well, yes. But also because a cheap Canadian bastard would attempt to bribe a police official in daylight," he said, laughing and clapping me on the shoulder again.

I decided—big surprise—to have another beer. I was in a whole lot better mood after Arty left. What I really love about a conversation like the one we'd just had is that you feel alive, connected, learning new ways to see things, to understand.

I also decided that tonight would be an off-night for Big Dave's. I sat of my porch, fired up the laptop, a smoke, and a tequila sunrise.

In my Junk Mail, I found a string of notifications. Very kind people with addresses like gnathite19688@fifthavenueheat.net  and lady-lilith@swedmoreFGF.ru were letting me know that I had "delayed mails cobbles," not to mention "missed emails sulphate," "missed mails slavish," and that "4 lost message has been restore."

And a big hats off to the arsewipe at bmo/MRKKLJDOQ@11103MILP. corp.prds1.centcollege.ca who let me know that "the funds you are at Bank of Montreal been frozen" even though I have never had a fucking account with the fucking Bank of Montreal.

I appreciated their vigilance but couldn't Google or Microsoft or the bank at least give them a company e-mail address instead of making them work at home?

This kind of illiterate scamming made me wistful for the days when I used to get urgent pleas from a Nigerian prince or a Tanzanian lawyer guaranteeing great wealth if I would only connect them to their unreachable accounts. I was honoured to have been selected but never got involved. I don't know how many fortunes I've passed on, but I was OK with it. Part of the charm of their attempted hustle was at least the effort of a detailed story.

That night, I also found a note informing me I was now registered for Friends of Paradise Regained.

I don't know what I was expecting—maybe a site that reminded e-readers of all the good things about the country. This was not that kinda site. Just to give you an idea, here are the headings that ran along the top: Land Scams - Expat Murders - Government Corruption - Police Corruption - Jail Horror - Smuggler's Paradise and Child Exploitation.

There are a lot of things I can't do. I don't only mean complicated things like quantum physics or accomplished things like mountain-eering. I mean ordinary everyday things that just about every fuck-ing human can do. I can't whistle, for example. I can't open a bag of chips without tearing the flimsy aluminum right to the bottom sending a cascade of greasy chips onto my lap. I can't seal or unseal those zip plastic bags of shredded cheese without resorting to using scissors. I can't roll my tongue into a tube. I can't dance or sing.

Life is messy, certainly the way I practice it. I do pretty much every-thing impatiently and incompetently which, if I were a brain sur-geon, I suppose might distress me—and my patients—but I'm not.

What I can do, however, is find my way around the Internet like nobody's business. I can comfortably crap on most of the new tech-nology that has only served to make life more complicated and trivial, but I can't fault the web for its ability to cram things into my wee brain, if you know where to look.

With all the subtitles and the reams of Archives before me on Paradise Regained, I ploughed into it.

The Mission Statement section kinda captured their less than subtle editorial direction.

*"We are a group of expatriates and proud Dominicans dedicated to unmasking the illegal and immoral activities of ALL Dominican institutions which throughout our history have shamed our country's reputation and impoverished our people. When the climate is safer, our dedicated volunteers will write letters, commence lawsuits, and bring knowledge of our website to the attention of regulatory authorities, international bodies, foreign corporations and investors, church and community leaders in the hope that internal and external pressure brought by these will bring about the institutional reforms this country desperately wants and deserves."*

They ended their preamble with a quote from Edmund Burke that pretty well summed it all up:

*"The only thing necessary for the triumph of evil is for good men to do nothing."*

At the bottom of the page was a shaded box headed by one word: *"Apology."*

*"We, the Friends of Paradise Regained, apologize for the need to remain anonymous. There are many forces—some domestic, some foreign—who would like nothing better than to silence us."*

I've been to a few conspiracy-type sites before. Mostly, I confess, because they amuse the fuck out of me. Holocaust deniers. Climate change deniers. Anti-vaxxers. And on and on.

Bruce, the real estate guy/conspiracy nutjob, had supplied me with a few URLs to "educate" me. What these sites did was entertain. They were filled with slender arcane "evidence" leading to wild conclusions that governments all over the world were running all these false flag operations (Sidebar: I think these guys just like typing the words 'false flag') on their own people, killing tens of thousands of their fellow citizens—that only this guy in his mom's Hoboken basement knew about.

But this, this was different. Each section was essentially a compendium of news articles from a variety of legitimate sources preceded and followed by reasoned commentary. No all caps shouting, no bold colours and bolder type.

What also struck me about this place: there was no pulling of punches when it came to naming names. The actual names didn't mean much to me but their titles sure did. Santiago Chief of Police, Assistant Director of Drug Enforcement, Senators, Magistrates, CEOs of sugar companies, heads of tourism associations, and on and on.

Apparently, they're *all* rotten bastards and they were all being called out. By name.

And that I decided could be a dangerous game they were playing, Sally was playing, just by being a member.

There was also a directory of forums stretching back to the site's apparent launch about four years earlier. Members—like me now— could toss in their experiences, their own two pesos' worth of opinion on any manner of subject.

If you've got the time and the inclination, something I had scads and oodles of—even though I have no fucking idea what a scad or an oodle looks like—you can start to form pictures of the anonymous posters. Who's an idealist, who's the resident curmudgeon. Who's the most enthusiastic contributor, who's the smartest, who has particular areas of interest and so on.

There seemed to be about a handful of regular contributors, each with their own special focus. SD Charger was one; he or she was big into unmasking corruption, who paid whom to look the other way, to grant re-zonings, to grease the wheels, to let government contracts to companies they owned, to free drug smugglers caught red-handed with more than half a ton of cocaine in their plane as it landed.

SD Charger made it his/her business to delve into corruption in government at any level. Mindful of my recent chat with Arty, I was amazed at the sheer amount of cases being reported on. They really were catching a bunch of the elected crooks.

Bob-o-link was big into the land scams, calling out hustlers and developers who were carving out large sections of empty beachfront, screwing the owners and, in some cases, re-selling land they didn't have title to. How could I ignore his description of Donald Trump's legal tussle with the local developers in Cap Cana who were wiped out when the real estate markets pretty well everywhere in the world tanked like the Washington Generals.

The DR—and any country with a decent climate and an airport— owed a huge chunk of its prosperity and its future to attracting middle-aged dilettantes such as myself. This was big business. But, as Bob-o-link detailed, expanding to accommodate North American and European retirees also attracted more than its fair share of grifters and land sharks.

Someone with the unlikely name of Angel was all over the Expat Murders section. I found this corner of the site to be problematic because for it to really make an impact, every death of an expat seemed to be included to, in effect, make the case that you were taking your life into your hands by just stepping off the plane. But there wasn't much detail as to circumstance. For example, a German woman named Greta, a resident of Luperon for 12 years, had been killed by her boyfriend, Oscar. Did that prove the DR was dangerous? Nope. It proved that Oscar was dangerous. I'd further suggest that the killing of spouses and lovers, current or ex, transcends borders.

BayahiBabe—a play on name Bayahibe, a small diving/sailing town on the south-east coast—caught my attention right off. She—if it was a 'she'—was particularly active on any forum dealing with smuggling, child exploitation, and the plight of Haitians.

Her entries really stood out because they were heavy-up on educated, passionate writing and had the look and feel of authority and expertise.

An added bonus to her writings was context, something the others didn't seem to believe in. BayahiBabe took great pains to demonstrate that there was no real difference between the DR's situation and that of a long list of other sunny countries—either the fast-developing ones like Peru, Guatemala, and Ecuador or the well-established old white fart retreats like Panama, Costa Rica, and Mexico.

Even better was her contention that, other than *appearance* of civility, there was no real difference between the DR and the US where dark forces were hijacking money and power through gerrymandering electoral districts, curtailing voter rights, locking up inner city kids in for-profit prisons for weed, and pricing pharmaceuticals or health care out of reach of poor people who fucking *died* as a result.

She allowed that the Haitian/Dominican problem was unique in the Caribbean because they shared one island—reminding us not to get all pissy by mentioning St Maarten/St Martin as both are relatively well-off. She also suggested that the tragedy of frightened Hondurans and Nicaraguans attempting to flee their murderous cities for Mexico and then trying to head north was the same-same as the Haitians slipping into the DR then looking farther afield.

Well into the new morning, after most of a bottle of *Cazadores Reposada*, a half can of Off!, and another pack of fast-burning Marlboro *blancos*, I was still reading.

BayahiBabe had some news articles posted, like the coverage of the United Nations condemnation of the legislation of the 2010 Dominican law requiring all Haitians born after 1929 to register with authorities and produce their paperwork proving their birth here. The catch-22 of all this, of course, is that most Haitians born here—many who had lived in the DR for decades, generations in fact—did not actually have birth certificates. BayahiBabe contended that the government of course knew this before they enacted the law which was precisely why they enacted it.

There were follow up stories of how this law was being implemented and its effects. Towns deserted, camps by the border, 10,000 "repatriated" last year and with the expectation that this year—being an election year—the number of deportees would soar.

The only distracting thing—and perhaps it's only distracting to anal former English majors such as myself—was the writer's frequent and unnecessary use of double exclamation points.

Just like Sally did.

I fought back my initial excitement. This wasn't conclusive proof the writer was Sally, I told myself. Lots of people use exclamation points on the Internet. It is the default way to emphasize emphasis without resorting to goddamned emojis or emoticons or whatever the fuck they're called that now pass for human feeling and writing intended to compel or persuade.

I went back over BayahiBabe's postings on the Smuggler's Paradise section beginning with the earliest ones. Four years of them. Scrolling through and scanning them I saw not a single mention of Las Terrenas.

That wasn't conclusive proof it *wasn't* Sally. Maybe, to further hide her identity, she made sure she never mentioned her home base.

I couldn't believe that opinionated and engaged BayahiBabe would restrict herself to one area of interest. I wandered through the other categories, scrolling quickly looking to recognize her photo icon. Bright orange sunset and a single palm in silhouette.

I stopped. A bright orange sunset and a single palm in silhouette isn't exactly a rare image for the tropics but something about it looked familiar.

I blew up the tiny image by 300%. It was all blurry—although maybe that was a function of a head full of tequila and lack of sleep—but what now was evident were three dark blobs in the sky on the right hand side at about leaf height.

That photo was in Sally's Facebook photo album. I toggled back there to confirm it. No question it was the same image.

CHAPTER TWENTY

Again, I weighed the facts. Again, they didn't constitute cast-in-concrete evidence. It was possible that BayahiBabe had seen the photo on her new cyber buddy Sally's site and grabbed it. After all they were members of the same group. But, c'mon, what were the odds?

What had Arturo said?

"Start with the possible things and, because many, many things are possible, we must throw them away one at a time until we are left with the likely things."

I went through her posts again, taking my time, looking for anything that might connect the anonymous author and the murder victim I had known, beyond an out-and-out mention of Las Terrenas. She chipped into virtually every forum. In response to an article entitled 'Russian, Italian Mafia money in Cap Cana', she had joined SD Charger in commenting at length, stating that she knew a Sascha Petrovic was spreading his particular brand of thuggery throughout the island.

Russians from the south? That was enough for me. Sally and BayahiBabe had to be one and the same.

I did another review of her postings, this time imagining her as she pounded them out on the keyboard.

I saw that there was a definite shift in tone. What started out as a reasoned, almost intellectual argument against new immigration laws had changed over time, beginning last fall and winter.

Her focus had moved away from the new laws and towards the effects—intended or otherwise—on the living, breathing humans who were impacted by them.

It was personal now. It was emotional. She dealt with the effects on individual lives, on the lives of people who were living in camps along the border, the lives which had ended at sea. Family loss. Permanent psychological scars. Daily vigilance and the continuous threat of arrest and deportation.

And, according to Sally, some did escape. For would-be emigrants in this corner of the country, it meant going through Samana town to stow away in trawlers or makeshift boats of their own design for the 200-mile trip to Puerto Rico or to head north through the Turks and Caicos and the Bahamas aiming for the US. Some drowned, many more were caught and deported back to Haiti. And many more just stayed in LT, mindful that with the looming expiration date to register, they were living on borrowed time and subject to being rounded up at any time.

Without citing sources—something she had been scrupulous about in her earlier campaign dispatches –the author described in detail three specific ocean trips—one originating in Samana, one in Puerto Plata and one in Punta Cana—which she claimed were human smuggling runs. For a rumoured price of $20,000 a head, some Haitians would sign on for an illegal cruise up the Eastern seaboard docking near either New York or Halifax, Nova Scotia. The price of that ticket didn't get you first-class but instead the privilege of being packed into the holds of shitty transports or kept below decks of a converted luxury yacht. 30 or 40 customers represented a take of upwards of a million bucks and there wasn't, I bet, much in the way of overhead expenses. Just the fuel and a small crew. Not a lot went to food for the passengers on what could be a four-day voyage of the damned.

I tried to imagine the effort it would take for a Haitian labourer to amass 20,000 US dollars. I couldn't. They had to have had something like sponsors—sympathetic foreigners maybe, or family and friends—collecting for years to send one of theirs abroad.

According to BayahiBabe, two of the three voyages—the Puerto Plata and the Samana ships—had ended in tragedy. She said one voyage had been widely reported while the other one had been ignored, although—she claimed—she had first-hand knowledge that the second trip had also been part of a human smuggling operation.

What happened was this: On the verge of being intercepted by US or Bahamian or Turks and Caicos coast guards as they navigated the archipelagoes between the DR and America, the sonofabitch captains of both ships had made the monstrously evil decisions to jettison their human cargos in open water.

To drown.

As the roosters started crowing, I sat their stunned.

If true, who does this? How can this happen?

I found one news story—four years old—telling of the Haitians who had left from Puerto Plata. The account fit what BayahiBabe had written. 28 Haitians had drowned when the captain of the Panamanian-registered *Esperanza* had forced his doomed customers into the water under cover of night off the coast of San Salvador in the lower Bahamian islands.

But I couldn't find any news mentions of the Samana expedition. The closest I came was a brief news story about two Haitian deck hands working a fishing boat out of Samana who had apparently been swept overboard during rough weather this past October. The ship's owner—Jorge Olivero—was quoted as being devastated.

It was the next sentence of the article that did a whole lot more than just catch my attention:

"Senor Olivero—a Las Terrenas businessman popularly known as "El Gordo"—has promised to care for the families of the drowning victims whose bodies were not recovered and who were identified only by their first names, Francois and Jean-Baptiste."

Jorge Olivero. El Gordo, the same Jorge Olivero who owned both nightclubs in Las Terrenas, the same Jorge Olivero whom Sally loathed and whom Tico had named a bad man. Well, of course it was.

BayahiBabe/Sally's comment after the article? "What bullshit from this piece of scum!! If someone had the courage to investigate, they'd find out El Gordo was behind the smuggling!! And they'd probably also find out that he was working with Sascha Petrovic!!"

I was too excited to sleep. Arty would want to hear my discoveries. It looked as though we had us the start of a motive.

'Perhaps' had turned into likely'.

# CHAPTER TWENTY-ONE

Sleepless but alarmingly caffeinated, I sat side by side with Arty in front of the computer monitor in his office, walking him through what I thought I had found.

I started with Sally's Facebook pictures, isolating the three-pelican photo, then switching to BayahiBabe's icon on Friends of Paradise Regained where I then scrolled through the stories and the editorializing—particularly concerning El Gordo—while supplying running commentary on sentence structure and topics of interest.

It took a while and at the end of it, Arty sat back and thought. And thought.

"It makes sense, *Ingles*. It is a good piece of the puzzle. Now what to do about it?"

"Start with Jorge Olivero. Sally had a real hard-on for him and; she mentioned him by name. So did Tico."

"El Gordo? I do not care for him. But on what basis to go after him? He is small time. He's running girls and he's running drugs through though his clubs."

"Isn't that enough?"

"It is not that simple. I have been here for six months and his name came up early. But he is smart. The girls will not complain, will not talk against him because he provides for them. As for drugs, do you think any of it passes through his fat hands? A bad employee, he says. I had no idea, he says. Once more, the employee knows better than to say anything."

"Alright. Then, he's dealing with the big-time bad guys. According to Sally, he's hooked up with this Sascha Petrovic."

"Evidence would be useful."

"Those two Haitians who drowned this fall."

"I was here then. The weather was bad that day. I remember. Olivero seemed very upset."

"But he couldn't give you their names?"

"He said he only knew their *pre-nombres*. I remember."

"And yet he said he would take care of their families. So how'd he find them?"

"Perhaps he did not. But perhaps it is not his fault. Perhaps they would not talk to him. Perhaps they were not their real names. We had the same problem."

"Did you try?"

"Of course I tried!"

"They wouldn't talk to you?"

"Wouldn't talk to me? They wouldn't even be seen with me! I went to Pétionville. Twice. The first time in a police car. No one was there. No one. The second time, I took an ordinary *motoconcho*. Again, they had vanished. Domino games not finished, beers not finished."

"So what about the smuggling angle?"

"It goes on, but not here. Not much, anyway. We are lucky."

"To have you as police chief?"

"Even luckier than that. It is what we *don't* have. We don't have a harbour. And sea is too shallow; we will never have a harbour."

"Meaning?"

"With no big harbour you can have no big boats, no yachts, no marinas."

"But they are good for business, no?"

"Good for many types of business. Much of it bad."

"How?"

Arturo explained that the DR had become a major transit country for drugs of all types coming from all sorts of places and going to all sorts of places. Cocaine, weed, crystal meth, oxy, the lot. That meant big business and that meant big out of town gangs—Colombians, Venezuelans, and Mexicans.

"They do not use airplanes very often now to deliver to *Norte America* the drugs you must have to get through your life. Private airplanes here must buy their gas from the National Police who now ask questions. Commercial flights are checked more closely. So the smugglers are back to the sea because boats are a different story. They leave from Punta Cana or Samana or Puerto Plata or Santo Domingo and they carry 10% of all the cocaine going to America. And now Europe as well."

"And you can't stop them?"

"The ocean is a big place. We get some. A small percentage. Like the Americans do, with thousands more men and billions more dollars. But it is not only the drugs that are the big problems. It is smuggling people."

Arty laid out how the smugglers' operations can work and how they differed based on the nationality of the smugglees. For some reason, the Cubans who try to get into America through the DR—instead of directly—have more money and, therefore, can make better travel arrangements. The aquatic versions of *coyotes*, after dressing up the Cubans as tourists, load them onto the larger fishing and excursion boats. From the air, it looks like they're on just another pleasure outing. Or pack the hold of yacht with a bunch of them and make $20,000 for a few hours work.

"For some of the rich people in Punta Cana," Arty said, "it is a sport. It is exciting, fun. For others, the Dominican boat captains, it is easy money with each of the passengers paying to get to Mona."

"Who's Mona?" I asked.

"Not '*qui*' but '*que.*' Mona is not a person. It is an island. An island owned by Puerto Rico and therefore an island of the United States. It is 200 miles from here but only forty miles from Punta Cana. You can hire almost every boat there for $500 each person. For $500 more, you can get to Mayaguez on the west coast of Puerto Rico about fifty miles past Mona.

"But it is getting harder so the costs are rising. They are using drones in the Mona Passage. To avoid them, as I said, the smugglers will sometimes dress their customers up as tourists on a fishing charter. Or sometimes they send one boat out first—with true fisherman— to be intercepted while another one circles around them to land on Mona or PR. If they get by the Coast Guard, it can take some time to find them on Mona for it is empty, a few park rangers, that is all. But, for the Cubans, asylum must granted. If they have just one foot on the island, they are in America forever if they want. Having become more expensive, these ways are not afforded by the poor Haitians and Dominicans. For them it is a *yola.*"

Arty described the boat used—an open air, really big old dory with a captain and an outboard motor and upwards of 50 people crammed onto it. There is no attempt to disguise them. They just take their chances.

"The sea can be rough, some of those old boats—all expendable costs of doing business—have capsized."

"And...?" I asked.

"Most Haitians, Dominicans are not great swimmers. But the sharks are."

I let that terrible image sink in.

"What happens to the rest?" I asked.

"The Dominicans and Haitians are deported immediately if they are caught on the water *or* on land."

"And if they're not?"

"They try to disappear on Puerto Rico if they can. But it isn't easy. They stand out, for most of them are black. They are subjected to the same racism with which they treat the Haitians here in the DR. I understand there is saying in Puerto Rico: "Being Puerto Rico and homeless in the streets is better than being Dominican.""

"Very nice."

"And of course, when the Puerto Ricans leave their island for America, they see the same racism against them that they use on the Dominicans and the Dominicans use on the Haitians. All based on your skin colour getting lighter and lighter."

It was true. I told Arty about how the kids I taught in the Bahamas once explained their complicated shading system going from the preferred white/bright white through caramel to coffee to black. Back in the late 70s—and perhaps still—one of their worst insults there was to call someone a "black Haitian dog."

"A wonderful world we live in, is it not?" said Arty, shaking his head.

We sat there for a bit, thoroughly depressed at the general and specific subjects we'd been talking about.

"We're not really any further ahead, are we?" I asked.

"Not true. We have a path to follow."

"And better questions to ask," I suggested.

"Ah, this small town causes many questions. But it may not be the place for answers."

"Maybe. But there is somebody we can talk to again."

"Tico," we said in unison.

## CHAPTER TWENTY-TWO

Arty and I agreed that I ought to talk to Tico first. I left the police station and headed for his worksite. To my surprise, he wasn't there, but Frank was. And he was pissed that his prized new hire hadn't shown. I almost didn't recognize him without his trademark smile, such was the effect of the project on his sunny ways.

"If you see him, fire him for me," Frank said.

"Now, now, Frank. Calm down. There must be a reason. He's the best worker you've got, isn't he?"

"Yes."

"Well, let him keep working, will ya?"

"This one time," he said and stalked off to berate a group of helmeted workmen yelling at each other and/or the old cement mixer that wasn't mixing.

No sign of Tico in the barrio. I figured it was too early for him to be out at Pétionville which left me stumped.

I crossed the street to talk to two Haitians I passingly knew: Philipe and August, art dealers extraordinaire.

On our main street there are several Haitian art shops. I say 'shops'; I meant wooden poles covered by—what else?—canvas roofs to

protect the colourful canvasses. You flip through the large paintings sitting on the ground the way we used to stand in record stores
thumbing through the LPs (vinyl for you youngsters). A flashing
kaleidoscope of Haitians fishing, cutting cane, going to church,
shopping at food stalls, groups of black figures brightly dressed in
brilliant colours that usually matched their backgrounds.

Two of these shops are side by side and Philippe and August, their
proprietors, shoot the shit and play dominoes all day until a pink-
ish foreigner approaches. Then they become mortal enemies as they
spring into action, cajoling, pleading for the tourist to examine his
wares. No, mine. No, mine. Et cetera.

Their operations were actually pretty sophisticated. In addition to
the indispensable calculators with the big numbers for haggling,
they both had credit card/debit machines, competing shippers who
would deliver worldwide, and a cottage network of artists who would
crank out the art, most of which was remarkably similar and bad,
like the pink-hued mountain lakes and lifeless still lifes that adorn
the walls above brocaded coaches owned by every aunt anybody ever
had. But every once in a while you'd find a strikingly original piece.

I knew both guys because I had bought a couple of the paintings
for the condo (one from each of them) and was always looking. In
Philippe's shop I found one, smaller than most—maybe 2 feet by
3—and different from the rest. For one thing; there were no people.
It was a beach scene at sunset (or sunrise). Fiery oranges and reds.
The sinking (or rising) sun dead centre. On the left: a palm tree in
silhouette and on the right: three birds flying across the sun. The
artist had titled it in fine black lines: '*L'Essence de Las Terrenas*'. It
was signed 'Thibeau'.

"Who did this?" I asked, well, demanded of Philippe.

"I have many artists—many more than August, the criminal."

"Who?"

"Thibeau," he said, pointing obviously at the signature. "Tico as he is called."

"Do you know where he is?"

Philippe tossed off one of those Gallic shrugs but he was looking at the back canvas wall.

I found a flap and entered another section of what amounted to a large tent. Five or six artists—Tico among them—looked up as one from the canvasses they were working on.

He seemed happy and embarrassed to see me.

"*Monsieur* Jake, *bienvenue.*"

"Know anybody named Thibeau?" I asked.

"*C'est moi.*"

"Frank is not happy *avec toi.*"

"*Je connais.* I will be sorry. I must *fini. Regardez-la,*" he said, proudly showing me his nearly completed painting.

Mostly blue and purples, the main subject was a boat on choppy dark seas. I counted twelve figures on board, all dressed in white with red sashes for belts, all looking skyward to a broad shaft of white/yellow sunlight that seemed to illuminate the imperiled ship.

Tico hadn't signed it yet but he had given it a title: "*Pour F-X.*"

Now I knew.

"Tico, we must talk."

He gestured behind him and we lifted another flap and were outside in a vacant, garbage-strewn lot.

He sat down on a cinder block; I perched on a wooden crate. We stared at each other and any trace of a smile faded, our eyes forecasting the conversation we were about to have. He did not evade my gaze, as if he were ready.

"You know where Xavier is, don't you?" I began.

"*Oui.*"

"The police will never find him, will they?"

"No."

"Because he's...dead?"

"*Oui.*"

"Xavier was the man called Francois on El Gordo's boat, wasn't he? Francois–Xavier, like the saint. "*Pour F-X*"."

"*Oui,*" he answered, first looking surprised that I had guessed right. Then, he started to cry.

That startled me. He was an emotional guy but this seemed over the top as a reaction to the death of an occasional workmate. Unless....

"Tico, was Xavier family?" I asked.

"*Oui!*" He blurted out. "My brother!"

Between sobs and in halting English and Creole, he told me what had happened.

A year ago, Xavier had just shown up in Las Terrenas looking for Tico. It wasn't completely surprising that Xavier had sleuthed out where his brother was. The Haitian community is a tight one. They know or know of each other. Where they are, where they're going. Xavier had learned of Tico's location and came, but, as Tico said, "not to be a family. He wanted only money and help."

Piecing it together from Tico's account, Xavier was five years younger and with no real skills beyond the ability to survive. From the
sounds of it, Xavier was a hard man, hardened by life alone in the
squalid rubble, in tent cities, in a ruined world where NGOs and aid
workers are to this day warned about "no go" zones, years after the
earthquake. Like Tico, he was desperate to leave Haiti but unlike
his brother, he had his sights set on Canada and the large Haitian
community in Montreal. But, without family there, he couldn't be
sponsored. So he was on his own getting there.

"You cannot tell a man like Xavier – maybe any man - what to do.
*Avec mon assistance ou non*, he was going. I tell Madame Sally. She
had *beaucoup sympathie*, she find the money, *beaucoup* money, and
she find a man with a boat."

"El Gordo?"

"*Oui.*"

"To take him to Canada?"

"*Non. En Floride.*"

"Only Xavier and one other?"

"No, no, no. *Un douzaine. Toutes sont mort.*"

A boat overloaded by greed, rough seas, and twelve humans who
drowned somewhere in Turks and Caicos waters in October just
passed.

It was pretty easy to imagine how Sally would have reacted. She
would have been devastated.

"She say she killed Xavier," Tico said. "But it was the sea."

I figured Sally would not have seen it that way. If she hadn't put up the money, Xavier wouldn't have died that day. It wasn't hard to imagine what Sally would have done about it. To salve her conscience and give voice to the drowning victims and to her outrage, she obviously had taken up the fight—starting with El Gordo.

"OK, Tico, OK. One question."

"*Quoi?*"

"Will you speak to the police? No," I corrected myself. "To the top police? Will you speak only to Chief Inspector Diaz? Tell him what you have told me. *Pour Madame Sally*?"

The Haitian thought for a bit.

"I am afraid. Haitians and police *pas bon*."

"Is it more than that?"

Tico went quiet.

"El Gordo?"

"*Non.*"

"Then who?"

"*...Les Russes,*" he slowly answered.

"The Russians?"

"*Oui.* One come to me. He have no Creole, no Spanish. He have machete. He show me. He say "Sally," then he do this."

Tico held up an index finger to his lips and hissed, the universal signal for silence.

"*Monsieur Jake,*" Tico said. "My life *pas grand*. But it my only one."

"Diaz will protect you. *Je promis,*" I said.

"OK. OK. I talk," he finally said, wiping his tears away with his forearms.

He looked at me with something like resolve, maybe relief that he had a path now, a way to unburden himself.

I helped him up and we entered the main store area.

"*Mon ami. Permit moi un secret, s'il vous plait?*" Tico asked in a formal tone.

"*Quoi, Monsieur Thibeau?*"

"Do not say about I paint."

"You should tell the world; you are *excellente*!

He smiled.

"Soon," he said. "I will be more *excellente*."

"*C'est* OK I buy this?" I asked after I had retrieved his sunset painting.

Tico's smile grew broader.

"*Oui! Oui! C'est parfait!* You buy!"

Standing on the sidewalk, I had to haggle a bit with Philippe, otherwise it would raise suspicion that a *gringo* had gone *loco* by paying the full asking price. With the painting tucked under my arm, I walked into the sunlight.

"You fuckin' owe me," I said, standing in front of our Chief Inspector with the painting on the paper-strewn desk facing him.

"You expect me to buy this?" Arty asked. "It is good but not to my taste."

"No. I found a Haitian who will talk to you," I said. "The guy who did this. Recognize the scene?"

It dawned on Arty that it was Sally's photo.

"Who?"

"Tico," I said leaning in and whispering.

"You spoke to him?"

"Yes. He has a lot to say."

"That would be good. So far, he has said little."

"Things have changed. But *only* if he talks to you alone. I gave him my word you'd keep him safe. I said that you were a good guy."

"Maybe that was unwise."

"Don't fuck me with me, Arty. This could be a big deal. You have to ask him about the Haitians who drowned in the fall. One of them was his brother. Xavier. The guy you were looking for."

"His brother?"

"Yes. Tico says El Gordo was trying to smuggle Xavier and a bunch of others into Florida. And he knows some Russians were involved."

That got Arturo's attention right quick.

"And he will swear to this in court?"

"I don't know. That's up to you to convince him."

"Where is he? I will see him now."

For an odd reason, maybe because he had asked me as small pay-back for the police interview he'd agreed to, I didn't want to tell him about Tico's moonlighting as an artist. Instead, I gave Arty directions to Tico's construction worksite.

"We will find him."

"What about El Gordo?" I said. "Maybe you could put some pressure on the fat fuck, let him know you're watching him."

"And scare off the big boss men—if there are big boss men?"

"I'm pretty sure there are. Why else would Tico say it? Remember all the shit I showed you on that website not three hours ago? Sally mentioned him by name and she insisted that a Sascha Petrovic was involved."

"I have no jurisdiction there. No, I must wait to see what Tico says. Thank you, *Ingles*. This is progress. But, you must know. I cannot protect him."

"What? Of course you can! You have to! I promised."

"It was not yours to promise, my friend. I can give protection at the workplace. But put Dominican police in the barrio? At Pétionville? How can I do that without big problems?"

"Lock him up?"

"My jail would be full of people with something to fear. And he must work; he must eat."

Arturo made sense. He always made sense. As I got up to leave I understood that I only had a hope and not a guarantee that Tico would be safe.

"Oh, and you should say some things on that website so you do not look like a spy," Arty said. "That should be no problem for you."

Arty was right again. So when I got home, Snake went into full rant mode on Friends of Paradise. Besides what I thought was a fairly well-reasoned argument for the government at least quadrupling its investment in education, I chipped in comments on the immigration laws, and on the need to re-examine prostitution laws.

Prostitution is legal in the DR, but, in, I suppose, a show of support for individual entrepreneurship, pimping allegedly is not. And hookers—again allegedly—had to be at least 18. You can write all the laws you want, but if you can't, don't or won't enforce them, guess what happens? So that means, of course, underage kids turning tricks and whole operations of bad guys running rings that pay the girls nothing while keeping them virtually enslaved.

And fuck that bullshit about it being a more "European" attitude towards sexuality, as distinct from North American prudery. Judging by the white guys hanging around the streets near the clubs, these are not free-thinking libertarian philosophers; they're middle-aged—or older—glassy-eyed perverts and predators who couldn't give a good goddamned about what happens to any of these girls as long as they get their aging rocks off.

I was exhausted and frustrated when I fell into bed. All this sickness was happening every hour of every day. And nothing was stopping the men at the top, men like Sascha Petrovic.

What had Arty said? He has no jurisdiction there.

Wait a minute, I remembered, I hadn't mentioned where "there" was.

# CHAPTER TWENTY-THREE

Christmas passed and with it, the pang that has accompanied the holiday for the last fifteen years.

I holed up in my condo, drinking and flicking through TV channels trying to find something that wasn't a Christmas special or a Christmas movie (little asterisk beside *Bad Santa*; I never miss that). That's been the way I've spent every Christmas since I decided to not be anywhere near snow five years ago.

But still.

Despite having passed through agnosticism into full-blown atheism by the age of 14, there was, is, and likely will always be the pull of the idea of family gatherings around statutory holidays. After Beth died, neither Halley nor I could bring ourselves to attend get-togethers of Beth's side or my side of the family tree. Instead, father and daughter built our own tradition of eating at a top-drawer Chinese restaurant with a lot of Jews and Arabs, then going home and opening our two presents. That ended when she went off to university after confessing her atheism to me.

Whatta kid!

But still.

# CHAPTER TWENTY-FOUR

The stores and restaurants were open for the Christmas week as LT experienced its first tourist throng of the year. The streets were jammed with foreigners from just about everywhere and Dominicans mostly fleeing Santo Domingo. Everything official was shut—government offices, schools and, it appeared, major crimes investigations. Arty disappeared for several days; I was told he'd booked off to visit his family but the desk officer wouldn't say where.

That Thursday night there was a knock at my door. It was late. OK, OK, late for me, which is pretty well any ol' time after nine.

It was Arty and he looked a little more than upset.

"Turn on the TV. Make it loud. Thursday Night Football."

"Browns/Bucs? Who gives a fuck?" I asked, not keen on quitting the fascinating documentary on Antietam.

"Do it, please."

I found the channel while Arty stood at the side of my sliding glass door leading to the balcony. He had pulled the curtains closed and parted them a bit to peer intently towards the street.

"Do you know," he asked, "you can see your television from the road when it is on?"

"How the Christ would I know that? If it's on, I'm not on the road, am I?" I shouted from the kitchen where I was getting us beer.

"I know."

"Oh, great, you've been spying on me," I said, as we sat down in front of the game.

"Maybe not just me."

"What the fuck is going on, Arty?"

"I am not sure, but I have a feeling that we are being followed, watched."

"What would you say: Where is the evidence?"

"You should be fucking off now, *Ingles*."

"Evidence?"

"Driving to LT last night. A car behind me the entire way. Three hours.

"You coming from Santo Domingo?"

"I was coming from a place that is no business of yours."

"You afraid?"

"Not for me. For you."

We stared at the truly inept football being played. I just couldn't bring myself to cheer whenever something monumental happened, like a first down, or Cleveland managed to put eleven players on the field at the same time.

"We—I mean—*I* spoke to Tico," Arturo announced.

"And?"

"He said what you told me. And much more."

"Can you use it?"

"Perhaps."

"There you go again with your fucking 'perhaps'."

"Tico had many details about what happened that day. He said that Miss Sally gave him 5000 US dollars and he took the bus with Xavier early in the morning from Las Terrenas across the hills to Samana town. He described the boat exactly and he said he counted at least ten Haitians on board, in addition to the two-man Dominican crew before he was sent away from the dock by some Mr. Muscolo."

"Well there. You have him! Haitians paying to crew a boat? Or Haitians laying out 50,000 dollars for a day fishing trip!"

"*You* know that; *I* know that. Think about the court, *Ingles*. It was El Gordo's boat but there was no sign of him. The defence lawyer will ask: 'Did you see Xavier give the money to El Gordo? No? Because he wasn't there? So who did Xavier give the money to? You don't know? Maybe there was no money. Bring forth Sally Bartlett to testify there was money. You can't? Or, if there *was* money, maybe you kept it, Tico. Did you see the boat sail away? Yes? You watched it from a distance? OK. Can you swear there were still at least ten Haitians on board? No? You know for sure they were Haitians? How?' And many more questions like that."

"That's a fuckin' shame," I said, knowing he was right.

"Perhaps. But for sure it is reasonable doubt. Here is more reasonable doubt: you say twelve men drowned. Where are the bodies?"

"Now that you mention it, why weren't bodies found?"

"El Gordo said that he didn't know exactly where the boat had sunk, only that it had been missing for a week. He said it was going to Inagua Island to fish. They didn't find the boat for another 10 days after that, almost 200 miles from Inagua, near the Turks and Caicos. There is not much left of a man in those waters. Sharks, lobsters, crabs are hungry animals."

We sat there, defeated, and not just by a shitty display of our favourite game.

"Did Tico mention Russians?"

"No."

"What?"

"I asked him specifically if anybody other than El Gordo was involved. He denied it."

"That's not what he told me! I swear, Arty. He said a Russian had threatened him."

"I believe you. But if he won't say anything, what can I do?"

"Sally named a Sascha Petrovic. Does that guy live here?"

"No."

"How can you be sure?"

"It is my business to be sure," Arty said, sounding a might testy that I questioned him. "I know of most, maybe all of the Russians who live here. There are not very many. And no one is named Sascha Petrovic."

"But they have their own restaurant."

"Some Russians here have purchased many condos. They advertise back home and bring airplanes full of tourists for a week, two weeks, a month. Here, and in Miches, Punta Cana."

"So they want genuine Russian food when they get here to go along with their genuine Dominican experience."

"As the Americans do. You know that hamburgers and French fries are not native to the DR, do you not? And Canadians—who knows what you people eat?"

I resisted the temptation to tell him about *poutine*. In the past, my attempts to describe gravy on cheese curds over French fries as covering off the major food groups had been futile.

"I also questioned Olivero," Arty offered up, during yet another interminable round of truck commercials.

"What happened there?"

"Not very much. He was not co-operating. He brought his lawyer."

Arty took a business card from his shirt pocket.

"Jose Ignacio Maria Gonzalez," he read.

"Yimmy is his lawyer?"

"You call him Yimmy?"

"Yes."

"Well, Yimmy did most of the talking. I would have done the same. We are being fishermen with him. And he knows it."

"So that's it? Just forget it?"

"No!" Arturo insisted. "I believe what Tico told me and I believe also that a man who is innocent does not bring a lawyer for simple questions."

"So what are you doing next?"

"The solid lead is El Gordo. I will approach it that way. I will go to Samana town. Some people might remember the boat, might remember the day. I will also go over and over the forensics. Maybe there is something there we have missed."

"Sounds like a plan."

"And what will you do?" he asked.

"I want to talk to the people closest to her again."

"I can do that also, *Ingles*. In fact, it is my job to do that."

"No. Please, Arty. Let me. I know them. And for different reasons, they're nervous."

"And you are not?"

"I hadn't really thought about it."

"*Ingles*, if you will not be frightened, then you must be careful. And thank you for the football game. But I cannot watch anymore."

"Comin' over this Sunday? Last games of the regular season,"

"Thank you but no. My vacation is over."

"Then for the playoffs?"

"I do not think so, *Ingles*.... It is better if we are not seen together."

"So look who's scared now."

"It is not that."

"Oh, I see!" I said in mock anguish. "I embarrass you, do I? So you're breaking up with me!"

Arty smiled for the first time that evening.

"It could never work," he said, playing along. "It is not you. It is me."

We were laughing as he left.

But I saw him glancing from side to side as he headed down the stairs.

# CHAPTER TWENTY-FIVE

Yeah, I had ruled out my drinking circle as a suspect pool. But that didn't mean they were clueless. Consciously or not, maybe they could fill in some blanks. Maybe they had seen or heard something, or they knew something that could get us on the right trail.

I wanted to start with Jose Ignacio Marie Gonzalez. Jimmy was El Gordo's lawyer, even though I was pretty sure he was a civil lawyer, which is why I was a little surprised when Arty told me he had accompanied EL Gordo to the police station. I knew he wouldn't be able to tell me shit in the way of details about his client relationship. That was protected everywhere in the world, well, most parts of the world, OK, OK, some parts of the world. But perhaps he'd say something that might help. I figured if he knew about all things legal in the DR, he'd also be pretty familiar with all things illegal.

I couldn't guess how important the expats were to his practice but I reckoned his foreign-born clientele supplied a good bit of his revenue. That's why I wanted to meet him at Big Dave's and not in his office. If he was tempted to be an asshole to me, he might do some calculatin' about how much alienating us furiners might cost him.

Sooner not later, I had the chance to have a beer with him. Well, I had a beer; he was sipping his customary Johnnie Walker Black, straight up. Jose Ignacio Marie Gonzalez was one of those guys who can make you feel scruffier and more slovenly than you actually are. His movements were precise, his manner graceful, his clothes and hair perfect. Nary a wrinkle in his black dress pants stretched under the table.

Before I could spring my line of questioning on him, he started quizzing me.

"You like it here, Jake?"

"Yes. Very much."

"You seem to fit in, get along with many people."

"I try," I lied.

"I must ask you: how it is you get along with that policeman?"

"Diaz?"

"Exactly."

"I guess he's a friend. We watch football together sometimes. Why do you ask?"

"No reason. It is just strange. I must tell you, Jake. I have never seen an expatriate with such a...a good relationship with a Dominican policeman."

"Is that a problem? He's a good guy."

"You misunderstand me, my friend. I like him too."

"You do?"

"I am not a criminal defence lawyer so I do not see him much. But I am a resident here so I would rather live in a safe place than not. And I hear his name around my office, around the courthouse. You will not often find defence lawyers saying nice things about the police but they tell me Inspector Diaz is a good man. Perhaps a great man."

"Any idea what a 'perhaps a great man' doing in Las Terrenas?" I asked.

"I believe he has damaged his career. He has arrested his superiors. He has arrested judges. He has fired many under him."

"So that's the reason for all his transfers?"

"You know about those?" he asked betraying a bit of surprise.

"Yes."

"But, despite being moved around, many people in the legal community—and outside—know of his abilities, his honesty. So he cannot be gotten rid of easily."

"But he can be re-assigned."

"Yes. It is a shame. They buried him with public relations about why they need him here. But he should not be here. He should be back in Santo Domingo. He should be the head of police. Maybe someday a man such as this will be the top policeman in the country, but not yet. And when we do get a man of integrity and intelligence, it will because of the honest men before him. Men like Diaz."

"And yet the gangs operate freely here," I said, trying to steer the conversation.

"They operate freely *everywhere* in the world. In the Vatican, for Christ's sake."

"But they are a really big deal here."

"No. They *seem* like a really big deal here. There is less requirement for discretion here. The Russian gang members, the Italian mob, the active ones at least, they do not have to hide their wealth. No one gives them a problem. They are protected, their houses are protected. I stress that I do not know this for a fact but I understand that there are not very many of them here. It looks that way, I know, but we are deceived. A handful of important gangsters, only."

"That's it?"

"The Dominican Republic is a station along the road. For the drugs and other things. All only passing through. There is no need for an army of criminals as they have in Italy, in Russia, in Mexico, in Venezuela, in America. *And* Canada. That is where the wars are fought. But here? Any assistance they need, they can—how do you say it?—subcontract it."

"To Dominicans?"

"Surely."

"Do you happen to know any of these Italian and/or Russian gangsters?"

His legs straightened up.

"I know *of* them. Who does not know *of* them?"

"But nobody actually *knows* them, is that right?"

"Nobody I know."

"Not even El Gordo? He's a client of yours, isn't he?"

Jose Ignacio Marie Gonzalez did not answer, but he also did not appear to be ruffled at all by me virtually accusing him of mob connections. Instead, he fired back the rest of his scotch and asked for *la cuenta* from Constanza, our server.

As he rose to leave, he put a generous tip under my beer bottle for her.

"I will also give you a tip, my friend," he said, clapping a manicured hand on my shoulder. "Enjoy yourself here. Only enjoy yourself."

I was getting pretty tired of being told to chill out. It takes the fun right out of something if you tell me to do it.

"What was that about?" Nick asked as he parked himself where Jimmy had been sitting.

"Fuck knows, man."

I recounted a bit of the conversation. The part about there not being that many gangsters in the DR. Nick thought that Jimmy was probably right.

"I mean, think about it: The heavyweights are here because of the sun. Period. They're businessmen. They can buy huge fucking mansions here for less than half in New York or Milan, or even Mexico City. But they don't actually have much of an operation to look after. No growing, no processing, no big sales network. No turf wars. No squads to protect them. Just shipping and receiving. Moving it all along to Spain or New York or Toronto. And a few bodyguards but a whole lot less than Justin Bieber needs."

"And any service they do need they can get locally. Anything for a buck."

"Anything for a buck is right. Jesus, most of the Dominicans in this—the ones I've met anyway – don't even think of themselves as soldiers in a gang or career criminals. A little guard duty at an airstrip or marina. Some loading and unloading from time to time. Some of them like to brag that they're *El Chingon de Chingones*—the badass of badasses—but that's all macho bullshit."

"That true for El Gordo?"

"He's a fuckin' piece of work. He's watched *Scarface* too many times. Absolutely a low-level wanna-be."

Just then, Miguel sat his lanky drunken Brit ass down at our table.

"So, gentlemen, what, I implore you, can you tell me about the state of the world today?" he wanted to know.

"Totally fucked, just like yesterday," Nick answered.

When Nick went on a pee break, I followed.

"Nick, I gotta ask you some questions about Sally. They're not easy ones."

"Sure, but not here, OK? Come to my place tomorrow. Any time before four."

"First street before Sally's?"

"Yeah, can't miss the place. Got a Harley sign by the gate. Villa de Hog, that's what I called the place."

"That's a really sweet name, Nick."

"Thanks. I wanted to catch that Caribbean vibe."

"I'll go out and entertain Sir Piss Tank."

"Fuck, I owe ya."

Nick left me to Miguel.

"I couldn't help but notice, old boy," the Brit said, "your negotiations with Philippe this week. He's a sterling fellow."

"You saw that?"

"I was passing by. At any rate, Philippe is one of those rarest of creatures—a Haitian who has been allowed to cross the divide into respectability and good standing in our community. August as well."

I said nothing. Miguel took my silence at his observation as permission to educate me further. He was obviously in the mood for one of his extemporaneous lectures. He droned on for quite some time about the unique relationship between Haiti and the Dominican. Did I know they'd been at each other more or less constantly since Haiti had become an independent country over 215 years ago? Or that their fussin' and feudin' had gone on well before that because the Spanish mostly didn't like the French anywhere? Was I aware that the Spanish animosity had trickled down to their slaves who thought they were a whole lot better than French slaves. Why, did I know that in a recent survey, 85% of Dominicans self-identified as having *Indio* ancestry when the real number of those carrying Taino Indian DNA was 10%? And didn't I find it interesting that 90% had African heredity but only 5% thought of themselves as being black?

Ol' Miguel could be rhetorical as hell but—and maybe it was because of his sonorous English accent—he actually *was* pretty interesting and it only cost me one beer.

At around noon the next day, I went on yet another walk (Note to self: slow down with this fucking exercise regime; you're not a young man anymore!) to Nick's place.

In the DR, with a sun that isn't at all like a Canadian sun, you have to choose your routes carefully, especially at mid-day. Along the beach, you've got welcome shade from the overlapping palm leaves, but you had to be under the full glare when you passed the cemetery and were on the open stretch of Playa Popy where the fishing boats came in. So you deke up to the coast road and you're back under the shade of walls and buildings, but inches from the stinking *motoconchos* whizzing by.

Nick's place was about 500 yards off the coast road, unmistakable for the motorcycle front end—tire, forks and handlebars and part of a gas tank—rising out of the thick, 8-foot high block wall that surrounded the large compound.

I rang the bell by the man-gate and heard a buzzer and a click. I made for the garage set apart from the three houses. Through the open bay door, I took in the oily shrine to all things combustion engine-related. The garage held at least six complete motorcycles and gawd knows how many others in various states of disassembly, plus a couple of ferocious-looking *Mad Max*-type dune buggies.

I found Nick squatting beside a motorcycle that looked bigger and newer than most of the rigs on the road. Jeff, the bike decorator, was watching as was a Dominican kid—maybe 10 years old. Being one of the more mechanically-challenged people I knew, I was betting that Jeff, for sure—and likely the kid—had a greater understanding than I did of the repair job underway.

Nick dropped his wrench and tried the ignition. The engine sprang to life and Nick kept his hand on the throttle, a big smile on his face as he revved the thing louder and louder.

Satisfied, Nick turned off the roaring.

"Let Ubaldo know that he can come get it," he said to Jeff. "1500 pesos'll do it."

Jeff left with the message and a cloud of dust from his bike.

"He'll tell the guy 2000 pesos," Nick explained, "who'll be happy to pay it and Jeff'll keep the difference as the middleman."

"*Chico, la piscina ahora!*" he then barked to the kid who smiled and trotted off towards the pool. We watched him struggle with the net pole and start skimming the surface.

"Great kid. His old man's in La Victoria and his mom has two jobs so he hangs around here a lot."

We walked towards one of three houses, Nick wiping off as much sweat and grease as he could with a filthy towel.

"Quite the fort you got here," I said.

"Lost a couple of machines when I first got here. Not gonna happen again. Beer?"

Yafrete was in the kitchen. Even when she was berating him in Spanish for apparently bringing his grimy self into their immaculate and tastefully decorated house, she was beautiful.

We went upstairs and out onto the second floor back balcony, settling into big, fat comfortable wicker chairs, clinking bottles then staring past the pool, over the compound wall and across the "protected wetlands." In the distance, on the other side of the rippling grass, we could see Sally's houses.

"Must be a bitch looking at those houses," I said

"That it is. What a fuckin' shame."

"You guys were pretty close."

"Yeah."

"Nick, I gotta ask: how close?"

"And I gotta ask: what fuckin' business is it of yours?"

"Easy, dude. I'm just trying to find out as much as I can about her. The cops need to know. They really want the guy who did this."

"We had...a fling. Sort of. One time. We were pretty loaded. Epic disaster."

"Did Paul know?"

"Yeah. Sally told him. I said it was a bad idea; she disagreed. That was four years ago. Everybody got past it. Even Paul."

"Sure?"

"As sure as you can be in things like that."

"Anybody else since?"

"For me?"

"No. Sally."

"I don't think so. She'd've told me."

"You sure?"

"Yeah, I think she started to look at me like her crazy little brother. So she'd confide in me. She told me she had the hots for Dave at one time but you know how she is—was. All loud and flirty. Don't mean nuthin'."

"Could anybody'd've got the wrong idea?"

"Maybe, but I doubt it."

"Dave?"

"Like I said, I doubt it. Dave's been living with this Dominican woman for years. Christ, they have a three-year old kid. Break your heart she's so goddamned cute."

"What? She's never been at the bar."

"Dave's pretty clear about that. Home is home; work is work, he always says."

"This girlfriend..."

"Wife, actually. Pilar."

"Is Pilar the jealous type?"

"I don't know much, Jake, but I do know everybody's the jealous type if the situation's right."

"Could she have...?"

"Thought about it and not a chance. For one thing, she's like four-foot nuthin'."

So that ruled her out on the spot. Arty had said the killer was at least five-foot nine.

"What about Sally and Bruce?"

"Fuck no! She could be all dramatic but she wasn't up for taking a ride to Crazy Town."

"Well, there must be something you can tell me."

"Look, I don't think Paul and her were getting along. Had nuthin' to do with me—or anybody else. They hadn't gotten along for some time. Money, her life here. You name it, they fought about it. Or at least she said they did. You know her. So much drama."

"Was she into anything else that might've got her in trouble?"

Here he paused.

"Nick?" I prompted.

"She was very into the Haitian thing. You know, how shitty they get treated. She was trying to help."

"How?"

"Well, that school she had. And on Christmas, she'd get all the expats to cook and she'd deliver meals to them, presents for the kids."

"Everybody knows that stuff. That didn't get her killed, for Christ's sake. What else?"

"Look, Jake, I've seen a lot of things. I've done a lot of things that

I'm not proud of. Being here. Free. It's the one shot I've got to put it all behind me. I can do some good things but mostly I can just start over."

"You're afraid aren't you?"

"Fuck, no! And cuz it's you, I won't kick the shit out you for saying it, but no, I'm not afraid of fuck-all down here. One phone call and I can get thirty bikers over here from Caberete, even if they're Angels. Another phone call to Jersey and maybe a whole fuckin' charter flight of brothers gets here. The Russians, the Mexicans, the Italians ain't got those kind of numbers here."

"Alright, alright. I take it back. But you're not telling me something."

"You *are* a little nosy fucker, aren't you?"

"Aw, Nick, what's it going to take? She was your friend."

"Don't play that fuckin' card, partner."

"Then don't be a wuss." (Note to self: Jake, you might want to tone down the name-calling to a biker—even an ex-biker).

"Put it this way: some people here are connected to a lot more people I knew in Jersey."

"And...?"

"I wasn't on the best of terms with the people from Jersey when I booked."

"People whose last names end in vowels?"

"Yeah, those people."

"Holy fuck! You ripped off the Mob?"

Nick looked half-proud and half-scared shitless.

"Them I *am* afraid of," he said. "It wasn't a lot of money. I mean, enough to get me started here. But these guys don't forget. And these guys can't afford to let word get out that some mutt took them to the cleaners. And these guys hire the best. So now I gotta keep my head down. Forever."

I flashed to *Sorcerer*. How could I not? After all the shit that fugitive Roy Scheider endures while being all courageous to get that dynamite through the jungle, he's in a bar in Managua waiting for his flight out. Spoiler alert: The last scene. From the outside you see two dark-suited goombahs sent from the States going into the bar to fatally settle up for what Roy did in the first place to become a fugitive. Roll credits.

"Look, Nick, I couldn't care less what you did. I'm not tellin' anybody."

"Alright, alright. You know the way Sally'd really get into something? Well, she was really getting into how all that smuggling worked. Who was involved, who made money."

"Friends of Paradise Regained?"

"That was just the start. She wanted me to join and I just couldn't. But she showed me her pages. She showed me the computers files she had. 'Holy shit,' I told her. 'You're getting into dangerous waters, sister.' She said she had a lot more info—just from digging around— and that she was going to go after them in a serious way. And fuck the anonymous shit. She was organizing a targeted campaign on them."

"She did think big picture."

"Exactly. She imagined starting a national effort if she had to, calling them out, you know the way people here are now protesting in the streets over corruption, over the price of electricity. She called it stirring the pot; I called it fuckin' crazy."

"And she honestly thought everybody'd all get pissed off over smuggling Haitians?"

"Not so much the public but about what'd it do the bad guys. It's the tip of the iceberg but it's their weakest link because it involves people, not product. These motherfuckers don't specialize. They're into everything: drugs, prostitution, sex slaves, extortion, guns, fixing fucking tennis and soccer games, for Christ's sake. House of cards, if the police took them seriously."

"Them? Sally didn't act alone?"

"Not entirely."

"Nick?"

"Margaret and Dot. Well, Dot for sure. And Sally was talking to people in Santo Domingo, Punta Cana, I think. Really, that's all I know. I didn't want to know. And I sure the fuck didn't want to get involved. So I had to tell her my story about needing to keep a low profile. She understood. Just like I hope you understand."

"Who the fuck am I gonna tell about you?"

"Well, maybe your cop buddy for starters."

"He couldn't care less either and, sure as shit, I don't."

Nick seemed relieved, although not completely convinced that Arturo didn't represent a threat to him.

I drained my beer and got up.

"Thank you, sir. For the beer and for the info."

"If I can do anything to help—ya know, on the down low—lemme know."

"Thank you, Nick; you're a good man."

I walked away thinking that was exactly right. He was a good man who had stopped doing bad things. A good man who had given me a good reason to talk to three people as soon as I could: Margaret, Dot, and Dave.

# CHAPTER TWENTY-SIX

Leaving Nick's, I re-traced my path home. The fishing boats were coming in Playa Popy and I had to watch.

The ocean was a bit rough and it was always uplifting to see the guys on the beach—who were busy cleaning their own catch—drop everything to help the next boat coming in. These boats were just giant, open dories and the pilot would gun his outboard timed to the rise and fall of the waves breaking on the beach. His already-landed brothers would leap up in the shallow water, grab the prow to push it down which would elevate the stern, thus saving damage to the motor props on the sand as she made land. Four or five sinewy laughing Dominicans hanging on the bow would also prevent it from being dragged back to sea by the undertow. Then everybody would haul the craft onto higher ground and return to scaling and filleting before the crowds turned up to start haggling for fish and shrimp that had only recently stopped showing signs of voluntary motion.

That night, I decided, was as good as any to talk to Dave.

Exercising the kind of self-discipline I have not ever been known for, I limited my beer in-take that night, sipping at a rate that shocked and surprised some people.

Pietro seemed encouraged, like I was reforming myself, inching towards membership in a temperance league that he hadn't joined yet either.

"If you stop, I will too," he vowed.

"Well, Pete, you better order yourself another beer, cuz I have no intention of stopping," I told him.

He seemed fine with that too.

Dave noticed my semi-sobriety too. I think it disturbed him.

"What's up, bud?" he asked.

"Aw, I'm taking some new meds. I shouldn't be drinking at all."

For the record, unless I've got a real good reason, like commenting on a woman's clothes choice in a store, I'm a piss-poor liar.

"You're a piss-poor liar," Dave remarked.

"Alright, alright. I need to talk to you after you close. And I wanted to be able to remember our conversation."

Dave had the knack, an astonishing talent actually, to dictate his bar hours by inference. He wouldn't just announce "Time, gentlemen" or "Get the fuck outta here, ya drunken bums!" or anything definitive, likely because he was a true hospitality guy who hated to offend his customers and just as likely because he preferred maximizing revenue from his cut-rate beer. But he gave off a series of signals. He'd just kind of go through the motions with his customers, lose interest in conversations, stack empty chairs, send servers home early. Subtle for our crew but it worked.

By eleven—a new record as far as I knew—the courtyard was empty. As ever, Miguel was last to leave. After the gawky drunk stumbled away, it was just Dave, me, the overflowing ashtrays, and a forest of big green beer empties.

We cleaned up, he cut the lights, and we sat in one corner, lit only from the street.

"So what's up?" Dave asked as we sipped our beer.

"It's about Sally."

"I figured that. What about her?"

"Well, I'm trying to get a handle on all the people she was involved with, what everybody was up to."

"Why?" he asked.

"Why what?"

"Why have you decided you should be doing this?"

A fair question that took me aback because I had only considered it something I *had* to do.

"I'm sort of unofficially working with the police."

That was one of those "bad fucking answer, asshole" moments. I have a lot of those. Dave set his jaw.

"Let me tell you something about that—as a friend," he said. "You're not doing yourself any favours by being mixed up with them."

"What the hell are you talking about?"

"I've been here the longest of any of you. Try running a business here and deal with the cops who decide that don't like you; it's a fucking nightmare."

"Diaz is different."

"Do you not fucking think that every cop who ever comes here doesn't swear he's different? That things are gonna change. Well, they never do!"

Dave was a bitter guy and I was pretty sure he had good reason.

"Dave, all I can tell you is I trust the guy. He wants this thing solved the right way. I think we all need to find out happened. Don't you?"

"What the fuck is that supposed to mean?"

"I've been getting waaaaay too much advice to leave this thing alone. And I'm not going to. Period. End of story."

That fell into the "good answer, asshole" category. Dave seemed mollified.

"Alright. I hear you. What do you want to know?" he asked.

"OK, tell me about El Gordo."

"He's a fat prick."

"Any dealings with him?"

"Not really. His crowd ain't the same as my crowd. He's got juice though."

"How?"

"Seven years ago, maybe eight now that I think about it, he fucked me. I had a beachfront lease—where Mojito's is now. Did you know that?"

"I heard you were on the water."

"Yeah, well, I'm absolutely sure he leaned on the property company to jack my rent by more than like double. I tried to make a go of it; I just couldn't."

"He had that much of a hard-on for you?"

"Don't think so. I think he just wanted the Cubans in there—I don't know why—because I heard the rent went right back down after I went bust and they took over."

"Bastard!"

"Bastard is right. But I'm doing OK and Ivan and Juan Carlos are good dudes, so it worked out."

"Anything else?"

"The Fat Prick pulls little shit. Like I know my beer order for the regular Presidente sometimes gets diverted to his clubs. I get the Presidente Light instead of *Normale*. That pisses me off cuz I sell more beer than he does. Thankfully, you fuckers—sorry, I meant to say 'my beloved customers' but it came out 'you fuckers'—can't tell the difference after a couple of bottles."

It was good to share a laugh with him. Other than the fact that he could pound the piss out of me, he's a straight-up guy and I liked him.

"I think the little power plays," Dave continued, "give a chubby to the chubby one. My wife, Pilar, used to work for him. I put an end to that when we got married. So maybe that still bugs him."

"Dave, I didn't even know you were married."

"No big secret. My first rule: work is work and home is home. You ever have a job?"

"Yeah, as a corporate PR slut," I said, recalling fifteen years of gainful and lucrative employment as the PR guy for a big computer services company.

"Did you bring your wife to the office all the time?" Dave asked.

"No. Never."

"Same deal."

"And you have a daughter?"

"Angela. She's a sweetie."

You could see Dave's eyes light up as he fished around in his wallet and brought out a photo. By the light of my Bic, I studied it. The kid was heartbreakingly beautiful, all smiles and big brown eyes. The supreme definition of cute. I told him that.

"She and Pilar are why I'm still here," Dave said. "And if I can get them into the States, we won't be. Now what else? "

"Don't get all bent out of shape but I need to ask about you and Sally."

"Nuthin' to tell. You know. She'd say anything that came into her head. And loudly. But she wouldn't act on it. And, just to be real clear here, I wouldn't either. Even though she's—was—about the same age as me, I was like a big brother I think."

"She needed protecting?"

"She needed someone to give her a little common sense."

"Did she listen?"

"Maybe a bit. She dialed it down a little. I did manage to talk her out of taking a TV camera crew and confronting El Gordo. She wanted to do the same thing to some Russians; I think I prevented that."

"My turn to ask. Why?"

"Why what?"

"Why'd you talk her out of it?"

"People like Sally. And Margaret and Dot, and even me in the early years think that everything here's like back home only with palm trees and lots of Spanish. It ain't. It just ain't. And why would it be? Forget when they got their papers as a country, a lot more of them have been here a lot longer than we've been in America. They got their way of doing things and it doesn't matter at all how fucked we might think it is. Now, we done?"

"We done."

At the street, now almost deserted, we left each other. But not before a firm handshake.

"Get these guys, Jake," he told me. "My money's on you."

"Why?"

"Near as I can tell, you're like...like the boy in the bubble. You got no skin in this game. So you aren't pinned by a bunch of other reasons like a lot of us."

"Thanks...I guess."

We split up. I stopped and yelled back at him.

"You live in the hills, by chance?"

"Are you kidding me? The way you fuckers tip?" he yelled back.

I headed towards the beach along the main street. Normally on my meandering walk home from Big Dave's, my full concentration is fixed on staying upright and moving in a more or less straight line. Being mostly sober on this night changed things. I was treated to a flood of conversations in my wee brain. It was sort of like the noise level in a high school cafeteria and with just as much coherence.

So is Big Dave bullshitting or was there something between him and Sally?

Good guy. See the size of his arms? Do not piss that boy off.

Is he running from something here or just tired?

I wonder where he aims to settle in the US. Plunk Pilar down in Nebraska? Bad plan.

What up with El Gordo? Just a petulant douche or is he trouble?

Was that Presidente *Normale* or Light I was drinking? He's right. I couldn't tell.

Halley really was a Nordic version of Angela, when she was a kid, wasn't she?

Jesus, the streets are empty. A couple of *motoconchos*, that's it.

Too much coincidence about El Gordo and the Cubans? It does explain why Ivan and Juan Carlos won't talk about how they got here.

Was El Gordo smuggling Cubans way back when or did somebody just pay somebody to get Carlos and Ivan the bar?

Can I really trust Arty? I don't know shit about him or how he might be—what did Dave call it?—oh, yeah, 'pinned.' My hunch says he's OK.

Maybe, but you ever have a bad hunch, asshole?

Dave outsells the two clubs in beer? Maybe. But how would he know? On the other hand, he probably doesn't move many Jagermeister shots.

But he does sell Johnnie Walker Black. To Jimmy. Fuck, I should've asked Dave about him.

Maybe I gotta look at just not trusting anybody from here on in.

Yeah, but what a shitty way to live.

I didn't just have to contend with disconnected thoughts and questions. Mini-movies were playing in my head—Dave and Nick in a fist-
fight. Pilar working for the pig as the disco lights flashed on his leering
beady little eyes, Dave packing up his bar on the beach, the Cubans
watching. Diaz cruising the town in El Gordo's Crown Vic, only with
a cop light bar on the roof. Angela looking all cute in a snowsuit.

Weird shit but I was used to it. I could blame all the chemicals in my
head—especially the ones I voluntarily put there in the 1970s—but
what was the point? Here we all are.

I took a left jog off the main street so I wouldn't have to walk by Jam
on the corner and continued to the beach. Once there, I gave my head
a literal and figurative shake and one by one the movies unspooled, the
unsprocketed film flapping against the take-up reel, the voices hushed.

In front of me was a somewhat lively and black ocean, its vigorous
waves capped in white phosphorescence lit by the half moon. I took
my flip-flops off and walked ankle deep in the warm splash of the
waves, staring only briefly at the groups of diners on the patios of
Fishermen's Village's restaurants as I passed them.

It was near to high tide and the beach strip was narrow at this point.
I had to be careful weaving among the tall curvy palms. On a night
like this some weeks ago, I had been coco-bonked by one of these
trees, knocked off my feet.

The rhythmic sound of the surf first muffled the music pounding
from Galaxy and then overcame it as I walked the last three hundred
yards or so along the darkened, empty stretch of Playa Ballenas in
front of my place.

I was glad my head was clear and I was focused on the sights and
sounds around me.

I don't doubt such clarity likely saved my life when the attack came.

# CHAPTER TWENTY-SEVEN

Even now I'm unsure how I came to be ready. Some amateur boxing training? Maybe. The fact that I'd walked this stretch of coastline scores of time and could—unconsciously—account for all the sounds and movements that were supposed to be there and weed out the ones that weren't? Maybe.

Blind, dumb luck? More than likely.

I just know that I caught some movement on my left periphery and reflexively ducked. A blade whistled over my head and I heard the 'thunk' as it embedded in the trunk of a palm tree. A fiercely whispered "*Yi-bat!*" in the dark from my assailant as he tried to loosen the machete and I was up and running, yelling at the top of my lungs as I sprinted towards the road and lights.

"Help! *Ayuadame! Aidez-moi!*" I shouted, which, in retrospect *only*, must've sounded pretty funny.

But my tri-lingual plea did the trick. As I reached the road, there was Né-Né, our night watchman, charging across the road towards the beach with his empty shotgun. Lights were going on in my complex.

Né-Né passed me as I stopped and tried to catch my smoker's breath. I turned and ran back to help him if he was set upon.

He didn't need my unarmed assistance. He stopped, levelled his shotgun at the dark seaside. To my amazement, the gun wasn't empty.

BOOM!

Christ, it was loud!

We stood side by side, watching bits of palm leaves that had been shredded from their tree flutter down.

And we heard a groan.

"Load it again!" I shouted.

"They give one bullet only."

I grabbed the gun by the barrel and held it like a club as we cautiously crept towards the darkness. There was another groan.

Away from the street lights, our vision got used to the night. We could see a figure lying on the sand at the water. I looked past it maybe twenty yards and saw the moonlight glitter on the machete blade still sunk into the tree.

'So now what?' I asked myself. 'Help the guy? Jake, would you help an injured alligator or great white shark?'

The quandary was solved jack snap when we heard the police siren. We retreated to the side of the cobblestone street and waited, feeling a whole lot safer as the siren got louder.

As the two cops poured out of the car, guns drawn, I realized I still had the Mossberg in my hands. I tossed it onto the street like it'd just bit me and we threw our hands in the air.

Né-Né explained in very loud and hasty Spanish what had happened, pointing at the beach. The cops looked dubious but they headed towards the sand and, with no orders otherwise, we followed.

We stood on the grassed lip of the higher ground. One officer had his flashlight flickering on the downed man. He was moving in pain, sort of rocking back and forth on his side. The other officer hopped down the three-foot embankment and flipped the groaner on his back.

"*Lo conoces*?" a cop demanded, looking up at me.

"No," I said but it actually was hard to tell if I knew him. The flashlight beam wasn't all that steady and there was lots of blood. Né-Né's blast had sent pellets raking the entire left side of the guy's face and shoulder.

"*Ilamar Inspector Diaz por favor*," I asked, thinking that Arty would want to hear about this kerfuffle.

"*Si. Si. Pero que pasa aqui?*"

How to tell him what had just gone on? I don't know if it was the adrenaline or the whole absurdity of what just happened but I got...I got silly. There's no other word for it.

My Spanish ain't near good enough to accurately describe what had just happened, so I pantomimed the whole thing under the headlights of the cruiser they had pointed towards the scene. One officer took notes while the other grinned like hell as I re-enacted my walking innocently along the beach, then dramatically crouching down, the swing of the blade into the tree and my running—in slow motion—ad libbing a bit to show my attacker trying to dislodge the machete. (Don't worry, I didn't touch the blade! Geez, I do watch crime shows, you know). I went back to my fake running up to the road then pointed at Né-Né who on cue picked up the action. He was in full Rambo mode, all tough and pumped up which got a laugh from the cops as the slender security guy fired a bunch of invisible rounds from what was apparently an invisible AK-47 assault rifle.

I had to hold up a finger and say "*Uno*." But other than that, the kid did pretty well.

One cop actually clapped. Meanwhile, the rest of our audience showed zero signs of appreciating our improvised performance; he just lay there on the sand groaning in pain. 'Fuck him,' I thought. 'He had just tried to kill me, so fuck him.'

Né-Né bowed and wanted to fist bump me. Fact is, he had saved my life. I gave him a big hug instead.

Arty showed up just about the same time as the ambulance. Things got a whole lot less amusing and surreal and a whole lot more business-like. He snapped on latex gloves and led the paramedics to the body. They were down on the beach for some minutes before Arty supervised loading the wounded guy onto the ambulance. For some minutes more he talked to his men and then turned on us. He was pissed.

"So I understand you gave quite a show," Arturo said and not in a happy way.

"I had to demonstrate—"

"Around my crime scene," he growled.

"Don't worry, I didn't touch the blade! Geez, Arty, I do watch crime shows, you know."

"In any of these shows, does the bad man who you think is down, pull out one of these?" he asked producing a clear plastic bag from his windbreaker pocket. The bag held a small, black handgun.

"You, *Ingles—et toi aussi—*" he said to Né-Né, "are lucky to be alive. That man's wounds are painful but superficial. The real injury was his broken leg, (Arty did a hand slash across his mid-thigh) "when he fell from the lip of the grass onto the sand. Otherwise you—*les deux*—would be dead and he would be gone."

That sobered me up right quick.

"We go to the station," Arturo said.

"Aww, Arty," I said, sounding like a petulant child not wanting to do the dishes. There was a bottle of Cazadores not a hundred yards away in my apartment, waiting for me, calling out to me.

"Now!" he added, putting the kibosh on any further pouting.

At the police station, they put Né-Né and me in separate rooms to give our statements.

I was flattered that the Chief Inspector himself grilled me as I wrote. And he took my statement in English which wasn't exactly standard operating procedure.

"Precisely what time was it? Did you see anyone else on the beach? Was there anyone strange hanging around Big Dave's? Did you order Né-Né to shoot?" Arty asked to get my ol' creative juices flowing.

I was scribbling away onto the next page when he stopped me, took the paper, and read it. He smiled for the first time that evening.

"It is rare for us to get a fucking novel," he said. "The waves were capped in white phosphorescence?"

"Sets the scene," I said just as he struck it out.

Fuck, I hate being edited!

He had me re-do the statement in a boring 'just the facts, ma'am' sort of style. I signed it and he left the room.

I had a cigarette by the open window. Then another. I saw my hand was shaking as I lit them (not 'lighted' them; no one ever fucking 'lighted' a cigarette!).

Arty came back and announced that I could leave, told me the much briefer Né-Né had already gone but that our statements had agreed.

I know I hesitated, fearing another walk home.

"Come," he said.

We drove in silence but he accepted my offer to come up for a drink. I wasn't entirely being hospitable. I did think it a good idea for a man with a gun to check out my condo.

"I am off-duty finally," he sighed.

"Tequila?"

"I think perhaps yes."

"Then I think perhaps I will make you a tequila Caesar."

My hands were still shaking as I prepared the drinks, taking a little longer than I usually spend making the drink which is, at the best of times, a whole lot more labour-intensive than opening a beer. Ice and then tequila, about half a lime's worth of juice then celery salt, clamato juice, some *salsa picante* drops, then stir, and, finally, a little sprinkle of more celery salt.

We settled into the tub chairs on the balcony and I settled into getting shit-faced.

"This drink," said Arty after his first sip. "This may become my favourite drink. Thank you."

A simple act that had gone a great distance to relaxing me. And Arty.

"Clamato's hard to find here," I said. "We Canadians are jonesing for it all the time. But I got a source."

"Where do you get this clamato?"

"You'll have to beat it out of me."

"As you wish."

"Funny. The guy who attacked me—did you get anything from him?"

"Not much. No identification, no co-operation," Arty said. "We do know he is not Dominican."

"What is he?"

"That I do not know. The nurse who was with him when they were pulling the pellets from his face heard him swear. But not in Spanish."

It came back to me.

"He's Russian," I said.

"How do you know?"

"He said '*Yi-bat*'. That's 'Fuck' in Russian!"

"Sometimes, you surprise me, *Ingles*."

"Sometimes, I surprise myself."

"He is handcuffed to the bed until we take him to jail for more questions—thanks to you—with a Russian translator. Maybe we can get something. But now, I must ask you more questions. I did not ask you at the station because I did not want them recorded or anybody hearing them."

"Let me get another drink."

"I will join you."

I fixed another round, already experiencing the warm buzz from a generous dose of tequila.

"Thank you," Arty said. "Now tell me what have you been doing lately that might cause this...this event?"

"Nothing. I swear! Just talking to my friends."

"Talking or interviewing?"

"I suppose you could call it interviewing," I allowed.

"Concerning?"

"Sally...El Gordo."

"Hmmm. For your health, I think your interviewing should be over."

"What happens now?"

"To you?"

"Of course to me!"

"I think nothing. I do not think there will another attempt."

"Well, I'm glad you're so sure."

"This man we caught is very young. A junior. If that is the best they have, they do not have many. They might not be able to afford to send anyone else."

"Why not get a Dominican?"

"A small mystery. Perhaps they did not trust one to do it. Perhaps they did not trust him to be quiet. And perhaps they wanted it done a special way to send a message. Perhaps they had no interest in killing you."

"Again with the perhaps!"

"Very well, *Ingles*. I will give you something *for sure*. If all they wanted was for you to be dead, you would be dead. A gun driving by on a *motoconcho* at any time. Or on this very night. Why not just shoot you in the back on the beach? Or wait for you here? No, they do not want attention. They wanted to stage a messy robbery so we would blame a local man."

"Like what happened to Sally?"

"Yes. And now they can't try to stage another so soon after."

"Well, they're not going to do that anyway. They'll know we got their guy."

"Which is why I think it was only to send a message to you. If it didn't work, they were willing to sacrifice this man, so there could be no mistake about who sent that message."

"Makes sense, Arty. You should do this for a living."

"Our next problem is the media," he said. "The events of tonight cannot be hidden. Sirens, ambulance, people watching from this building, this cannot be a secret."

"Need some public relations advice?"

"You have such advice?"

"Tell the newspapers it *was* an attempted robbery. A poor—unidentified—tourist was not hurt. There is a man—also unidentified—in custody. A drunken Canadian—that would be me—and a brave security guard—that would be Né-Né—prevented the robbery. The police came right away and the streets of Las Terrenas are safe again. End of story."

"And the ambulance that was seen loading up a man?"

"A precaution. The poor tourist was in shock."

Arty considered the explanation and smiled.

"Makes sense, *Ingles*. You should do this for a living."

"There are a couple of loose ends. Your men—"

"My men will not be a problem."

"And Né-Né. He was pretty pleased with what he did. Better talk to him."

"We have. The *Haitian* has a good reason to be quiet," he said, emphasizing Né-Né's ethnicity.

"You threatened him with that?"

"I used the tools I had."

"You are a bastard."

"You would be wise to remember that, my friend," he said as he drained his glass and got up to leave.

At the door, he turned to me.

"To be safe, *Ingles*, you should probably stay in your home for some days."

"Even though you said another attack is unlikely?"

"Even though I said that."

As I tried to get to sleep, one scene played over and over. Establishing shot: Close-up of section of thick palm tree trunk at night. FX: whistling sound. VIZ: Machete blade burying itself in the wood. Camera lingers on blade quivering in place. Fade to black.

# CHAPTER TWENTY-EIGHT

For a short while, staying inside or near apartment—I allowed myself visits to the pool bar, reasoning that Alejandro, the World's best bartender™, would protect me as a matter of course—wasn't much of a hardship. Watching TV, drinking, lying in the sun, and fucking around with writing wasn't exactly a big departure from my usual routine. I am at perfect peace with wasting my time. But I can't stand it when somebody or something wastes it for me. My house arrest wasn't completely voluntary so it bugged me. And after a couple of days, it made me downright claustrophobic.

No harm in an afternoon visit to Big Dave's, I told myself. That was a crushing disappointment. And continued to be a crushing disappointment every time I showed up there. For one thing, being a committed chickenshit, I had determined to stop going out after dark so the bar was almost deserted when I dropped in. I'd be there in mid-afternoon timing myself to leave by 7 at the latest. That would be before sunset and the real evening rush.

For another, I was shunned by my now suddenly former drinking pals who did turn up. It was as if I had dropped—and continued to drop—the loudest, longest, stinkiest fart in the history of flatulence. For Christ's sake, even Miguel turned down my offer to buy him a beer.

Obviously, Arty's attempt at covering up my attack as a clumsy attempted robbery convinced exactly no one in the small expat community.

To be fair, they did nod and wave and smile, but they had zero interest in getting very close to me physically. I assumed they weren't keen on becoming collaterally-damaged bystanders in any news account describing how the courtyard at Big Dave's turned into a bloody kill zone.

Only Nick, bless his ballsy heart, would sit with me; but he wasn't there that often during the day. He confirmed to me that the rest of our crew's behaviour was "nuthin' personal" but I was seen as being potentially injurious to health and happiness.

During about a week of this excommunication New Year's passed—but with no pang because I have never celebrated it. But there loomed the possibility that I might make a resolution—no, not a foolish pledge to give up smoking or drinking. But I was close to reaching a Rubicon-type decision point.

Why not just fuck off back to Canada?

Not forever. But at least until everything got solved and cleaned up down here.

Or, then again, maybe forever.

Why not? My old man had a wonderful expression to signify the unnecessary and annoying. "I need this like I need another arsehole." Nothing seemed right anymore. The warmth and charm of the place had evaporated. I was getting crusty—OK, OK, crustier. I got fixated on the irritating aspects. The litter was more irksome, the *motoconchos* louder, the garbage and sewage smellier, the language more confusing, the bargaining more exhausting.

I was actually reduced to writing out a list of pros and cons. I set aside financial considerations, mostly because I bet they'd be a wash. No gain, no loss. I'd get my money back but not more, meaning I had had a place to winter for the absurdly low cost of the condo fees.

Under the reasons why I should go back to Canada, I wrote SAFETY in caps and underlined it. I didn't include all the little sensory things that were pissing me off because, I reasoned, the picky list on the Canadian side of the ledger would be longer and include shitty slow drivers, shitty ever-present bureaucracy, shitty nickel-and-diming banks and cable companies, shitty drinking and smoking laws, shitty taxes on everything I liked consuming.

Under the column persuading me to stay, also in caps, I wrote: NO SNOW and MURDER NOT SOLVED.

Just then, the phone rang.

"Diaz," the voice said.

"No," I answered. "You've reached Jake Lydon. But you sound awfully like Chief Inspector Arturo Diaz yourself. Did you know that?"

Apparently Arty wasn't in the mood for my juvenile fucking around.

"There is news. Paul Bartlett sent us e-mails of the campers. We sent his picture to them. We have five answers. All say it was him that was with them. And we have the tests back on the machete you—with luck—did not touch. It was the same one that was used on Sally. We found her blood. I thought you would like to know."

Click.

Not much of a conversation but it was all I needed to make me rip up my little list.

I may have suspected it before, but now I knew for sure that this whole shitshow was one giant connected Lego set.

Whether they wanted me to or not, I had people to see. Reckoning that I was still a pariah dog among the Big Dave crowd, I decided to go a-calling, something I just about never do.

If you want an idea of how obsequious and accommodating I can be,

I accepted and actually drank some of the fucking organic Emerald Spring Lung Ching green tea Dot offered me as we set up in her jungle-y courtyard ringed by her multi-coloured guest cabins festooned with seashell wind chimes, stone replicas of Taino fertility gods, and crude *papier mâché* parrots looking as though they'd been drunkenly fashioned by Grandma Moses if she had pulled a Gauguin and fucked off to Polynesia.

Setting aside the tea, which I eventually did, the whole scene was pleasant as hell, except Margaret was all fidgety because she had a million details to look after and Dot was so blissed-out that I suspected she was on the verge of talking about the galaxy—that'd be infinite space, not the local nightclub.

That is until I brought up the reason I was there.

"So ladies, I was wondering, hoping really, that you could shed some light on Sally's interest in human smuggling."

That wasn't the icebreaker I was aiming for. More of an icemaker. They stiffened up, looked at each other nervously, and I thought I could see Margaret's piercing grey eyes suggest to her partner that silence was in order.

They didn't want to talk to me and I didn't blame them.

"Jake, you've got to understand," Margaret said. "We're close to getting our citizenship. We've been here seven years. We can't rock the boat."

Dot was a little more forceful.

"You have no idea! None! What it's like when you get the government's attention. Ask Jimmy."

"The lawyer? What's he got to do with it?" I asked.

"He understands. Look, when we set up the inn, he handled all the banking, the paperwork with *Registro Nacional de Contribuyentes.* We had wanted to call this place La Mariposa Azul," Dot said, pointing to the office building's large stained glass window of a royal blue butterfly, pretty well the same design Tico put on Sally's pool. "He talked us out of it. He said that using that name would bring to mind the Mirabal sisters—the Blue Butterflies they were called—who raised holy hell against Trujillo. Three of them were murdered. Since then, they've come to represent violence against women."

"We knew all that; that's why we picked it," Margaret added.

"Jimmy thought it best to avoid anything that sounded like protest," Dot continued, "because you never know what ticks someone off. And then, your paperwork just gets lost."

"OK," I said, "then tell me this: was Sally afraid?"

"She should've been but she wasn't," Dot said. "At least she said she wasn't."

"Naive?"

"No. Well, maybe a bit. But she believed that one person could make a difference. Could spark others. Could start something. But, she said, to do that, you had to be fearless."

"Like the Mirabal sisters?" I said.

"Yes. Let me tell you how we met her. What was that, dear, five years ago?"

"Six," Margaret answered.

"She was driving this small Jeep-like thing she had rented in Caberete, where she was staying at the time. Paul was back in the States and she was out exploring, driving the coast road. We met her when she pulled into the parking lot at Luis' Restaurant on Playa Coson as we were walking to our car. She was all by herself and we got to talking. She was laughing when she told us she'd got her car stuck, backing out of a narrow dead end some miles from the restaurant. One wheel hung up. She spoke no Spanish then but she'd been able to convince six or seven Dominicans, strong young men, to come, and help. They lifted the vehicle out and off she went. That could've been dangerous, I told her. There she was in the middle of nowhere, a blonde *gringa* alone, with some layabout young men. She looked incredulous that I even would suggest she could be in trouble."

"What Dot's trying to say," Margaret said, "is that Sally couldn't have cared less about the power these people have. And she should've."

"Who are 'these people'?" I pressed on.

Margaret gave Dot a more pointed warning look. Translated into words, it would have read something like "I love you, Dot; you know that. But talking about Sally's activities—even to a dissipated douche such as this guy—just isn't a smart thing to do."

Dot—bless her blissed-out heart—snapped to immediate attention.

"For God's sake, Marge, do we just sit back and do nothing? Hide our heads in the sand? Nothing changes, that way! Nothing gets better. You know and I know, it's getting worse because no one stops them!"

"Them?" I asked.

"Who really knows? We've been here long enough to know it's not the street cops. There must be 1000 cops dismissed for being involved in small stuff. Never mind the port workers, the airline workers, boat owners. That's all penny ante. These guys are occasional foot soldiers because they're so goddamned poor. But they're not organizing anything."

"Then who is?" I asked.

"It used to be home-grown. Colonels and majors in the army, head of the drug force, airline owners, senators, all the way up the line."

"Used to be?"

"It's changed since we've been here. What's everybody talking about now? The global economy. It's the foreign gangs now. Mexican cartels, Colombians, Venezuelans, Russians, the Mafia. You know, the same ones operating in the US, Canada, all over the world."

"You read about the two Canadians who were just arrested at El Catey airport?" Margaret asked.

"Yup."

"They had 25 *pounds* of cocaine in their bags! How'd they know to come to this little town to get the drugs? Who'd they know here? Who's waiting for them in Montreal?"

I admitted I had thought the same thing when I read the news.

"And it's not as simple as good guys and bad guys. It's competing bad guys," Dot added.

"How do you know all this?"

"...I read. I watch. Look, I was born at night, but not *last* night," Dot said.

"Please, Jake. Keep us out of this," Margaret said.

"I will, ladies. I promise."

Walking back home I replayed our conversation. Yes, I had gotten a clearer picture about Sally but not much more beyond there were big forces at play. I had already figured that.

I also remembered something Dot had said, an expression she'd used that sounds kinda nifty the first time you hear it but that becomes real tiresome and trite very soon afterwards.

'I was born at night, but not last night.'

I knew I had just heard that recently. Rather, that I'd read some-where. It came to me. On the Friends of Paradise Regained website.

There was no Search function on the website so it took me a while—hours actually—to find Dot's expression.

There it was, in a contribution from SD Charger to a comment trail in one of Sally's postings, the one that named El Gordo and Sascha Petrovic as the pricks behind some disastrous people smuggling.

'Right on, Bahayibabe,' SD Charger had written. 'These vermin are killing this country while pretending to be upstanding businessmen. Oh, sure they are! (sarcasm). I was born at night, but not last night.'

Again, here we had way too much coincidence. So Dot was SD Charger. Another piece in the puzzle. I didn't know what I could do with it or even if it mattered. Not yet anyway. It's like those 1000-piece landscape jig saw puzzles. What I had with my discovery was one of the bits of plain blue sky. You know you'll have to eventually use it, but you also know you can't until you fill in a whole lot more.

# CHAPTER TWENTY-NINE

I checked my e-mail when I got home.

Just two messages in my Inbox, from my two favourite women. My daughter Halley—she a detective sergeant in the Metro Toronto police service—and Alexandra—she my late-stage love interest.

Alex's note set off some complications. While she apologized for the last-minute timing, she invited me to be her guest at a Pan Caribbean economic development forum slated for two weeks from now in Havana, on the next island over. She was pretty excited. With the US starting to lighten the fuck up over the Castros, it would be her first chance to go there. She knew that in a previous life, I'd visited Cuba several times. Quick images flashed through my wee brain. Images of walking the Havana *malecon* with Beth, attempting to dance at the intoxicating Buena Vista social club with Beth. Snorkelling at Cayo Coco with Beth. Strolling the beach at Guardalavaca. With Beth.

Like I said: It was complicated.

As diplomatically as I could, I wrote Alex back, passing on the chance. For days, the cyber silence would be deafening. And for days, I did nothing about it.

Halley's note was simpler; she just wanted to firm up her vacation plans.

For two weeks of my winter stay I spoil myself. My trusty bowling bag and I take a ten-minute *motoconcho* ride east along the coast road to the one of the few all-inclusives in the area. Fourteen days of not carrying groceries and beer, no fucking mosquitoes to defeat, no converting pesos in my head, no whine and roar of the *motoconchos*, and no beds to make. And on top of that there's an omelette guy who enthralls me with his artistry.

My daughter Halley usually comes down from Toronto to join me for a week and I get my temporary neighbours all intrigued by the dirty old man down the hall.

Yeah, I know, I know. How financially dumb can you be, you ask? She could just fly down and stay with you, you point out. Back off, will you? She did that once and it wasn't much of a holiday—for either of us. For one thing, she actually cares about what she eats. I don't. So she can always find something healthy-ish at the *El Trougha* buffet hall at the hotel without inflicting her dining choices on me. Also, she is a neat freak—obsessively so in my opinion—whereas, I am equally obsessive about being a slob. Much friction ensued. This way, I can limit her orderliness and cleanliness fetish to a 300-square foot hotel room.

At any rate, she insists on paying her own way down here which I like. But on the one night we go into town, she lets me buy her a dinner at Paco Cabana or Le Terrasse and I like that more.

I wrote her back, telling her that the middle of March would be the best time. I figured I'd be out of this shit I'm in by then.

As with just about every other aspect of my personal social planning, I, of course, figured dead wrong.

# CHAPTER THIRTY

I thought that Arty would want to know about my visit with Dot and Margaret. After all, he had asked to be kept informed. OK, OK, it was another excuse to get out of the house.

Diaz wasn't at the police station. It was 7 a.m. so I wasn't really expecting him to be there. I told the officer on duty that I'd wait.

"You wait for long time. The Chief Inspector is at a crime."

"*Donde?*"

"Pétionville."

I hailed the first *motoconcho* I saw and we putted along to the next lane off the beach road after Sally and Paul's. The bike bounced along the potholy road for maybe three-quarters of a mile then came to an abrupt stop as the police cars came into view in the distance.

"*Aqui. No alli,*" said the driver, pointing father down the road he had no intention of travelling.

At the best of times, the guy probably wasn't going to take me all the way to the club as Dominicans and Haitians usually kept a distance from each other. The cop presence made his decision a whole lot easier.

I walked the rest of the way, skirting the muddy puddles from last night's rain. The crowd of on-lookers was entirely black. They were not happy to see me. Apparently my skin pigment caught someone else's attention as Arturo made his way through the crowd.

"You must go, *Ingles*."

"Who?"

"It is Tico. He is dead."

"What! How?"

"Like Sally. Now please go; one of my men will take you."

Stunned, I got into a cop car, managed to give my address. We rode in silence. I stared out the window, the beachside palm trees flashed by. The ocean was being the ocean. And nothing registered. Nothing seemed real.

Unlike Clint's assertion in *Unforgiven* that "kid, we all got it comin'," some people, lots of people, don't. Tico was one of those people. And I was responsible. You can, of course, argue—as I did and continue to do after all this time since his murder—that the only person liable was the son of a bitch who swung the blade but there was no getting around it: I had helped get him killed.

I had spent the majority of my life governed by the good one line—a motto, a saying that seems to sum up a stance or explain away an action. Once said to myself, it erases any need for further analysis. Popeye's "I yam what I yam," Doris Day singing "*Que sera, sera,*" Whitman's "Do I contradict myself? Very well, then I contradict myself." A particularly pointy arrow in my quiver of self-justifying mantras had always been Pete Townsend's declaration: "I don't need to be forgiven."

On this night, I sat on my balcony and considered its utter hollowness.

'I'm sorry, Tico. I know you can't forgive me. And not that it matters a whole bunch, but I know I can't forgive myself. I also know that all I can do right now is find the motherfuckers who did this and make them pay as dearly as I want them to.'

CHAPTER THIRTY-ONE

Some days passed before I left my apartment. Booze-fueled inertia and a long wallow in sadness, self-pity, anger, and recrimination can do that. Overriding this mess of emotions is the huge sense of unfairness. Death—whether accidental or intentional—disrupts what you take to be the order of things. A nine-year old falls off a Ferris wheel, a 40-year old on vacation drowns in a rip tide, a 22-year old urban kid gets gunned down over an imagined slight—all of it is so fucking unfair, all of it means that these people didn't get their shot at a full life, seeing and feeling and loving the moments that fill you up.

Tico's death had not created much of a public ripple in my small pond of acquaintances. No news story on-line, no discussion at the grocery store, and no one at Big Dave's who acknowledged it beyond Nick.

"That was a fuckin' good guy," he said.

Tico would be mourned in his community. That much, I knew. I had ruled out attending his funeral. Why distract and likely enrage people in grief?

I checked in with Arturo. He was obviously trying to be helpful, and kind.

"We interviewed the man who found Tico," he told me. "He said that when he discovered him he was still alive, mortally wounded but alive."

"And he didn't get help?"

"It was too late. Believe me."

"So what do you have?"

"Very little. He was attacked on the road. We know he left the club alone. Perhaps two in the morning. From behind. Someone was in the bushes by the side of the road. One swing to the neck."

"That's it?"

"The witness—a Marc-Philippe Tousaint—told us that when he found him, Tico said one word—"*Espada*"—before he died."

"*Espada*?"

"Blade. Sword."

"What do you think?" I asked.

"I do not know. It was the thing of his immediate concern."

"Connected to Sally?"

"Yes. That is my assumption."

"And mine."

At home trying to sleep, I kept turning that one word over and over in my mind.

*Espada, espada.* It made no sense to me at all. Why would Tico's final word be a description of the weapon that was killing him? If it was, why wouldn't he have said 'machete' and not 'blade'? More than anything—why would his final word be in Spanish? To another Haitian? Why not the French *machette* or *lame* for sword?

Using Arty's sliding scale of probability, it just wasn't likely, or even possible. It *had* to mean something else.

Restless, I got up, went to the balcony, and fired up my shitty laptop.

What followed was the shortest Google hunt I had ever been on.

"Espada Dominican Republic." Hit Enter.

The first full page of the instant results had only one topic of my search. Punta Espada, the luxury golf course in the equally luxurious Cap Cana in the south-east corner of the country. If I knew/ cared/ was even remotely interested by/ followed golf, I might've made the connection a little earlier.

I noodled around with all things Espada for a while. The golf club site, the reviews for the attached hotel. As I tend to do a lot with new places, I also checked out the various real estate sites selling the high-priced homes around the golf course and marina. You could tell the sales agents—crisp-looking guys with names like Skip and Darryl—knew their market. A bunch of the house descriptions were in Russian only. These barns were two million and up.

On any topic, most searches first turn up a long string of self-promotion sites. So you only get one side of things and there is never just one side of things. Take whatever your search word was and add 'Critics of' and you get a different view of the same subject. After a couple of hours, I had wandered through a host of negative comments on everything from the golf course lay-out and price to the quality of the club house restaurant to the string of sub-developments within Cap Cana that went bust in 2008 and stayed bust right up to the current depressed real estate prices.

But really, only one unanswered question stood out: Why the fuck would a Haitian labourer in Las Terrenas care or even know about a prestige golf course community on the opposite coast of the island?

While a lot of people had been helpful in supplying bits and pieces, I had only one—well, two—candidates who I believed could help me connect the dots: Dot and Margaret.

I showed up again at the Mariposa B&B. And again, it was plainly evident that I hadn't shed my leper status. As sweet as these two ladies are, I had to get at what they knew.

"Margaret, I need to find out if Sally had anything to do with the Punta Espada Golf Course?"

"She didn't play."

"You know what I mean."

"Margaret?" I prodded.

"She knew that that's where Sascha Petrovic lives."

"How?"

"She said she'd been there."

"Did she tell anyone else?"

"I don't know."

"Did she tell Tico?" I asked.

"...yes."

"Margaret!" said Dot coming up to us. "She didn't just tell him! She went to Cap Cana *with* Tico. She told me that place was the start of the evil. You know how she was, Jake. She tried to barge her way in."

"Wait a minute! With Tico? Are you sure?" I asked.

"That's what she said."

Tico had neglected to mention that trip. That's how frightened he was of the Russians.

"Did she meet Petrovic?" I asked.

"I don't know..." said Margaret.

"No, she didn't," Dot said. "A goon stopped her at the gate, told her to stay away."

"Was she trying to bust Sascha?"

"No. She was trying to get passage for Tico's friend."

"Xavier," I said. "And, by the by, he was Tico's brother."

"Brother? I didn't know," Dot said and I believed her.

"And Petrovic wouldn't take her money?" I continued.

"He knew who she was."

"BayahiBabe?" I said.

That was a jolt for Zen Dot.

"How...what..?" she mumbled.

"Look, if I could figure it out," I said, "anyone could, Dot. Or should I call you SD Charger?"

Double jolt.

"OK, so now you know we're in pretty deep," Margaret said. "And you know we're in as deep as we can afford to be."

"What's the connection with El Gordo?"

"After Petrovic ran her off," she went to El Gordo. "Paid him a lot less. The plan was to get Xavier to Florida and let him take his chances from there."

"That's why there was all that cash was in her apartment. It was supposed to go to Petrovic."

"Yes."

"So you knew about it then?"

"Yes. I'm sorry," Dot said, "but what was I supposed to say?"

"I don't know. Maybe something."

"She got the money from Paul in the first place; it's not like her pension was enough, so it was going back to where it belonged," Margaret said.

"Why El Gordo?"

"He wants to get into the big leagues. He started as sort of a local small-time thug. Running girls, drugs through the clubs. Sally knew he wanted to expand the business."

"But Sally—BayahiBabe—said he was hooked up with Petrovic."

"Yes, but El Gordo told her he was doing this for his own business. On the side."

"I didn't think Russian gangsters let you moonlight," I said.

"So now you know as much as we do," Margaret said. "Please, Jake, leave us alone."

"I'm sorry, ladies. I really am."

That night, I kept turning Burke's quote over in my mind.

*"The only thing necessary for the triumph of evil is for good men to do nothing."*

You either do something or you don't. There is no half measure here. It's like sort of being pregnant or sort of liking the Rolling Stones. You're in or you're out.

I didn't have a view of myself as a good man. At best, I figured I was an OK man but I needed to do something. I could just turn over everything I knew to Arturo, wash my hands of it, and order a double T&T. But that'd be worse than chickenshit. It would be willful rather than automatic cowardice. And besides, Arty just couldn't crack the expat world like I could.

But there were no swelling horns, no flag (Canadian or Dominican) snapping in the wind for background. Instead I tried to talk myself out of it.

'Jake,' I said to me, 'leave it alone; it's not your country.'

'Oh, fuck off, Jake,' I replied. 'If things work out, you'll be here for 20 years, for about the same time you spend in Canada every year. And hey! It's not the Russians' country either.'

'But fucking around with crime gangs? That's crazy dangerous.'

'So's smoking two packs a day.'

'Did you stop to consider that you can't plan my way out of a paper bag?'

'Then I guess it's time to use that great fucking brain, isn't it?'

I'm pretty adept at imagining how things might play out. How it would look as a movie. But logistics, details, and execution, not so much.

I started with: 'Why, I'll just march into Cap Cana and confront

Petrovic. And he'll feel so bad that he'll admit everything and turn himself in. Foolproof. Ironclad. Sure fire. What could possibly go wrong?'

'Think harder, Homer,' I told myself.

The problem is I tend to over-think, over-decorate. When I was trimming Christmas trees, you could barely see the fucking tree. Same goes for my cluttered mind.

So for some days I walked around in more of a daze than usual, constructing these elaborate, Rube Goldberg-type plots with lots of moving parts, lots of actors and events that had to happen just so.

Their only common characteristic: they couldn't possibly work.

# CHAPTER THIRTY-TWO

That Sunday was Super Bowl Sunday, the best day of the year. I took a day off from my grandiose planning. There were three of us in my apartment. Nick, Trevor, and me.

Nick, I could see—even if he's a fucking Giants fan—but Trevor asking for an invite was a bit surprising.

"I can almost understand the game when you explain it, yeah?" he told me.

Both declined my offer to show up at my place at noon for six and a half hours of pre-game shows. Fuckin' fair weather fans. Odds makers take a beating again, but I was half-lit when they turned up and fully illuminated by the final whistle of what—again—wasn't much of a game. But the ads were good.

"Well, mate, seems to me it's all about the bloody money, idn'it?" Trevor said.

In retrospect, I suppose that comment from Trevor (fuckin' cynic!) got me off my complicated scheming.

Of course anything I was going to do had to be simple. And nothing's simpler than money. If I came to Petrovic with a proposition, a deal in which he could make some big money, he might go for it. And I might hang him with it.

The simplest of all would be a significant drug buy. Say, half a million dollars of cocaine in transit before it gets stepped on would probably be classified as significant. But, I reasoned, that Petrovic might only be the middleman, if he touched the deal at all. The powder on the island more likely flowed through Colombian or Mexican or even Venezuelan fingers.

And besides, more outrageous to me was the human trafficking. I didn't have a ton of sympathy for anyone who had volunteered for the drug wars. I figured that cartel foot soldiers in Sinaloa or Monterrey or wherever the fuck had some inkling about the work-place environment when they signed up.

Whereas the Haitians were complete innocents who wanted nothing more than a decent life. Yeah, yeah, poverty and hopelessness were also no doubt powerful incentives to join drug gangs. But hooking up with outfits that routinely butchered families, decapitated students, murdered journalists and politicians, and plopped humans into vats of acid is a pretty clear moral choice.

And besides besides, ordinary people dying to get to another country was what had really mattered to Sally.

And to Tico and Xavier.

I determined that I would pose as a Canadian businessman interested in middle-manning a deal to move illegals to Canada.

Owing largely to my exposure to false identities just this last summer, I still had a fake ID of my very own. Glen Johnson was my pseudonym, a boring-as-fuck insurance company clerk from Toronto.

All the counterfeit papers created for me by a whiz bang computer hacker—now on the lam—still existed and I knew where. In an evidence storage locker at the Metropolitan Toronto police department, the same cops my daughter worked for.

Armed with this paperwork, I could resurrect Glen Johnson, a former insurance minion turned international human smuggler. I needed a back story, something persuasive about why boring ol' Glen was pulling the Monty Python 'Lion Tamer' routine. I had time to make that part up.

I figured Halley wouldn't want an e-paper trail on this so I called her at home that night and, after laying out the situation, I told her what I'd planned to do and how she could help by couriering me the fake paperwork.

Negotiations with her were just a little bit on this side of delicate.

"Dad, are you out of your fucking mind?"

"I got this, Hal."

"You don't 'got' anything. You don't have a fucking clue what you're getting into."

"That's what everybody said about the clown show this summer. That turned out OK."

"You were shot!"

"When did you turn into such a petty detail person?"

"You nearly died, dad!"

"Operative word being 'nearly'."

We chatted amiably like this for a bit. The conversation ended—rather abruptly, I thought—with her saying "I'll see what I can do!" followed by a loud click, oh hell, let's call it a slam.

But, on the plus side, she hadn't flat-out refused to send me the papers.

Cash was the next order of business. I had access to some. Even with the fucking killer exchange on Canadian currency, I could probably get my hands on $200,000 US, representing a huge chunk of what I had set aside for my encroaching decrepitude. If things went sideways, there wouldn't be any more sunset years for me anyway, so what the fuck?

But there had to be more coin to make sure Petrovic was interested. Even though I have never understood it, there is everything to the notion of big round numbers (50th Anniversary? Why not 49 or 53? How about the Top Eleven?). A million bucks sounded way better than 200K. I wouldn't need the whole nut. I had looked ahead to negotiations and decided that I'd show 500K in actual cash with the rest to come after the boat made land.

The fact is, I can't sell shit to a fly. But I was definitely incented to canvass the expats and Dominicans I knew. At least the ones I thought I could trust and that I reckoned had some money.

It took me about ten days to rustle up the money. A week and a half of discreet one-on-one meetings with the gang from Big Dave's. I didn't want to go outside this group and approach the better-heeled crowd living up in the villas. I only knew one villa resident and even though Jimmy the lawyer was probably the wealthiest among us, his connection to El Gordo ruled him out. Approaching complete strangers didn't make sense. I wouldn't know who I was talking to, who I could trust. And I ruled out a bunch of people in my own little circle who I thought either didn't have the money or the discretion. Miguel for one. Jeff, the motorcycle decorator, was another.

My elevator pitch—even though there aren't any elevators in Las Terrenas—was simple. I was going to carry on Sally's work. Not by opposing the new immigration laws or outing the bad guys, but by getting as many Haitians as I could out of the Dominican before they were deported back to Haiti where they were going to have really shitty lives instead of mostly shitty lives here.

Everyone wanted to know how I was planning to pull this off. I refused to give details. Mostly because I didn't have any. But telling them that "The less you know, probably the better" made it sound like: A) I was concerned for their welfare, and B) I had a fucking clue what I was doing.

Nick was the only one who was interested in performing due diligence. He wouldn't commit to a donation unless he approved of the plan. Sitting at a table at Dave's, I gave him as much as I had—OK, OK, there was some embellishing going on. He seemed to think the Glen Johnson ruse was brilliant.

Vlad, Nick, Big Dave, Margaret and Dot, Frank, Mad Tim, and even paranoid real estate guy Bruce all kicked in. Pietro declined, explaining that his allowance from his wealthy Venetian father wasn't that generous and what was left over each month was committed to his pastor/swindler and his super church in Tulsa. For a lot more secular reason, Sergei passed too, explaining that re-selling dog-eared Grishams for a buck wasn't nearly as profitable as everybody thinks.

I found Sally's Denver phone number on my old rental agreement and called Paul, reckoning that he should be invited to join in.

"What are you going to do?" he asked in response to my money begging.

"Get as many Haitians out of the country as I can."

"How?"

"Apparently there's a Russian dude in Cap Cana who does this sort of thing."

"Who?"

"Sascha Petrovic. Heard of him?"

"No. You sure he's the one?"

"Dead sure. Sally found him."

I outlined the plan such as it was.

"Jesus, Jake. I'd love to—I want to—but I'm flat broke. All our money is tied up in the houses down there and they're not selling. Plus I'm mortgaged to the hilt up here. I'm tapped out."

I didn't push it. Paul asked to stay up-to-date and apologized again.

I was happy that almost everybody else I pleaded with had come through. Nick had US cash—I didn't have to ask where he got it from. His was the biggest contribution, almost 100K in crisp, sequentially-numbered US tens and twenties. The rest came in the form of bank drafts and piles of pesos. All in, just over half a million worth of US dollars.

I reckoned that Petrovic wouldn't want great piles of brightly-coloured pesos as the Dominican currency isn't exactly an international standard. Converting most of it to US dollars took time. At the current exchange rate of 45 pesos to one dollar, that was a lot of paper. I went to all the *cambios* in town—the glassed-in kiosks that handled money changing. Then, with Tim at the wheel, I took short day trips to Nagua, Gaspar Hernandez, and Caberete along the coast to hit the *cambios* there.

I was a little nervous about getting challenged at these places because you have to show ID. I figured that if Halley came through—and I was betting she would—I could use the Glen Johnson passport if my real one eventually raised suspicions. But none of these places recorded anything; they just wanted to see my passport.

So there I was, with a half-assed plan and my trusty bowling bag stuffed with US cash. Now I needed a greedy Russian to want it.

I went to Sergei's bookstore early one morning as he was opening up.

"Do you know Sascha Petrovic?" I asked.

"Everybody knows Sascha Petrovic," he replied without missing a beat.

"But do you *know* him."

"Please stop, Jake. You are not a bad man but you are annoying now."

"That's probably true, but do you know him?" I persisted.

"I do not. I do know he is *not* retired, and neither is his father," he said, looking nervously around at a couple of customers who had come into his small shop.

"His father?"

"Nikolai. I know he is the big cheese. And I also know you must be quiet now."

"Are you threatening me?"

"Oh, for fuck sake. I'm warning you. As any friend would do."

"Thanks for the thought, but I still need to get in touch with Sascha."

"Why?"

"I have a business proposal."

"What is it?"

"That's between Petrovic and me."

"So he will call you because you asked him to? Is that your belief?"

"OK then, tell him he needs to know that I have a million reasons to call me and fifty passengers for his travel service."

"Give me your phone number."

"E-mail's better."

"Give me both. I'll see what I can do."

I handed him the contact info.

"Glen Johnson?" he asked.

"Don't ask," I said.

The telephone number was no problem; I had determined that for the few times my phone ever rings, I would only answer "Glen Johnson" until this thing was over. I also had given Sergei the fake e-mail address I had created for the bogus me.

I wasn't exactly convinced that Sergei could deliver the message or if he had suddenly turned accommodating to get me the fuck off his tits. I needed a back-up and there was only one man whom I was positive knew Sascha Petrovic.

Time to have a little chat with El Gordo I decided. I don't know what—if anything—I could learn or what he could do, but for sure it would help get the word out that I wanted to play.

# CHAPTER THIRTY-THREE

I hoped he'd be at his bigger club—Galaxy. It was mid-afternoon when I walked into the place.

There is something very weird about a dance hall or bar that's all lit up and empty of cheek-by-jowl patrons. I walked across the darkened disco light floor below the mirror ball. Halfway across, I was intercepted by a very large goon who had moved towards me with surprising grace. He didn't put his hands on me but I reckoned that was only a matter of time. And not much of it.

"Just a word, *senor*!" I yelled, hoping the sound would travel around this well-dressed muscle mass.

A pause and I heard a gruff "OK."

El Gordo was sitting around one of those red-cushioned circular booths. ("And, boy, was he sitting *around*!" Ba-boom. Rimshot. "Thank you very much, ladies and germs. I'm here all week. Try the veal!").

He was a wide load, having presumably been enjoying the fruits of his labour. Although a relatively young guy—maybe late 30s—he'd already run to overindulgent flab, cloaked in an open-necked silk shirt, several gold chains, topped off by a pudgy face decorated with a pencil-thin moustache. I actually had to stifle a laugh at this unintentional retro fashion statement that made him look like an obese 70s porn star.

He had a pile of paper spread out on the table and an astonishingly beautiful woman was turning the pages over for him. She wasn't doing this so he could display his power and laziness and excess. A more practical reason lay behind her assistance. El Gordo was unable to thumb through the paperwork himself because at the end of each arm was a very large plaster cast completely enveloping his hands.

Well, that settled the question about Russians allowing side jobs, I thought.

"*Que?*" he barked.

"*Senor* Olivero," I said. "I would like you to take a message to Sascha Petrovic."

"*No lo se.*"

"I think you do."

I gave the page-turning beauty a scrap of paper with my contact info.

"Business," I said.

"*Vamos!*"

He waved one clubbed hand. I wheeled and left as fast as I could.

The last part of the plan—such as it was—was to get my hands on a listening device. A bug. If I got a meeting with Petrovic, I knew I would be searched pretty thoroughly. I needed something undetectable, something Q would come up with for James Bond.

You'd be pretty amazed—I know I was—flipping through website after website at all the high-tech spy thingies on the market. Remember those secret decoder rings that used to come in cereal boxes when you were a kid? You can buy real ones now. Supply a working credit card and, poof, you're in the espionage biz.

From a California company, I ordered a teensy microphone/trans-mitter that was built into a shirt button and a wireless receiver with a range of a mile. What the hell, I ordered six matching dummy buttons. I then spent extra to double the recording capacity to three hours and extend the range to two miles. All for 450 bucks—with free shipping.

Outside of Santo Domingo there is absolutely no postal system of any kind in the country. There's the illusion of mail at some of the hotels which sell postcards to their guests who like to send them home to rub their friends' and family's collective nose in the fact that they're sipping apple martinis by the pool while their loved ones are freezing their asses off back home. The hotels bag the cards up and drive them to Santo Domingo for their eventual dispatch to the US or Canada or wherever the fuck and nobody seems to mind that they get to their destinations weeks after the returning tourists do.

For everyone else, it's courier companies, big and small. And none of this overnight delivery either. Judging by what other people had told me, the timeframe in which I could expect parcels to turn up was somewhere between the day after *manana* and the 12th of never.

The last job on my immediate things to do list was to tell Arty what I was up to. I didn't relish this conversation; I wasn't expecting much in the way of encouragement from him.

The wheels were in motion and I had nothing left to do for a while but wait. Which I fucking hate doing. For anything. Wait an hour for a table at a restaurant? You're suggesting that I line up for food? Not a chance. Well, maybe if it was a soup kitchen and I was starv-ing. But other than that.

My meeting with Arty went, I supposed, as well as could be expected.

First, I wanted to furnish him with all the bricks in the wall, recount-ing the mounting evidence that, while maybe not a lay-down for a jury, was pointing more and more towards Sascha Petrovic as the man behind the death-dealing in Las Terrenas. The Punta Espada connection, Margaret and Dot's inside skinny, the works. This wasn't me just casually fingering Petrovic. I mean, this was two of those giant yellow hands pointing at him.

Arty listened patiently. I expected to be interrupted by a few of his judicious reality checks, but I wasn't.

"So," he finally said. "You appear to have proved your case, *Ingles*."

For some reason, he didn't seem all that thrilled that I had done so. Or maybe I was just being too much of a compliment whore.

"And now it is up to me to act?" he asked rather than said.

"Not necessarily. What if I could bring him down?"

"What if I had enough money to buy a yacht *and* the Packers of Green Bay?"

"I'm serious, Arty."

"You go there and do what?"

"I have a plan."

"Why, that is the most wonderful thing I have heard today."

"Just listen, will ya?"

To his credit, Arty did listen, interrupting only occasionally. But there was something distracted in his manner, like he was going through the motions of listening and caring.

"Arty, did you know Petrovic when you were in Punta Cana?" I finally asked.

"I knew his father, Nikolai. Sascha was a teenage punk. His father was the boss man."

"You couldn't charge him with anything?"

Arturo paused.

"I could have done so. I did not."

He was looking out his window. Before I could ask why he hadn't nailed Nikolai Petrovic, he spoke again.

"Two of his men visited my family while I was working. It was late at night. They suggested to my wife that my investigation of Petrovic would not be healthy to her family. Maria left me after that; I did not stop her. I did not try. She took Paulo and Juanito and left. To be safe. She returned to her father's house in Puerto Plata."

"Sorry to hear that."

"I was eating alone at a little restaurant one night and Nikolai, the father, just sat down at my table. He didn't say anything, just stared at me. His eyes, they sparkled, maybe like a wolf. Then he said only one thing."

"Which was?"

"*Calle* Juan Lafy."

I looked at him puzzled.

"The short street in Puerto Plata where Maria's father and mother live. I knew then, my wife, my children would never be safe."

I could see his eyes watering. At his impotence. At the thought of losing his family.

"What is it you expect to do?" he asked, becoming focused again.

"Get him talking about his operation."

"This will be only your word against his."

"Leave that with me."

"Why would he trust you? Why would he even see you?"

"The best reason of all. Money."

"You have money?"

"Half a million."

"Pesos?"

"Dollars."

Arty looked surprised.

"Cash," I added.

"And what will you do with this money?"

"Buy something from him."

"What?"

"Leave that with me too. The less you know, probably the better."

"I can do nothing to help, *Ingles*. You understand this?"

"I do. Wait; there is something you can do."

I told him about the mail I was expecting. My packages would most likely be coming through El Catey airport. Because shipping a foreign passport —a counterfeit one at that—and hi-tech surveillance equipment might arouse some interest, I asked Arty to smooth the way at customs. He agreed, and said he'd drive to the airport himself to ensure that a thick envelope from the Metro Toronto Police

Service and a small package from Sentry Electronics of Pasadena were to be let into the country unopened.

A few days later, I found this in Glen Johnson's junk e-mail folder:

*Send passenger list here.* My reply was to be directed to info@ OdessaTravel.com.

Fuck! I hadn't counted on that. Clearly, Petrovic wanted to vette the travellers or at least confirm they existed. I also realized that Sergei had somehow been in touch with him; I hadn't said a word to El Gordo about why I wanted to talk to Sascha.

So now what I needed were customers. Real live Haitian customers en masse. I toyed with the idea of just faking up a passenger list but discarded that notion. The deal would be dead before it even started if Petrovic found out I was bullshitting. And I assumed that with his reach he could find out.

Going door-to-door in the town barrio didn't seem like a swell idea either. I needed to talk to them in a group and the only gathering place I knew was Pétionville.

My only connection to the Haitian community which had learned centuries ago that trusting white people wasn't a real good move was Ricky, Tico's former right hand man.

He was working for Nick now, tending to the needs of Nick's three-house compound. I went to see him, explaining what I was trying to do. Ricky had zero interest in joining me; I understood why he refused. Tico had been involved and now he was dead. We who know nothing about physical threats ought to be a little more understanding of people who know—unequivocally *know*—that their lives are in danger.

"For Tico," I said, trying a little emotional blackmail. I was desperate. I had no other way in.

Still no dice.

Mercifully, Nick came out and I explained the situation to him while Ricky stood off a bit watching us with a very sullen look. Nick went over to him, threw a meaty arm around him, and went for a stroll and a chat with his new employee. Even though Nick is pretty much a pussycat, he was fearsome when he got cranked up. I figured he had supplied Ricky with a much more immediate sense of danger. Reluctant or not, Ricky agreed to take me.

That night, Ricky and I set out, not saying a word for the 45-minute walk.

Off the main road, we were in inky blackness. I couldn't see it but I had to pass the spot where Tico died. A wave of sadness rolled on me. And gave me something that felt like determination.

You know that scene in the westerns where the stranger flings open the saloon doors and everything just stops? The piano, the eternal poker game, the laughing and glass tinkling and fightin' and cussin' crashes to a halt. Well, it was a lot like that.

Dancers stopped dancing, drinkers stopped drinking, and the clack of domino tiles went silent. Instrument by instrument, the house band quit.

'What the fuck,' I thought. I got up on a chair.

"*Qui veut aller au Canada*?" I shouted.

There was clamoring. Definitely there was clamoring.

Ricky organized them into a ragged single file and I signed them up.

Yes, they had a few questions.

"*C'est legal?*"

"*Non.*"

"*C'est dangereuse?*"

"*Oui.*"

"*Vous allez a Mona?*"

"*Non.*"

"*Ma famille va avec moi?*"

"*Oui.* Tell me how many—*combien?*"

"*Qu'est ce que le cout?*"

"*Nada, zero, rien.*"

And Jack Snap I had thirty names and a few personal marks on a sheet of paper. Totalling up the number of family members listed, I had 53 potential passengers. I marvelled at the fact they were all willing to gamble on a risky boat trip, even after I had answered their questions as honestly as I could.

Through Ricky, I told them I couldn't guarantee when they were going—or even *if* they were going—but that they would hear from Ricky one way or the other within two weeks. I felt badly that I had aroused hope, however slim. But there was absolutely no other way.

I had involved enough people in this escapade. From now on in, I was going to do this alone. Or so I thought.

I went to Mad Tim's to rent a car. He refused.

"What the fuck? Why not?" I asked.

"I don't trust you, boyo."

"I'll repeat: what the fuck?"

"You don't know your way around and you're an easily distracted wanker. I'm not letting you destroy a major feckin' investment of mine."

"But I've got to go."

"Then hire me, ya cheap prick."

"You up for a road trip?"

"Always. Where to?"

"Punta Cana."

"Shithole."

"You ever even been there?"

"I have. Knocked around there a bit a few years back. That's how I know it's a shithole."

"But I thought Las Terrenas was the shithole."

"'Tis. Punta Canada's a bigger shithole."

"Punta Canada?"

"Crawlin' with you feckin' Colonial bastards. That's why it's a bigger shithole."

"Can you squeeze in an overnighter?"

"Let me check my feckin' schedule—Yes. Wait a minute! I see your game. Get an innocent Irish lad drunk in the big city, you filthy arse bandit!"

I tried to negotiate a price—not including his likely staggering beer tab.

He wasn't having any of that.

"Sally was a friend of mine too," he said. "Help out with the gas, get us a place to stay."

I asked to fill out the rental paperwork but he told me there wasn't going to be any.

"Are you sure you want to go there?" Tim asked.

"I *have* to go. I need to talk to some people."

"What kind of people?"

"Cap Cana people."

"If it's all the same to you, mate, I'll wait in the feckin' car."

# CHAPTER THIRTY-FOUR

That night, Arturo showed up at my place.

He was in full Lt. Castillo mode, not saying anything but he plopped two packages onto my counter. One from Toronto, one from California. The final pieces.

Arty asked about any progress I had made. I told him about my visit to Pétionville and my guest list and about my trip south in a couple of days.

"I cannot forbid you to go there, *Ingles*. I wish, but I cannot."

That was about as encouraging as Arty had been. Maybe because I was getting all jacked up and nervous about putting a theoretical plan into practice, I was getting frustrated with his—I don't know— lack of enthusiasm.

"Arty, can I ask you something?"

"Of course."

"Are you coasting on this?"

"Coasting?"

"Taking it easy, not wanting to push it."

I expected some angry blowback. There was none. Instead, he stared intently at the lit landscaping.

"You knew what Tico meant when he said *"Espada"*, didn't you?" I asked.

"I suspected...yes," he answered, not taking his eyes off the gardens.

"And you hoped I would just forget about all this, didn't you?"

He turned to me.

"Yes."

"Why? Are you paid off?"

"No."

"Then why?"

"I was afraid of them. For what they could do to my family, Yes, me also. And now you."

*"Was* afraid?"

"Truthfully, I still am afraid. But I am more afraid of you doing something very stupid to get yourself killed. I cannot be involved. But if you were willing to risk so much, then, at the least, I can help."

"How?"

"I have someone you can talk to. His name is Enrico. You will find him on the beach. He sells boat excursions. And other things."

"You trust him?"

"With my life."

"How about with mine?"

"And with yours."

"And I find him how?"

"He will find you. Wear the shirt you have on now," he said, pointing at the bilious bright red, yellow, and orange number I was sporting. "Go to the place called Bibijagua along the beach. You must be alone."

"OK, and what will this Enrico do for me?"

"He can make the connection you seek. He can tell you the situation."

"What about the local police?"

"There are many good men in the area. I served with some of them years ago. But that does not mean all the men around them are also good."

"So I'm on my own?"

"Completely."

You could tell this whole thing was really stressing Arty. A man of action, a guy in charge of other men with guns and here he was, standing idly by, cowed and letting a middle-aged, overweight, alcoholic, chain-smoking *turista* carry the load. I think he didn't feel right with that.

I didn't either. I was scared shitless.

"*Ingles*, understand you are breaking the law. I cannot know about it. And if you are caught...You will have problems."

"I understand."

"Do you think you can do this?"

"Yes."

Arty studied my face for a few seconds, looking for proof—one way or the other—about the truth of my claim.

"You will carry a gun?" he asked.

"No. They'll search me. That's the first thing that'll happen—if I see him."

"I was going to say that. When will you leave?"

"A soon as I can. A couple of days, maybe."

"Tell me before you go."

Tom Petty's right; the waiting really is the hardest part. Mad Tim had to get his business in a leaveable state and I didn't have much to do beyond sewing on my mic buttons and staring at the bowling bag o' cash sitting on the bed in my spare room.

I figured some hard drinking might help pass the time. So I did that. They used to give kamikaze pilots a shot of ceremonial sake before their doomed flights. Fuck that. If I was going to crash and burn, I'd need a whole lot more incentive to get into the cockpit.

Two days later, after I left a message for Arty, Tim and I set off early for the five-hour drive. First, west along the newer and spectacular coast highway to the El Catey airport where we cut south on the even newer four-lane highway through the heart of the country.

I absolutely love going on long bus or car rides in a foreign country—just as long as I'm not driving. I offered but Tim declined, being rather protective of his new Toyota 4Runner.

"You'll just kill the pair of us before we even feckin' get there."

Anyways, it was delightful cutting through the magnificent country seldom visited by outsiders other than well-meaning missionary groups who every winter descend upon remote villages to do and build good works. We were honking along just fine past a series of villages and towns that decades, maybe centuries ago had served as the economic drivers when Spain ruled the island and its slave-grown sugar cane, coffee, and tobacco were sought by the world. In between the settlements, were mountains and valleys, palm-lined ridges and overwhelming green, green, green.

From time to time, I'd break the silence between us by tossing out an observation or news item that was intended to within seconds make Tim climb up on his crazed soapbox.

"Did you see where the World Health Organization just listed the DR as the single most dangerous country in the world to drive based on traffic fatalities per 100,000?" I innocently asked.

That brought on an animated five-minute tirade about the complete incompetence of the drivers, the government system that keeps them incompetent, and the utter failure to regulate or see that drivers had licenses, never mind insurance or road-worthy vehicles.

Which led to another five-minute rant after I noted that 80% of the deaths involved two-wheeled vehicles.

Not too surprisingly, all the main highways in the DR lead to its main city. That meant you couldn't get there from here without passing through Santo Domingo, unless you were prepared to figure out and then brave the spaghetti web of local and mostly unmarked roads that snaked up and down mountains haphazardly joining tiny villages and farms.

Mercifully, we didn't have to go right into Santo Domingo, picked up Highway 3 heading east to Higuey and the south-eastern tip of the island.

The land was predominantly flat and covered with sugar cane fields as far as you could see.

Mad or not, Tim was a wellspring of knowledge even if it was always tinged (well, dyed black) by his spirited editorializing.

"You want to see what slavery looked like in America two hundred years ago?" he said, sweeping an arm out the window at the fields. "Right there by the feckin' roadside they've got acres of re-enactors, tens of thousands of them they illegally truck in from Haiti for the harvest. Poor bastards working ten, twelve hours a day, seven days a week, breakin' their backs swinging machetes. Livin' in *bateyes*— which is Spanish for concentration camps. No water, no electricity, feckin' guards 'to keep the peace,' they say, and they take away what few papers they have. And for what? Two feckin' dollars a day! That's the rate. And the poor bastards are happy to get it."

"That's the real problem, isn't it? Haiti is way more fucked."

"Yes and no. Because you can get dirt cheap labour, doesn't mean you have to. Brazil pays its cutters about five times as much. I looked it up. Bastard cartel here could at least double wages."

Tim fell silent, then shook his head.

"Dachau with palm trees," he said.

As we passed Higuey, Tim got verbal and serious again but not in his usual loud, spitting-mad way.

"We still can turn around, my son. Go back to LT and you can feckin' do what you were doing, what you *should* be doing. Six months of sand and sun and beer and leave all this shite to someone else."

"Time's past for that, Tim. I can't unring the bell."

"I figured you'd say that. I had to try, like that question at the wedding: ya know, if any man knows a reason why this feckin' couple and so on."

"Tim, did you know Sally came to Punta Cana with Tico late last summer or early fall?"

"Christ, no! She rented a little Kia SUV, piece of crap. I assumed she was going to Santo Domingo again for another shopping trip. That's what she said, anyway. And there was no Tico when she picked the car up. Must have stopped for him on her way out of town."

We actually drove past the turnoff to Cap Cana and straight towards the centre of Bavaro to the hotel room I had rented on-line. From the airport on in nothing looked familiar. Almost twenty years ago, Beth and I had been to Punta Cana, at a time when there weren't that many hotels. We hadn't gone off-resort then, beyond walking the miles after miles of superb and mostly empty beaches.

My, my, things had changed. Grand entrances to a bunch of places that weren't there the last time I was. Paradisus, Barcelo, Dreams, Be Live and Catalonia, never mind the stretch of hotels farther north than where we were going, all with great stone walls flanking bubbling fountains and elegant signage. The omnipresent barriers and guard stations blocking the wide entrances.

Our temporary home—Hotel Azul—was not one of these places. It was, to use the technical term, a toilet. But a toilet with double beds. And a roll-away cot.

"Mr. Big Spender," Mad Tim said, surveying the room.

"Last room available, so get off my back."

"Ah, spring break. Dumps like this were built for drunken Yank college students. Everything's bolted down and they can just hose the place down after the kids leave. Make half their feckin' money in a month."

"And the rest of the year?"

"By the hour."

We unpacked, and I stowed my trusty bowling bag as best I could. It would be way too much irony to have the money ripped off before we put it to use, but we had to leave it in the room.

We walked to the beach and stood there, I think a little stunned at the activity and large amounts of humanity, so unlike the usually empty beaches in and around Las Terrenas.

The beach was packed, the hotel loungers all full and spaced about 4½ inches from each other. And it wasn't just on land you saw the hub-bub. My god, you couldn't count the boats off Punta Cana. Fishing boats, dive boats, party boats, boats for pulling giant inner tubes or parasailing tourists aloft, and not one but two fake pirate ships with crews duded up in swishy buccaneer drag.

Add to that, the noise of numerous helicopters running loudly over-head, charging, I imagined, a hefty price to watch all this human leisuring from above.

"So what's your plan, Sherlock?" Tim asked. "Walk up and down the feckin' beach asking strangers if they're human smugglers?"

"I have somebody to meet. And it has to be alone."

"Where?"

"A place called Bibijagua."

"Well, you better pick up the pace, lad. That's about a feckin' mile south, maybe more, from here. "

"Fuck!"

"I'll be long gone before then."

We trudged along, our conversation limited to *"No, gracias"* in response to the many vendors who assailed fair-skinned Tim.

This was the one place where my gaudy Hawaiian shirts actually fit in. Oddly, I had bought this shirt on another beach in the DR, this one at Sosua, more than 20 years earlier. Something about the black palms backlit by these garish colours had attracted me. And for ten bucks? It had worn like iron.

"There's Now Larimar," Tim pointed. "That's my stop."

"Why there?"

"Used to spend time there."

"Why there?" I repeated.

"They made a great feckin' big deal of not using those coloured plastic bracelets to identify paying guests like branded sheep. Must have cost them a fortune for that distinction."

"Why?"

"Grease the guards, grease the bartenders a bit and you can eat and drink all feckin' day for nuthin'."

"You cheap Irish bastard! That's fraud, or theft or something."

"Tell that to the cheap Canadian bastards who let me in on it. And, me boyo, maybe not get too high on yourself. I'll put money that nobody in that crowd has a bag full of half a million dollars to do an illegal smuggling deal with a feckin' Russian mobster."

"Point."

"Now run along. You're meeting is just past the Melia Caribe. I'll be waitin' here."

At least the sand wasn't loose; walking was easy, although, with that sun, I was sweating like a pig and I couldn't afford to take my shirt off.

The deeper the tan, the less frequently you are preyed upon by the beach hustlers selling excursions, massages, hookers, hair braiding, weed, or just trying to drag you into their stores/grand shacks interspersed among the five-star hotels and bearing hand-painted signs like Wal-Mart, Macy's. They figure—correctly—that if you've been burnt brown in March, you're more or less a local and not the one-or two-week vacationers who are their bread and butter.

It's why I was a little surprised when a short Dominican, broke off talking to two really, really pink tourists and approached me, carrying a huge three-ring binder.

"I like your shirt, amigo," he said, falling in by my side.

"I do too," I said not breaking my stride because if you slow down you're hooked.

"And Arturo Diaz, he likes this shirt also."

That stopped me.

"Enrico?" I asked.

"Now listen. I will pretend to sell you an excursion and you will pretend to argue."

We sat down on the sugary sand of the broad beach. From a distance, his fellow salesmen clustered around beached fishing boats, watching us with bemused looks.

Slowly, Enrico began turning the laminated pages, pointing at my various entertainment options, whipping out the omnipresent calculator with the big numbers—the main weapon in Dominican deal-making, along with exclamations of "Cheapie! Cheapie!"—making a big show of proving to me what a bargain he was giving me. I made an equally big show of refusing each offer to send him back to calculating as we spoke.

"What can you tell me?" I asked shaking my head at the outlandish price for a half-day party boat tour which according to the photos featured passengers who'd all need fake IDs to get served back home.

"You are looking for a man, no?" he said.

"Yes, Sa—"

He cut me off pointing forcefully at the photo of mud-splattered dune buggies.

"No names! We know who you want."

"Will he call me?"

"I think yes."

"Will he try to fuck me?"

"He is *muy loco* but no. His father would not allow it. He has a reputation in business to keep."

"Does he suspect me?"

"I think no. He will be careful. The son, who can say?"

I gave Enrico the name of my hotel and room number.

"Now you will wait," he said.

I loudly signified the end of our haggling over excursions, even though the VIP Snorkelling Trip to Saona Island looked mighty tempting and I had knocked 50 bucks off Enrico's outrageous price.

As Enrico loudly cursed me and returned to his fellow hustlers who ragged his unsuccessful ass, I got up and strolled back, found Mad Tim almost where I'd left him. He had migrated from the beach to a bar by the main pool and was so completely immersed in drinking beer and ogling that I startled him.

"You done?" he asked.

"For now."

"Let me buy you a beer."

"You mean get me one for free, speaking of cheap bastards."

It was pleasant as hell, sitting by the sparkling pool—or maybe I was desperate for it to be pleasant as hell. Drinks before the war, as Mr. Lehane puts it. And it had to end because of a telephone call I couldn't afford to miss. I don't much care anymore for things with a time limit. Especially when I had to be the one blowing the final whistle.

Neither of us was in a good mood as we trudged back to our shitty hotel to wait.

The room phone rang just as we were finishing a dreadful order-in pizza.

"It's Sascha," a voice said in perfect English. "I will send my man in one hour. Have the money."

"If that's the way you want to do it, we won't be here," I said.

"What?"

"I have a driver. I will go to meet you."

"No! You don't get to fucking tell me how this goes down!"

"Then no deal."

I hung up.

Sounds cool and decisive, right? I was shaking like a palsied jitterbug.

"What the feck have you done?" Tim asked.

"Trust me."

"What do we do while I'm trusting you?"

"Wait."

I was being perhaps a little overconfident but I was sure—well, sort of sure, definitely hopeful, at any rate—that Petrovic would call back.

We waited.

And waited.

At least his call had given me the chance to test my recording device. Clear as a bell.

After listening to the brief phone conversation again, Tim piped up:

"I'll say this: you got balls. Not much in the way of brains. But you got balls."

"Or maybe I'm just a fucking moron."

"I'm not ruling that out either."

We waited some more and time crawled until we finally fell asleep.

The last thing I remember Tim saying was: "At least I got to see this feckin' shithole again."

In the depths of sleep, I heard the phone ring.

# CHAPTER THIRTY-FIVE

The LED clock on the nightstand said it was 12:17.

"Come to main gate at Cap Cana. One hour," Sascha said and hung up.

"We're on, Tim," I said as I woke him from his snore fest. "Do you know how to get to the main gate at Cap Cana?"

"No problem. Half an hour maybe."

Groggily, we left Bavaro and were soon on the deserted new highway running south past the airport.

"Now, we watch for the bandits," Tim said, which sort of put me into another panic, on top of the one I was already in regarding early morning visits to murderous gangsters. What with it being one in the morning and us having half a mill in cash in the backseat and all.

A few minutes later, a siren and blue and red flashing lights filled our car.

"What'd I tell you?" said Tim as we pulled over. "Can you sound Russian?"

"*Da.* I even know a few words."

"Good. Make it loud and pissed off."

Tim waited patiently for the two cops to saunter over to his window. He spoke politely in Spanish for a bit.

"Vot ees it?" I thundered.

That got their attention right quick. As they peered across at me. I thought: in for a kopek, in for a ruble, as somebody maybe says.

"Why you stop me? *Te svenyas*!" I demanded, keeping my spitting rage going, but wondering if I had overreached by calling them pigs.

Tim was trying to tactfully translate but I was yelling over top of him.

"Vot are your names? Queek!"

 When Tim pointed at their badges and asked "*Como se llaman*?" the lads reflexively covered their shields with one hand while tapping the door signifying that we were free to go.

"I gotta remember that," I said.

"Works around here but gets you a thumpin' in other places."

We pulled up to the elegant guard hut. On the other side of the barrier sat a silver Hummer. Two very large human beings got out. One approached the hut as the regular security guard turned away from the scene and began fiddling with his phone.

"He stay," said one of the behemoths, pointing at Tim. "Car stay. You come."

"You can't leave, Tim; sorry," I whispered. "You'd be out of range. And no matter what, don't replay it. Boris or Dmitri or Alexei or whatever the fuck his name over there would hear you."

"Got it."

"Hope you two kids make friends," I said to Tim as I took my trusty bowling bag from him through the window.

"Get fucked, me boyo," he said which I took to mean 'Good luck' in Irish.

I left Tim smoking in the SUV, and walked past his hulking Slavic shadow who stood impassively by the gate. I got into the passenger side of the Hummer. My driver had to scrunch down so his head didn't scrape the ceiling. On a fucking Land Rover that was designed with extra headroom, presumably to allow for the silly hats Brits wear on safari.

We drove down empty and winding well-lit boulevards. Through the impressive border gardening I could make out the fairways and greens of Espada, the white sand traps virtually glowing under the bright moon.

I will admit to being distracted from ogling the lifestyles of the rich and criminal in moonlight. As we drove farther from the guard hut, I was thinking that we might soon be out of range of Tim's receiver.

Predictably, the house we rolled up to was spectacular. A massive ersatz Italian villa with illuminated fountains, wide cobblestone steps and what must have been a football field's worth of tile on the patios that spilled out like Travertine ponds from the main house.

I stood briefly in front of the place, apparently admiring its unabashed opulence. What I was really doing was giving myself a last-minute pep talk. From here on in, I had to be on automatic pilot, assuming the role of a tough guy negotiator, an amoral prick with money to make. I couldn't think of Sally or Tico or the massive cruelty visited upon them by the sons of bitches on the other side of that door. I knew I had to be one way: confident, calm, and above all non-chatty. In other words, the very opposite of the way I normally am. It was a role I had to play, the sum of every gangster movie I had ever seen.

The large piece of well-dressed muscle led me through the ten-foot oak and wrought iron front doors. In the tiled foyer the size of my condo, he searched me. I want to say he gave me a pat down but what I got was a slap down. I then got a wanding from those metal detector sticks they use at airports. It set off tick-tick-ticking as he ran it over the first metal button of my shirt. He stopped briefly and then was satisfied after he passed the wand over the rest of the buttons and got the same noise.

The goon then took my trusty bowling bag and started rooting through the stacks of bills. He checked the lining, the straps.

As I was being manhandled, I looked around the house, a Tuscan wet dream of over-decoration. I was ushered into a great, great room where a young and very jumpy man was pacing the huge Persian carpet in front of a grotesquely-carved fireplace, all gargoyles and curly-cues.

I put him at maybe 25, just under six-foot, well-built, with watery blue eyes, perfectly jelled hair, black designer jeans, and a black silk shirt, for fuck's sake. A Caribbean hipster dude who I quickly found out wasn't interested in small talk.

"Sascha, I presume," I said.

"You have all the money?" he demanded.

"Half."

"Half? What's this bullshit?"

"Half now; half when the boat returns."

"All now!" he said as petulantly angry as any ill-raised teenager.

"That's not how it's going to work," I said.

"All of it now," he repeated becoming a little more agitated. He was either coming off or getting on some kind of dope jag. Or maybe he was just a jumpy asshole.

He hurled my trusty bowling bag across the floor, and some bundles of 50s and 100s went spilling out.

"Sascha!" a deep voice boomed. I turned to see a beefy-looking guy in his mid-fifties. He looked an awful lot like Robert Shaw in *Jaws*, only dressed in a silk smoking jacket.

"But, papa, he's trying to fuck me!"

"Leave us!"

"But..."

"Now!"

Sascha stalked off. Presumably to inhale a line or two of white-powdered comfort.

"I apologize," Nikolai said when we were alone. Well, alone except for the giant stationed at the front door. "My son does not yet understand the proper way to conduct business. Please to sit. We will talk."

"Talk about what?" I asked as I perched on the end of a giant leather sofa that must've cost five or six cows their futures.

"I will ask some questions. There is much that depends on your answers."

"Shoot," I said, almost laughing out loud at my hugely inappropriate suggestion.

"First, what should I call you? Mr. Lydon? Mr Johnson?"

"You choose."

"In Las Terrenas, you are Jake. I will call you Jake."

"Fine," I answered, more than a little bummed that my elaborate Glen Johnson identity had been a complete fucking waste of time.

"Now you tell me if you are alone in this operation."

"Yes. I do have a driver who knows enough not to ask questions."

"OK. Next, I will ask you about friendship with Chief Inspector Diaz."

"He is just that. A friend."

"I must worry about police friends."

"We both know why Arturo Diaz will not be a problem for you. Or me."

"You have no obligation to anyone?"

"No."

He gave off a 'harrumph' or some Slavic equivalent.

"Not your daughter, the police woman, not that stock trader in Boston? Not your reporter friend Stephon? Not your neighbour, Carl?"

I bore down on myself as though I were in a dentist's chair having a root canal without anesthetic, summoning the big, big effort to remain calm as he rhymed off the people close to me.

"I care for them, but I don't owe them anything," I said.

"So, if they were all to die. Perhaps at the same time. You would be OK?"

"What the fuck kind of bullshit is this?" I demanded, hoping my sudden and very real anger covered my equally real dread.

"Be calm. I meant nothing by mentioning."

"The fuck you didn't! Do you not think I know you could have them all killed with a wave of your hand?"

"And still you are here."

"And still I am here."

"Now you will tell me, why you are doing this?"

"It's simple. These Haitians are getting screwed. You have a way to get them off the island."

"Only that reason? You want to help them?" he asked, looking at me like I was fuckin' nuts—which at that moment, was a notion I couldn't dismiss.

"And...a friend of mine died trying to help them," I added. "I owe her that."

"Who?"

"Sally Bartlett. Did you know her?"

"No."

"Did Sascha?"

"I think no. He does not often visit Las Terrenas. Why would you believe Sascha knew her?"

"I don't. I was just asking."

I let it go. I couldn't imagine he was about to confess to murder right off the bat and me calling his son a liar was a low percentage shot this early in the match.

"You obviously checked me out. Besides knowing those close to me, what else did you find out?" I asked.

"You are quite famous. Last year. Newspapers everywhere talked of you."

"It went away."

"You made money from it?"

"Some. I gave most of it away."

"Ah, yes. You bought fire truck for Las Terrenas."

"So?"

"Sorry for my surprise. I do not see many idealists in my business."

"Yeah, I'm a fucking hero."

"You keep some money?"

"No. Fucking fire trucks cost more than you might think."

"And if we make deal, nothing for you?"

"Call me practical. I need to cover my expenses. You understand. Let's say 10%."

"How you say, for shipping and handling?"

He chuckled, I think pleased with his joke and to see a mercantile side to my idealism.

"Satisfied?" I asked.

"Yes."

"Now, can we discuss the details?"

"Yes."

"I turn over half a million dollars and deliver fifty Haitians to you."

"Twenty-five."

"What? I was told the price was 20,000 a person."

"You were told wrong. The price has gone up. My overhead is high. Fuel, crew, a good boat. They are using drones now."

"Well, I'm sorry for wasting your time, Mr. Petrovic," I said getting up to leave, although I wasn't at all sure I could make it out of there with the money. Or my life, for that matter.

"Sit!" he commanded.

I stood. He smiled at my impertinence.

"You bring me thirty Haitians," he said.

"Forty."

"We know this end at thirty-five."

"Yes, we do," I said, offering my hand. He was smiling as he shook it. And damn it, I was smiling too.

"And I bring them to you—"

"At your expense," he interrupted.

"At my expense. Now where am I taking them? Here?"

"No. Bayahibe."

"When?"

"I will send message. One week. Maybe ten days."

"And where are you sailing to?"

"Canada. Nova Scotia."

"You guarantee their safety."

"No. I guarantee to *try* to keep them safe."

"You have to do better than that."

"I cannot. But for this business to succeed for me, I must deliver or people like you will not call me."

"But not like El Gordo guaranteed their safety."

He started.

"What do you know of El Gordo?" he asked.

"I know he lost at least two Haitians last fall. A simple job and he fucked up."

"We talked to him about that. Not me. Viktor over there spoke to him," he said, indicating his bodyguard.

"You did that?"

"Besides no longer playing piano, he is no longer in business for moving people," Nikolai said.

"You call me when the ship leaves Nova Scotia," I said, "and I'll deliver the rest of the money."

"Within 12 hours."

"Within 24 hours."

"Is this only one deal?" he asked.

"Maybe. I don't know. If it works out, if they are delivered safely."

"You can get more of them? More money?"

"Yes."

"When?"

"I said we should see how this deal works."

"Smart."

"Anything else?"

"No. Easy deal. Easy plan. I like easy."

"You going to count the money?"

"No. Insult to me. Insult to you. You will not fuck me."

"No, I will not" I said, knowing that, with the recording, I already had.

"You will be my guest tonight," he said, sweeping a beefy arm around the gaudy great room.

"Are you asking or telling me?"

"Asking."

"Then thank you for your hospitality, but no thank you. I have a driver at the gate. I have things to do in Las Terrenas."

"Understood. A drink then? Cheers to our deal."

"Why not?"

"Champagne?" he asked.

"Beer?"

He laughed.

"A man of conviction!" he said.

"Actually, a man of habits."

He laughed again.

"Sit now! Presidente?" he said as I eased myself back into the chair.

"Aw, what the fuck. Do you have Dos Equis?"

"Viktor!" he roared. "*Dva* Dos Equis!"

I settled back in an ox blood leather and metal-studded wingback, as Vast Viktor padded off. I don't know if I audibly sighed with relief but I wanted to exhale with wind tunnel force. After a couple of soft poo moments at the outset, my tough guy wheeler-dealer act appeared to have worked. I was now in business with one of the top gangsters in the country. And more importantly our transaction had—hopefully—been recorded in indictable detail. One drink and I planned to be very much outta there.

Except, as it turned out, it wasn't quite that easy.

*Quelle* fuckin' surprise.

# CHAPTER THIRTY-SIX

The beer in chilled mugs arrived. We toasted as I offered a *"Naz zdarovya"* which made him smile.

The elder Petrovic had a disconcerting habit of staring right at me the whole time we spoke. I saw what Arty meant when he described his wolf eyes. I wasn't off the clock yet and knew I couldn't let my guard down. I stared back even though meeting someone's eyes isn't a long suit of mine. He seemed to find the answers he was silently looking for and he appeared to relax.

"You do not gamble in the casinos here?" he asked out of fucking nowhere.

"No."

"I did not think so."

"Why do you ask?"

"Tell me you are careful man who cannot lose what he have. No insult."

"I am an old man who wants to keep what he has earned. And no insult taken."

He sort of grunted, appreciating I hoped the slight shading on my answer.

Just then Sascha emerged from his private drug den.

"I'm going out!" he announced.

"Where?" his father asked.

"What do you care?"

"Where?" Nikolai demanded.

"Coco Bongo. OK?"

"Be safe."

Sascha looked at both of us with what amounted to hate. That expression might have been caused by different reasons, but, for sure, it was hate. He snorted, only without the coke this time, wheeled, brushed past Viktor, and left. The massive front door slammed loudly.

Hard to imagine, but the hardened crime lord across from me looked embarrassed.

"I envy you," he said.

"What?"

"You do not have son. When sons fuck up, they fuck up very much. Daughters is rare for them to do that."

At this point, he had taken his eyes off me and was staring at the bank of opened patio doors. We could not see but we could hear the surf pounding on the black shoreline beyond the huge illuminated infinity pool.

"I envy you two times," he said.

"Why?"

"You can do this deal or not. You maybe do another one. Or not. Such is not my situation."

"Are you sure?"

"I cannot quit. Another beer?" he asked, then signalled to Viktor without an answer from me.

I hadn't intended to turn into some kind of gangster life coach but that sort of statement asked, nay, pleaded for an answer. And besides, another beer was on its way.

"You must have enough money. Just walk away, if you want," I said.

"Not possible. I have responsibility. Not just to my son. To organization I made. It would all go to shit. He would all go to shit if I fuck off."

"So what?"

"Easy for you to say. Not easy for me to do. Many people need me. I do not cause anything to happen. I do not make people buy from me. I meet demand. All the things that are demanded – the drugs, the guns, and, yes, the shipping of Haitians – are illegal. So I am illegal."

The Dos Equis kept coming and we kept talking.

I thought of Tim, imagined him dozing or chain-smoking. Or both.

I have a very short list of talents. After four plus decades of more or less continuous practice, I can drink a lot—a great lot—of beer without becoming sloppy and stupid, particularly if I'm talking about more than the Raiders. Despite his bulk, Nikolai did not share this ability and I could see his movements slowing, his speech thickening up.

At moments, I had to remind myself that I was pounding brewskis with a vicious killer. It was like drinking with a bike gang member, something that's eventually unavoidable if you like dive booze establishments as much as I do. It always works out just fine as long as you mind your manners. After it's over, you can get all indignant about having had to defer based on an unsaid and uncivilized potential physical threat that drunken bikers can pose. But, at the time, it's still a pretty good idea to defer.

"How old are you?" I asked.

"I am fifty this summer."

I told him he ought to read Jimmy Buffet's book, *A Pirate Looks at 50.*

"I will look it up," he said laughing. "By way, I bought your book."

"Get the fuck outta here!"

"No. I did. I look into you. Find it on Amazon."

He rose unsteadily from his chair, made his way to a sparsely populated book case on the other side of the great room and brought back a well-thumbed copy of *On the Rails,* based on stories my father told me about the Dirty Thirties.

"You will give autograph," he said as a statement of fact.

"Of course."

Like I had a fucking choice.

He presented the book and a pen to me, almost bashfully, the same look I remembered at a signing I did in a bookstore years ago, an experience I likened to being a cross between a carny barker and an Amsterdam hooker. The difference of course was that none of my few customers back then likely was a billionaire Russian mobster who could put two behind my ear without even thinking about it.

"Did you read it?" I asked.

"It took many nights, many words I must look up but, yes, I read it."

"Why?"

That seemed to take him aback.

"I like to read. Also, for business, I must learn about my associates."

"....And?"

"I like it. Depression more bad in Russia, but I like it."

I would suspect all writers are sluts for praise. Even totally obscure ones, such as myself.

"Do you like what you do?" I asked.

"It was very much fun at one time. A thrill. Making deals, commanding men, demanding respect, building something...and, of course, money. Always the money."

"And now?"

"Everything has become...old. You know what I hate now?"

"The killing?"

"No," he said, looking for the first time in a while pissed-off at my directness. "That is business. That is what everyone understands. Rules of game. No, it is how stupid everyone is. Some, they know business good, but none of them are...are..."

"Interesting?" I ventured.

"Yes! All is boring."

"Like piss on a plate."

He thought about the image then laughed.

"See! Writer make good joke."

He turned serious again.

"And the business is now crazy. Very hard today. You think perhaps I am cruel. I am pussycat compared to new ones. They are nothing like old Russians like me, or even the old Italians."

"Because you have all that honour among thieves bullshit?"

"No. That is for movies. We have belief in rules. Follow rules. It is simple. Pay for things you bought. Deliver things you make promise. Do not use product. Respect your partners. Fuck your enemies. But use the force only when you must."

"Like with El Gordo?"

"Yes. See? No need to kill him. He will remember me. He will never fuck with me. But the Mexicans, the Colombians, here now. They kill for...for fun. They are brutal beyond words. Even the young Italians, and Russians."

"Like Sascha?"

Now I was pushing it, now my tightrope was getting narrower.

He seemed to be deciding between considering my remark or having Viktor pound the piss out of me. He sighed heavily.

"Like Sascha." he admitted quietly. "Do you know what it is like to look into your child's eyes and not see you in them? "

"No."

"That is right. Your daughter is police. And you have no son. I told you, I envy you. Sascha is not stupid. He wants business of his own. Not his poppa's. I understand. But I take years to have this. He will wait only days. And he will make quick deals with people who he should not make deals with."

"Like who?"

"Like Dominican gangs."

"Here?"

"Yes but also Trinarios and DDP in New York. And they have business not just there and here but in Spain, Europe. He brags to me he has gone into many other businesses, with many other people. I am racist, he say because I deal with only Russians and a few Italians but no one else. That is not the world today, he say. He brags he has people working for him in United States, Canada too. All the way to Rocky Mountain and soon California. He is good with computers. He find them all there on black net."

"Dark net?"

"Yes. Dark net. They do many things I do not know about. Steal cars to send to Russia. Fake credit cards. Fake land deals. More than that."

"You must be so proud," I said, but he ignored me.

"But he cannot keep it all in his head. Sometimes he does not get paid, sometimes he does not pay. When everyone is fucking everyone else, there will be bad problems. Of course, he will not listen. I am a *staryy pes*—old dog. To my face, he say that! That is why he made deals with that El Gordo. That is why he spend much time in Las Terrenas."

"So he *did* know of Sally Bartlett."

"Yes....And me too. I was not truthful earlier. She came here with that Haitian."

"His name was Tico," I said.

"She came here with...Tico and money for me to take his brother to Canada. I send them away."

"Not worth it?"

"Not worth it, yes, but also Sascha found her on the computer. That Paradise Regained. He believe she was trying to trap me."

"So you had my friend killed?"

"No! Sascha show me what she write. Big deal. So someone talks about Russian mob on Internet? Who is to give a fuck about that? We are everywhere—books, movies—everywhere. It is always bad Russians do this, bad Russians do that. But bad Russians have no need to attack outsiders, to bring police."

"Then who did? Viktor?"

"No. I say stay; he stay."

"So who did it?" I asked.

"Sascha and another man went. Very stupid. Very bad."

"So you didn't try to kill me?"

"Fuck, no! Swear."

And I believed him.

"And then that Haitian...Tico. Sascha say he was talking to others, to police, making trouble, telling people what happen. So Sascha went by himself."

"And you did nothing?"

"I found out after. What should I do? Kill him? My own son? Give him to police? What?"

What followed was a lengthy silence. I was thinking about Sally, Tico, Xavier, the way they died. That they died at all. And for what? Maybe he was thinking about his evil son, about what he could do. Maybe he was thinking about packing it all in.

"I am sorry, but my friends meant more to me than your batshit crazy son," I said.

"It is opposite for me. Understand?"

I heard the front door open. Sascha re-appeared, granting us a contemptuous stare before disappearing again somewhere in the house.

His father and I watched the little shit but said nothing. Nikolai shrugged as if to say: "See? What I tell you?"

Something occurred to me.

"I don't think Sascha could find Sally on that site. It took me hours. And I knew her."

"Sascha make one good deal. He found old British man in Las Terrenas. Paid him a few pesos to be on computer. It is he who found her and tell Sascha."

Fucking Miguel! Fucking "Anything for a buck" Miguel! I choked back some display of outrage while Nikolai continued.

"The world you live in, grew up in, is different from mine. I was a young man—like Sascha—when Soviet go away. Poof! Crazy time. After that and still, you must take what you can. To survive. Like here, like many places where law is not problem. You Canadians or the Americans know nothing of this. But all my life, there is only weak and strong, only winners and losers, and most of losers must be dead. I learn early. I learn when a competitor tried to kill me."

"What happened?"

"He did kill my Mischa, Sascha's mother."

"I'm sorry."

"The Russian mind, Russian heart is different than yours. There is no room for pity, for mercy, there is only winning."

"If you look around, you'll see this isn't Russia."

"You are right. More palm trees here."

"I still think you can walk away if you really wanted to. The hills around Las Terrenas are full of retired gangs-I mean businessmen. Imagine thirty or forty years of doing fuck-all, just enjoying yourself. You could grow tomatoes, learn to scuba, take up tennis."

"Not all the old men live so well, without problems. Jean-Louis Vignault. He is one."

"I don't know the man."

"I think maybe you hear of him. The French who died in your town last year. His life end much sooner than he want. This I know. Because I end it."

Holy shit! Holy shit! Not only had he fingered his own son for Tico and Sally's murders, he had just confessed to ordering a hit himself on the poor son of a bitch who rather violently shuffled off the mortal coil last fall.

"Why did you do that?" I asked.

"He was associate of mine, many, many years ago. In Marseille. He fucked me out of much money over some Kalashnikovs. I found him there and now it is OK."

"Winners and losers."

"Yes. Do you not think there are many who would do same to me?"

"With Viktor over there as part of your retirement package, I doubt many would try."

"Perhaps," he smiled. He *was* thinking about it.

I stared out the window, believing that everything that needed to be said, had been. Time to go. It was late. By my calculation, the tape—if it had worked—must have been on the verge of running out by now anyway. When I turned back, I saw that Nikolai had fallen asleep.

Unsure of the etiquette in these situations, I pushed my trusty bowling bag stuffed with money to his feet and headed towards the front door.

"Go now?" I asked the ever-vigilant slab of a human named Viktor.

"Oh, Mr. Lydon, don't leave us just yet."

I turned to the voice and saw Sascha, still all jumpy. His only new features were a long machete he was twirling in one hand, and a rather large handgun in the other.

# CHAPTER THIRTY-SEVEN

"What the fuck?" I said. "My business with your father is over. We have a deal. So I'm going now."

"I don't think so."

We stood there facing each other, maybe eight feet apart. Viktor formed the third point in our little triangle. I knew he'd be armed but there was no sign of a gun. I was sizing up the situation; Sascha seemed to be enjoying our little stand-off. In seconds, I'd done the math. I was slightly taller and more than slightly heavier. He was armed with one weapon that could take an arm clean off and another that could put a sizeable hole in me. On the other hand, if I could get inside the arc, not give him any room to swing the blade, maybe I could grab the gun. I might even be able to bust some of the little fucker's ribs with body shots. And on the other other hand, there was a good chance that Sascha was fucked up on something which made him unpredictable.

"Daddy dearest doesn't have all the facts," he said. "And stay where you are, Snake."

"Let me get this straight, *you're* calling me a snake?"

"Not 'a' snake, The Snake...from the website. It took some time, but I found you! Actually, Miguel found you."

"Big deal. I put that shit on the website to make it all look real."

"And what you said to the husband, that was shit too?"

"How do you know what I—"

'Fuck!' was all I could think of to say to myself as it dawned on me that Paul Bartlett was in on whatever Junior had going.

Sascha just stood there with a smirk on his face, a smirk that I'd give just about anything to wipe off. Violently. I tried to recover.

"Of course I was bullshitting Paul too!" I said. "I needed to raise the money. I figured that would help."

"Nice try. That is what my stupid father said you had done when I told him. He said that you were only interested in the business deal, that you weren't trying to trap him. And I finally had to tell him about Paul Bartlett. Bartlett's part of my business, has been for two years. He has helped to open up Colorado. No marijuana of course, but a big market for coke and crystal meth. And with all those cattle farms, they need cheap labor—cheap Haitian or Dominican or Cuban labor."

"You're fucking lying! How would you even know him?"

"You, Inspector Diaz, even my beloved father are concerned about mostly what happens here. You all forget there's another end to this. You need a distribution network, someone to receive goods, to sell the product. Your shitty little town is full of expatriates and they have connections all over the world. El Gordo doesn't get around much but he knows everything that goes on in your shitty little town. I was looking to expand; he had a name, a few names actually. Ask Viktor."

I turned back to the king-sized version of Dolph Lundgren. From the expression on his broad face, it was obvious that the little prick was telling the truth.

"Why Paul?"

"Old KGB recruiting trick my father taught me. Find a man with a problem. Two men in this case. Miguel and Paul both had money problems. Paul's were mostly because of her. He was all whiny about her taking twenty grand from their bank account after she'd already blown the wad on the new house."

It was a nasty piece of irony that Margaret and Dot had returned most of Xavier's unused passage money to Paul a few weeks ago.

"Oh, but wait! It gets soooo much better," Sascha continued, excitedly rattling on like a drug-fuelled high school kid explaining his science project. "On top of that, his wife was a becoming a problem with her campaign against us. So I told him that he needed to handle it. Otherwise he was finished in my business. I also told him that she would fuck anything with a dick and two legs down here while he was back home working. That sealed the deal. The dumb shit believed me. So I sent our private plane to Denver, beat the storm, and returned to our little airport here. No questions, no customs."

"Paul was in the hills. The campers were interviewed."

"His brother. In snowsuits they look alike. Now...where was I? Oh, yeah. As soon as he got here, the four of us drove up to Las Terrenas."

"Four?"

"Bartlett, me, and two of these little beauties," he said, holding the machete's blade on its edge at neck height, admiring it. "Bartlett went in first. A surprise visit, honey! And he quietened that fucking dog. He swung as she came to greet him. Can you picture that? But he was a pussy with the blade. He barely scratched her. Then he completely lost his nerve, and was useless. He needed a man to finish the job so I stepped up."

"But he was devastated, completely fucked up when I talked to him!" I insisted as if I were trying to argue against what I now knew to be true.

"With guilt, not sadness. Apparently, they look the same. And he then wouldn't touch the Haitian. So I had to do that too. Which was OK with me because – you know what? – it was fun."

"Why Tico?"

"You can blame Diaz for that one. A Haitian talks to the police a bunch of times and still is not arrested? He was dangerous. To me. To El Gordo and I did owe that fat fuck a favour. And while you're at it, you can also blame Diaz for the little incident with you and Dmitri on the beach. You should pick your fuckin' friends a little better."

"How would you know who either of us talked to? El Gordo?"

"No, the fat fuck is not very reliable but that old British guy is. I thought you were harmless at first. It was Miguel who pointed out that you were getting serious. He overheard you talking about this Glen Johnson crap. The website, all those chats with Diaz. And then, leaving your shithole condo to actually visit people? You never do that, Miguel told me."

"You listened to that piss tank?"

"He's smart, he's poor, and no one really notices him. Perfect for watching and reporting."

"Yeah, well that kid Dmitri fucked up."

"No. He did as he was told. The Bartlett bitch was a real problem. The shit she had on her computer was going to be trouble. You were just annoying. But you surprised me. I thought you would turn chickenshit if we threatened you. I didn't want to kill another expat. Dmitri only fucked up because he got shot."

"And you're father knew about all this?"

"After it happened. By then, what could he do? The problem with my father is he's not just an old dog, he's a blind one. He doesn't see a threat unless it shoots at him. Like what happened to my mother. He doesn't get it. You have to be worried about everything all the time these days to protect your business."

"Or," I said, "Here's another theory: you have to be worried about everything because you're a pathetic, little, paranoid, piece of fuck, cokehead punk."

Well, didn't that set off pathetic, little, paranoid, piece of fuck, cokehead punk.

"Viktor! Grab him!" he shouted.

Viktor didn't move.

"This man has deal with father," Viktor said.

That made Sascha even more bullshit. He rushed past me and up to the giant, waving his gun in Viktor's face.

Enraged, Sascha was focused on the man-mountain when I punched the little puke as hard as I could in the back of his head, sending him into Viktor's arms.

That was my cue for getting the fuck outta there. Or trying to. With the front hallway occupied I bolted across the great room and through the patio doors, past Nikolai who had been awakened by the brouhaha.

Owing to my willing slavery to nicotine, my normal running range is ten, maybe eleven yards before I'm on my knees horking up bits of lung. Pumped with adrenaline I became superhuman—for me. I made it across the patio, down the steps and onto the beach as the bullets started flying.

Going straight ahead into the water wasn't much of an option, so I right-turned it, and ran south towards the dark rocks I could see breaking up the sandy beach.

You know those movie scenes when a bunch of thugs stand there with automatic weapons spraying an area and the good guy somehow doesn't get hit? On some authority, I can tell you real life ain't quite like that.

A bullet caught me in the side, spun me around in truly remarkable pain. But it didn't drop me. I righted myself, stumbled on until another slug ricocheted off the first rocks I'd passed, sending fragments zipping into my arm like stone darts. I rolled into a crevasse.

Sascha reached me first. He was standing over me, like some kind of modern-day psycho pirate, a gun in one hand, the machete in the other. In the bright moonlight, I could see the manic glitter in his eyes just before I made my bold defensive move of shutting my eyes and pointlessly shielding my face.

In nanoseconds, I thought of my daughter, of Beth, of Alex, and I was aware of the ocean washing in, washing out.

# CHAPTER THIRTY-EIGHT

I didn't see the impact of the short burst of gunfire. I didn't feel it either. Instead, I felt Sascha fall on me, heavy and lifeless and bathed in blood and fleshy, gutsy bits of himself.

I could see Viktor lower his rifle. I could hear Nikolai wail.

The father did not approach his son, as I heaved the kid's corpse off me. One look would've told that Sascha's tattered, bloody body was lifeless. He turned instead to Viktor and raised his pistol. Viktor lifted his rifle. They faced each other for some seconds. Viktor no doubt imagining the hard choice of shooting the man to whom he had sworn  blind allegiance for all his adult life, Nikolai perhaps considering the value of that loyalty and the probability that, when it came right down to it, his employee had taken care of a problem that would only worsen.

Simultaneously, the men lowered their weapons. Nikolai turned and approached me.

"There must still be rules", he said, standing over me. "Somebody must pay. Understand?"

"Rules are made to be broken," I managed.

"Not this time. You disappoint me. You think you could catch me?"

"What about me?" said a voice behind me. A voice I recognized.

I painfully twisted around. It was Arturo, all swaddled in black, his revolver pointed at Nikolai. I could see at least five other Dominican ninjas crouched around the rocks.

Nikolai looked up, long enough to see the man who would kill him. Diaz fired as the Russian was raising his gun. Petrovic's head snapped back and there a brief flash of spray illuminated by the moon, crowning his head like a fatal red halo.

Instantly, Viktor's assault rifle clattered to the rocks and his hands were on his head, as he doubtless made a quick career decision. No boss, no need to die.

"Tim! Got to get to Tim!" I shouted.

"He is safe," Arty said, kneeling beside me, cradling my head. "But you...you are hurt, *Ingles*."

"No shit, Sherlock."

He barked orders in Spanish and right smartly I could feel cloth being pushed into the holes in my side.

That was a real ouchie.

The adrenaline subsided, the agony exploded.

I did the only sensible thing.

I passed out.

## CHAPTER THIRTY-NINE

I woke up in a completely white room. But no black curtains. On one side of the hospital bed was a bank of beeping machines and an IV. On the other side was Arty, looking all concerned.

"You are OK, *Ingles*?"

"Asking or telling me?" I croaked.

"You lost much blood. But it was replaced. Hah! *Now* you are a true Dominican."

"In that case, gotta smoke?"

Arty, bless him, produced a fresh pack of Marlboro *blancos*.

"Gotta beer?" I asked as he lit me up.

"You push it, *Ingles*."

"Don't you fuckin' talk to me about pushing it! You left it a little tight back there, Arty."

"Viktor is quick. He beat us to Sascha by a second maybe. One of my men told me he watched Viktor shooting before. Not at you. He was aiming at the moon. If Viktor's AR bullets had hit you, we would not be speaking right now."

"So Sascha shot me?"

"Yes. Small calibre. No big deal."

"For you maybe."

"We have the early match for Sascha's fingerprints on machete. The same one for Tico."

"That was quick."

"Ah, computers and scanners."

"Not that it matters much now."

"It matters to me, *Ingles*. Now it is all proved. Now it is over."

"No, Arty, it's not done," I said. "Sally's husband was in on it."

"You will not let this go, will you? We have confirmation from the campers in the snow."

"That was Paul's brother. He's gotta be involved too. Listen to the tape. Sascha confirmed it all."

"We have. It stops when you are talking to the father."

I lay there trying to think of something, anything else, that could prove Paul's involvement in killing his own wife beyond the say-so of a rabid – and very dead – Russian punk.

Arty's talk of fingerprints set something off in my wee brain. I remembered.

"Where were the husband's prints in the house?" I asked.

"You still may be under the drug effects, *Ingles*. It was his house. His prints were everywhere."

"Did you find them on the kitchen counter?"

"What?"

"Did you find them on the kitchen counter?" I repeated.

"Yes, of course."

"How about the bedroom furniture?"

"As well."

I sank back onto my pillow.

Now it was over.

"You said yourself that Paul had not been back to the DR in over a year. Since last December," I said.

"Yes. We have the records from the airport customs."

"Sally had Tico change the kitchen counter this past spring. She didn't like the original one. So how did his fingerprints get on it? And the furniture was just about the last thing she bought. Again, in the spring."

"You are sure?"

"I am completely, 100 per cent sure."

"Fuck!" Arty said.

"Petrovic smuggled people out of the country. But he could also smuggle them in."

"Fuck!"

"And...and the machete. You said two swings—one backhand and one forehand."

"Yes."

"No. It was two *people*. Sascha had the killing swing. He's right-hand-ed. Paul had the lighter first swing. He's left-handed."

"Fuck! Paul is gone."

"Don't worry; I bet he thinks he's in the clear. He's not going any-where. Get the Denver police to show his picture and his brother's to the campers. See which one they thought was Paul. And while they're at it, the cops should search his house or find a warehouse or storage container he might have rented."

"It will be done."

"When can I leave?"

"The bullet was through and through. You will have a full recovery. Two or three days here and then you will go home and go back to your easy life."

"That's it?"

"For you, yes. You must be out of all this. You know that."

"Yeah, you want to be a media star grabbing all the glory; I get that."

"Now would be a good time for you to be fucking off. There would have to be too many explanations. You broke many laws. We need many pure news stories from this. These gangs must know they can-not always be safe."

"And you have the recording."

"Yes, but with Nikolai dead and Sascha dead, we will not be using it. So it must be as though you were never in the house."

I sank back in my pillow, relieved. Yeah, I was pissed off a bit that all my pseudo-planning hadn't meant much.

Arturo explained how his side of things had worked. He had called some of the men he knew from his days in Altagracia province, and took two officers he trusted from Las Terrenas with him. A top secret operation. They didn't want to come by land; alarms would've gone off by the time they had breached the gate. Instead, they'd used rubber rafts launched half a mile down the coast while two officers took care of Igor Goonovich at the main gate.

"You were in there a long time, *Ingles*. We watched. Everything was calm until you tried to leave. We were preparing to assault the house when you came out to join us."

"How did you even know exactly when I'd be at the house?"

"I understand a police car pulled you over on the airport highway."

"You did that?"

"We had to be certain you were on your way. We had the license plate from the rental store."

"You crafty bastard!"

Ol' Arty was looking pretty pleased with himself.

"What happens now?" I asked.

"There will be a fight to take over the Petrovic's operation. Some bad people will probably die. And at the end, there will not be much to take over. The first night we knew the real prize was Viktor. He is being very co-operative. He knows many people who were in business with Nikolai or Sascha. We have Mexicans, and Venezuelans, Dominicans and, of course, Russians to pick up. That is happening now. For the ones who haven't left the island."

"Viktor is fucked."

"He has a chance. He knows he almost died on the beach. The FBI has said they will pay to hide him in witness protection."

I tried to imagine Viktor working in a bowling alley in Des Moines.

"Speaking of paying, do you happen to know how much I owe here?" I asked.

"The hospital has asked for a passport and a credit card. I almost gave them your Glen Johnson papers."

"But you didn't?"

"No I did not."

"So how much do I owe?"

"The *Nacional Policia de Republica Dominicana* is pleased to pay."

"Thanks, Arty. Where's Tim?"

"He said he will be at Now Larimar until you are safe to travel."

"And the money?"

"Returned to you when you go back."

"Thank you again, Arty."

"I cannot believe how much you now must repay me."

"Oh, I'm sure you'll collect it all... with interest."

After three days in hospital, I was going mad with boredom. *The Simpsons* in Spanish is entertaining for only so long. About the only words I picked up on were: '*Ay Carrumba!*'

I did manage to borrow a less than shitty laptop from a sweet nurse so I could try to resume my browsing, find out what had actually gone on in the rest of the world while I was otherwise occupied.

And I did write to Halley telling her that she could relax because I hadn't used the fake papers she'd sent after all, which was sort of true. Thanks to fucking Miguel, Petrovic had known instantly that I wasn't Glen Johnson.

While I was at it, I sort of lied some more to Halley by mentioning that the Dominican police had decided to take over the investigation putting my one-man crusade out of business. I even sent her the link to the *DR1* webpage with the news story that contained no mention of a nosy fucker from Canada.

She wrote back expressing her relief that I hadn't done anything more foolhardy than smoking and drinking excessively. She added a P.S.:

*Dump Glen Johnson before coming home. He's a pain in the ass for you.*

I thanked her for her swell tip and wrote that "*I got rid of Glen*", assuming that she'd know that I had already realized how a random search at Canadian Customs might turn up the counterfeit me, creating a bit of instant unpleasantness. I sort of lied there too. I planned to get rid of the bogus ID package in a safety deposit box at Banco Popular as soon as I got back to Las Terrenas. Never know when he might make a return visit to the island.

In a separate note, she forwarded her e-ticket for the Bahia Principe El Portillo for next week, starting the 21st of March.

My, my, time flies when you're being shot. I had five days until the 21st to miraculously recover and meet her there. Plenty of time. Well, not really. Unless I wanted to wear grandpa pants cinched just under my armpits for the whole week she was down here, I'd have to explain yet another hole in my body. Five whole days to come up with a story. Where's the challenge?

Tim finally did come by, on the third day of my convalescence.

I thanked him for his concern.

"Feck off, mate. Inspector Diaz told me you were fine and I hate hospitals."

"Probably not as appealing as a Punta Cana beach during spring break."

"It was heart-warming. But now it's time to get out of this shithole."

"You got caught at Now Larimar."

"I did, indeed. The jig's up."

The ride back was a whole lot less pleasant than the trip down. Bumps in the road—which I swear Tim was hitting deliberately—painfully jarred me. He had made up for my highway torture by bringing a cooler full of Presidente along for the ride. It had magically and tragically evaporated by the time we hit the exit to Sanchez.

"Tim, what say we skip the new coast highway and take the old road through Sanchez and up the mountains?"

"Suit yourself," he said, veering off the four-laner. "We save the toll and the old road has fewer shitty feckin' drivers."

As usual, there was the spectacular and spectacularly slow ascent and then the free-wheeling hurtle down the other side of the mountain—a ride that, depending on your point of view, is either exciting or harrowing. Well, the way Tim drove, it was both. We slowed down somewhat as we cruised into my town. Because that's how it felt again. My town. I had only been gone from Las Terrenas for four days but I was absolutely delighted to be back.

Not that I was there very long as my vacation with my daughter was imminent.

Even though most of the money wasn't mine, I felt like fucking Santa Claus giving it back to the various donors from Las Terrenas. Of course they were happy to just get their cash back but there was something else. I knew and they knew that it made possible the downfall of a major crime family. None of that appeared in the papers or on-line news, but my 'investors' knew.

And I felt real shitty making another night time visit to Pétionville, this time to tell the would-be immigrants they wouldn't be. It was something more than that, however, that bothered me. What I had done —what I had set out to do—was fuck up a murderer. But I had also eliminated a source for illegal immigration for some Haitians somewhere who might somehow scrape up the cash and/or sponsors.

Ricky escorted me again. He was no more chattier than he ever was, but at the door of the rickety dancehall and social club he said: "*C'est OK. Monsieur Jake. Nous sommes heureux que vous avez essayé.*" They were happy I had tried.

Other than a pretty small circle of friends who were used to keeping secrets, my half-assed involvement went unnoticed. I really liked the anonymity during the aftermath of my little outing to Punta Cana. The papers kept it going for quite awhile, as long as the arrests and trials kept coming. Repercussions would continue, rippling out and enmeshing any number of bad guys.

One of them was Paul Bartlett, Arty told me. Denver police and the FBI had scooped him up and emptied out a storage unit of illegal pharmaceuticals. In a touching display of international co-oper-ation, they would allow the DR to extradite him to face a raft of charges here first.

"La Victoria will make him miss camping in the snow," Arty said.

Neither Arturo nor I were under the illusion that all the arrests and sentences had magically transformed the DR into a crime-free par-adise. But it had made a dent and, for sure, a message had been sent.

But nothing can change what had happened. Sally was still dead. So was Tico, his brother Xavier, and scores of others whose only desire, whose burning hope was to make life better for themselves, their families.

For that they risked it all. And that is what they paid.

## CHAPTER FORTY

Arty was a fucking hero which was fine by me for the simple reason that he already was a fucking hero in my books for having saved my Canadian bacon. Plus, it gave me something to ride his ass about because he had turned down the offer to promote him back to Santo Domingo. He was staying put and I was even happier about that.

I had an absolutely delightful time at Bahia Principe El Portillo with my daughter. Halley came down all stressed from work and fish-belly white. We had a grand week. She's been a goddamned dolphin in the water since she was a kid so it was a pleasure to see her—in pool or ocean—cutting the water with her crisp and sure strokes—so unlike her old man's near-drowning thrash.

She did gasp a bit when she saw the red-pitted marks on my upper arm and the ugly wound on my side. But she seemed to buy my story about my recent ill-fated snorkelling trip that saw rough waves throwing me into some staghorn coral that impaled me and thank you, dive master, for getting me out of the self-chummed water before the sharks showed up and wasn't that a close call, but everything's fine now, thanks for asking, care for another mojito, daughter dearest?

I was pretty goddamned proud of myself having tricked my daughter, what with her being a cop and all.

After that, we ate and drank and laughed and the week just flew by.

I bummed a ride on her chartered bus out to the airport to see her off. The little witch could not let her father get away with anything. Just before we hugged good-bye at the check-in counter, she had to say:

"Oh, and dad, I do know what a small-calibre through-and-through looks like."

"I'll tell you all about it someday."

"Pretty sure I don't want to know."

I then made a return trip to the hotel for my week of solo all-inclusivity which was also delightful. It was all peaceful and I was relieved that no one threatened to hack me or shoot me—although there was a German tourist who got pretty pissed when I told him to shut the fuck up as he was loudly berating my magic omelette guy for adding too many green peppers.

After an indulgent week of pampering, I was glad finally be back at my place. Alejandro, the world's best bartender™, was gladder still.

"You *vamos* for so long," he chided me. "The Tanqueray *es malo* I think."

Given that the DR starts to really heat up by the beginning of April, I felt duty bound to reduce his inventory.

After one such pleasant afternoon, I was sitting on my balcony when the phone rang. With a bit of effort, I got up to answer it.

"You bastard!"

"Why, hello, darling. How are you?"

"You bastard!" Alex said again. "You couldn't call and tell me?"

"Well, unless you have some advanced medical training I don't know about...and just imagine our chat: 'Guess what I did today, honey. I got plugged by a Russian mobster! Bye. Have a nice day!'."

"That's not the point."

"Sure it is. Look, I appreciate it. I do. But you'd just worry and get all upset. Why would I do that to you?"

"So...how are you?

"Fine. Great, in fact. Halley called you? That rat."

"Yes. She's worried about you."

"See? Now you are too."

"For Christ's sake, Jake! That's two gunshot wounds in—what—six months!"

"More like seven. I'll stop, I swear."

"What happened? Even Halley couldn't tell me."

"Not much to tell and anyway, I'd rather explain in person."

There was way too much pausing going on for my liking.

"Alex?"

"I'd love to, but work...you know. There's this huge report I'm putting together on generic drugs..."

"Sure."

"OK?"

"Sure."

"Why don't you come to Boston?"

"Snow on the ground?"

"Yes, but...oh, forget it."

Fuck! I thought after we'd hung up. We both sounded like pouty, wounded puppies. I hate that. She's not coming here because of a stupid thing called work and I'm not going there for the even stupider reason that I don't like snow. And yet...and yet it felt somehow enlivening. As if it showed me a glimpse of how much we cared about each other instead of bundling it up in the casual, practiced flippancy we both used whenever we veered towards honest feelings.

The two of us had a chance together. I knew that. But I didn't know much else. I didn't know what it looked like. Maybe she'd just walk away from stock picking and helping small companies grow. But on the other hand, maybe I could put on my big-boy pants and get over my juvenile obsession with the Endless Summer, only without surfing. But on the other other hand...

Fuck!

When in doubt, I say: Obliterate! And get obliterated.

But even that was going to be messy, I thought as I turned the corner of Big Dave's courtyard and was reminded that I had one last piece of business to tidy up. The only fly in the proverbial ointment was a skinny, old, alcoholic insect, sitting off in one corner of the patio.

I didn't know until that very moment but apparently I have a rule against kicking the shit out of septuagenarians—by the way, it's a rule I hope eveybody'll adhere to should I make it that far. Staring at Miguel, I knew that as much as I'd like to, I couldn't lay a beat-down on him.

I sat with Nick but stared at the gawky Brit. Nick wanted to know why I was so fixated with Miguel, so I told him.

I told him just before Miguel rose and lurched over to our table.

"No hard feelings, old boy," he said, extending a trembling bony hand for me to shake.

I was pretty sure Nick hadn't heard of any post-70 beating ban as he got up and into Miguel's face.

"You're leaving now, fuckwad, and you're not coming back. Ever," he hissed.

There was some blustering and harrumphing from the Brit that subsided as soon as Nick laid hands on him and steered him less than gently out onto the sidewalk.

It was all rather discreet and understated until Miguel, after standing and weaving there for a while, made some elementary decision that he wanted at least one more beer. He started back into the courtyard.

Jack snap, Nick was up and livid.

"I will fucking kill you!" he bellowed.

The force of his threat stilled the crowd and, after a couple seconds, Miguel's synapses started firing long enough to convince him that self-preservation was a smarter choice than self-pickling at this particular drinking establishment. He wandered away.

I felt bad. Not for Miguel but for Dave. He'd just lost an important source of income. I explained the situation to him, how Miguel had, whether he intended to or not, for a few pesos, contributed to Sally's death, probably to Tico's, and nearly mine. Dave vowed that as long as he owned the bar he would never serve Miguel again and Nick and I vowed to do everything in our power to replace his lost revenue stream.

# EPILOGUE

On April 6, the Weather Network told me it was snowing in Toronto and points north-east.

Fuck that. I decided to stay in LT for at least another three weeks just to be safe. I wrote to Alexandra explaining my travel plans. She wrote back—within the hour. I know because I checked and re-checked my in-box for 49 friggin' minutes.

*Boy, what a crazy coincidence! I have to be down there next week. New rice crops are coming in and I have to verify bushels per acre yields.*

I replied. *Crazy, crazy coincidence. Advise arrival. Stop. Bring sandals. Stop. Love, Jake. Stop.*

OK, OK, I agonized a bit typing out the L-word. But, I gotta admit, it looked right on the screen. It felt right. More than right.

Bonus: She was coming south and I wasn't going north. Early April in Boston was bound to be only a bit warmer than Mississauga Lake. And I knew what that meant.

Thoreau once cautioned us to "beware of all enterprises that require new clothes." I got my own wrinkle—as it were—on that sage piece of wisdom.

Beware of all enterprises that require the wearing of socks.

I still fucking hate socks!

# ACKNOWLEDGEMENTS

I need to—yet again—push a heap o' gratitude towards Glenn Torresan and his Hangar 13 Art & Design shop for making this book possible as a book. Despite his mistaken—but spirited—praise of the Beatles, Glenn's cover design, photography, and lay-out (as well as his deep affection for tequila) are much appreciated.

Thanks too to Ron Corbett for being a swell publisher and writer. And for his life-long love of words—many of which he has arranged in compelling sentences.

And speaking of 'yet again', thanks to Maggie—yet again—for her love, support, and ass-kicking.

And for all you fact-checkers out there, you won't find any between these covers. I make shit up.

## ABOUT THE AUTHOR

John Owens has written two mystery novels, *Connecdead* and *Machete*, starring Jake Lydon who bears absolutely no resemblance to his creator and who is a role model for exactly no one.

Owens is also the author of two works of historical fiction. *On the Rails*, a cross-Canada Great Depression-era saga and *The Sixth String*, the story of a flamenco guitarist caught up in Hitler's Germany.

He lives with his wife, Maggie, in Morrisburg, Ontario on the banks of the St. Lawrence River and Indian Rocks Beach, Florida.

He faithfully rotates his tires.

If you're inclined, you can find him at johnowens.ca or on Facebook.

www.ingramcontent.com/pod-product-compliance
Lightning Source LLC
Chambersburg PA
CBHW020357260626
47156CB00007B/2159